ALAN ORLOFF

SANCTUARY MOTEL

A Mess Hopkins Novel

First published by Level Best Books 2023

First edition

ISBN: 978-1-68512-397-0

Cover art by LEVEL BEST DESIGNS

This book was professionally typeset on Reedsy.
Find out more at reedsy.com

Chapter One

When I thought of an inn, I pictured a solid structure, built with chiseled stone or sturdy weathered wood, situated on the side of a mountain or on a bluff overlooking a craggy shoreline, the kind of homey place where a rosy-cheeked lady wearing a cable-knit sweater checked you in and escorted you to your room. Fireplaces abounded, along with freshly baked muffins—or better yet scones—and everyone spoke in revered tones about the place's rich history.

On the other hand, a motel was an eyesore slapped together from cinder blocks and cement, a utilitarian rest spot on the side of the road luring weary travelers with promises of free HBO and low, low rates.

The Fairfax Manor Inn was all motel. Without the HBO.

I should know; I'd grown up around the place, and for the last ten months, I'd been running it.

The Inn was built back when clean, no-frills, economy motels were the rage. It stood in the northern part of the City of Fairfax in Northern Virginia, on a stretch of Route 50 dominated by chain restaurants, gas stations, and car dealerships. Weirdly, there were three other independent rinky-dink motels within four miles.

My parents had owned the motel for the past twenty-two years, but then had gotten the traveling bug and stepped away from the business abruptly, tossing me the keys to the front door. Our arrangement was simple: I ran the place and whatever money I earned, after paying the expenses, was mine to keep.

I also got to live there.

Now I was performing my every-other-day ritual—cleaning up the grounds. I pushed a garbage can on wheels across the parking lot, stopping every five paces to pick up trash, hands protected by a pair of yellow rubber dishwashing gloves. Old tattered newspapers, soda cans, cigarette butts, and things much, much more disgusting.

I couldn't imagine anyone actually liking trash pick-up duty, but it could have been worse; I could have been inside poring over last month's profit and loss statement, trying to figure out how to eke some profits out of this place without sacrificing my on-going mission.

A figure waved at me from across the parking lot. I stopped my trash collection and waved back, thankful for the diversion.

D'Marvellus Jackson strode my way. He stood a few inches taller than my six feet and he had an athletic gait—a former Division I college point guard whose career had been derailed by a knee injury. Vell and I were best friends, despite being different in many respects. He's Black; I'm White. He's wiry and scary strong. I'm a couple of pounds overweight and struggle on pushup number eight. He's got his pulse on the latest trends; I still wear cargo shorts. He's eight years my junior—a mere child—and never lets me forget how out of touch I am.

We bumped fists, but he skipped further pleasantries and got right down to business. "I need a room."

"For who?" I stripped off my gloves and tossed them into the garbage can. It seemed I had more important matters to handle. When Vell said he needed a room, he really needed a room. And it wasn't for him.

"Woman in trouble. And her son." Vell cared deeply about others. Our common ground.

"How do you know her?" I asked.

"Friend of a cousin's boyfriend's sister's hairstylist."

"In other words, Mama sent her to you." Vell's mother knew practically everyone in the Metro area, especially those living in the margins.

Vell nodded.

"Where are they?" I asked, looking around. "And where's your car?"

Vell hooked a thumb over his shoulder. "I parked them all—mother, son, car—at Denny's. Grand Slams for everyone. Wanted to make sure you had a room before I brought them in."

"What's the woman's name?"

"She says it's Nicole, but I'd say her name is Scared."

"Come on, let's talk with Cesar and see what's available."

* * *

When my parents handed me the reins of the Inn, they imposed one stipulation. I couldn't fire my biggest expense, the motel's operating manager, Cesar Ruiz. They'd hired Cesar early on, and he was the one who kept the place running. He made sure the rooms were clean, he balanced the books, he handled the front desk, he ordered supplies, he updated the website, he insured that maintenance was conducted on the appropriate schedule. Organized, efficient, dependable, and fiscally responsible. In short, Cesar was everything I wasn't.

And it was nice that at least one of us was concerned about the welfare of the motel.

We got along okay. I let him run things, and he didn't tattle to my parents about some of my less-than-wise choices or philanthropic activities. I considered that a win-win.

Now, Vell and I scuffed across the parking lot to the registration office/-manager's suite, where Cesar lived with his husband, Diego, and their ten-year-old son Abie.

We reached the stand-alone A-frame office, and when I opened the door, a bell above *ding-a-linged.* Eight seconds later, Cesar appeared behind the registration desk, impeccably dressed in a blue suit and red rep tie. What was that saying? Dress for the job you wish you had? I think Cesar dressed for a job at the Four Seasons, not the Fairfax Manor Inn, where a stained sweatshirt wouldn't have been out of place.

"Evening, boss." Cesar's smile dimmed as he addressed Vell. "And a good evening to you, too, Mr. Jackson."

"Good evening, Mr. Ruiz.," Vell said, a little more formally than the situation called for.

Cesar tipped his head slightly. "What can I do for you, Mess?"

When I was five, I got sent to my room after misbehaving. Rather than serve my sentence quietly like a good little boy, I pulled everything out of my drawers, my closets, my tiny desk, and threw it on the floor in an epic tantrum. My older sister started calling me Mess, and the name had stuck like crazy glue. "What have we got tonight, roomwise?"

Cesar shifted his attention to the registration computer and hit a few keys. The motel had fourteen units, excluding the manager's suite. I lived in Room Thirteen and used the adjoining Room Fourteen as my office. Griff—our security guy—more or less lived permanently in Room Seven. The other eleven units were available to rent.

"Rooms One, Four, and Ten are occupied with paying customers. I can furnish you with their departure dates, if you wish."

"That's okay."

"All the other rooms available?"

Cesar stared at me for a beat. "No sir."

I stared back. "Okay, then. What rooms are available?"

Cesar consulted the screen. "The two young ladies you checked in Sunday night are still using Three. And the elderly gentleman you invited to stay with us two nights ago—I believe you said his name was Rocko—is still occupying Eleven. Plus, he invited a few of his closest friends to join him." He arched one eyebrow. "I didn't catch their names."

Rocko was homeless, and every month or so I brought him in for a couple of days. "Okay. That leaves a few extra rooms. I'll need one. How about Eight, where Griff can keep a close watch on them?"

"Indeed." Cesar's fingers were already moving on the computer to generate a keycard. "And the name of your guest?"

"Nicole."

"Last name Smith or Jones?" Cesar asked. "Or perhaps Williams this time."

"Let's go with Jones," I said.

"Of course. I assume the room is comped."

"You assume correctly," I said.

"For how long?"

I glanced at Vell, who'd been mercifully quiet so far. He shrugged at me. I shrugged at Cesar.

"I'll put her down for a week," Cesar said. "To start."

* * *

Vell had picked up Nicole and her son, Kevin, from Denny's and we'd gathered in Room Eight. Nicole sat on one bed, Kevin lounged on the other, attention fixed on his phone, while I leaned my butt against the dresser. Vell had taken off, now that his charges had a safe place to lay their heads.

"Vell didn't give me any details about your situation, and that's fine for now—you can fill me in later. Maybe there's something more I can do for you. What's important is that you two have a safe place to stay for a while. I gather you want to keep under the radar?"

Nicole nodded, gaze averted. She was petite, with slightly mottled skin, and wore an expression of hopelessness I'd seen on too many people lately. The edges of a purple-yellow bruise peeked out from under some heavy makeup below her left eye.

"You haven't told anyone where you are, have you? Mother, friend, neighbor?"

Nicole shook her head.

"Good. For now, let's keep your whereabouts undisclosed, okay?'

"Okay." Nicole's voice was almost as tired as she looked.

"This is what I tell all my guests. You're welcome to stay as long as necessary, but most people move on—to a more permanent situation, in a safe place—in a week or so. If you're hungry during the day, feel free to call Sandy at the bagel café next door and she'll run something over to you." Sandra Beech owned Hole Lotta Love, and Cesar liked to refer to her as our exclusive room service provider. I pointed to the nightstand. "The number is there, on that laminated "Amenities" card. She keeps the place open until about eight o'clock. Just tell her to put it on my tab."

Nicole raised her head, met my eyes. "That's very kind of you."

"Any friend of Vell's ... Or Vell's mother, I should say."

Nicole offered a small smile. "Amen."

"Also, next door is a man named Griff. Big guy, scary-looking. Don't be alarmed, he won't hurt you, but he will hurt anyone who comes along trying to start trouble. If someone like that does come along, just bang on the wall—he's right next door in Room Seven." I pointed to their shared wall.

Throughout my spiel, Kevin hadn't glanced up from his phone. I figured he was taking it all in, teenagers were adept at multi-tasking, but was too cool to show any interest. At least I hoped he was listening—it always helped when everyone knew the score.

"Any questions?"

Nicole shook her head. Even though I wasn't yet up to speed on the specifics, I could only guess that this was one of the worst days of her life. Running from home, from an abuser, from someone she probably loved—or still loves—couldn't have been easy. And with a child involved ... maybe that did make it easier, knowing you had to protect your kid, no matter the personal cost to you.

"Okay, I'll let you get some rest. Of course, you're free to come and go as you please, but it might be a good idea just to stay close. We can talk more tomorrow, if you'd like. In the meantime, if you need anything, give me or Cesar a call."

"Thank you, Mess." Nicole turned to her son. "Kevin, don't you have something to say?"

Kevin remained glued to his phone.

"Kevin!" Nicole said.

At that, he glanced my way and grunted something I couldn't quite make out.

I took it for *thanks*.

Nicole shrugged and mouthed the word *sorry*.

I shrugged back and started to leave, but stopped when Nicole's phone rang. She glanced at the caller ID and a look of panic flashed across her face. She quickly turned the phone over and put it on the bed next to her.

"Nicole?" I asked. "Who was it?"

"Nobody." She looked as if she were about to cry. She looked about fifteen years old.

Her phone rang again a second later. This time, she answered it. "Hey honey." She listened for a moment. "Listen, we're at Aunt Ginny's. She's having a rough time, so we may end up staying a couple of days. Sorry I had to leave on such short notice."

She bit her lip as she listened to the reply.

"Okay. I'll let you know. Gotta run." After she disconnected, she closed her eyes and tried to get her breath under control. I imagined how difficult it must be trying to be pleasant to someone who'd abused you and forced you from your home.

"Nice going, Nicole," I said. "Looks like you bought yourself some time."

"Maybe."

"What?"

"I'm not sure he believed me."

"He doesn't know where you are, so even if he doesn't, he can't find you." We were only a few miles from their apartment, but we might as well have been in the next county. As long as no one slipped up and told him, of course.

"He'd better not find us," she said. "Because he won't be happy. And when he's not happy, we're not happy."

Kevin snorted, without looking up from his phone. Then he said, "Todd can rot in Hell as far as I'm concerned. Then *I'll* be happy."

Chapter Two

The next morning, I darted into Hole Lotta Love for a blueberry muffin and coffee. On my way to the counter to order, I spotted two of my guests in a booth having breakfast. I detoured to their table.

"Good morning, ladies." These two twenty-something women—sisters—had come to the motel earlier in the week, needing a place to stay. About a year ago, the younger sister, Rona, fell down some stairs, suffering a traumatic brain injury. Her older sister, Avia, had been taking care of her since—their father had died when they were little, and their mother was a raging alcoholic—but lately had to miss so much work that she'd gotten fired. Eviction followed, and, fortunately, they heard about me from someone at a shelter. I wouldn't wish their troubles on my worst enemy.

"Good morning," Avia said. Rona simply smiled.

"Getting by okay?"

"Better than okay. I've got a few job interviews lined up."

"That's great," I said. "Fingers crossed."

Rona repeated, "Fingers crossed."

"Thanks, Mess," Avia said. "I just paid Cesar for tonight's room, but hopefully we'll be out of your hair soon."

Some guests wouldn't accept outright charity, so we had a very flexible sliding scale. I think we were charging them $12.50 a night. "Don't worry about that. You just worry about nailing those interviews, okay?"

"I will," Avia said.

"She will," Rona said.

I said goodbye and went up to order. Sandy wasn't in, so I gave her daughter Crystal a heads-up about Nicole opening a tab and grabbed my food to go.

I was already late for my monthly meeting with Uncle Phil.

I drove to the posh suburb of McLean, over hill and dale, past mansion after mansion, until I arrived at Uncle Phil's. It wasn't the largest castle in the neighborhood, and I bet that ate at Phil, although any normal person would be impressed by its neo-grandeur.

Whatever. Material riches didn't impress me, although if someone tried to pay me off to be impressed, I'd listen.

I rang the bell and some fancy chimes sounded within. A moment later, Uncle Phil himself answered the door, decked out in a designer polo shirt and spiffy yellow pants—which he probably called slacks. His outfit cost more than my entire wardrobe, if you excluded my leather bomber jacket. Maybe the butler had the day off.

"Late, as usual. Come in, Benjamin."

Uncle Phil was the only person on earth who still called me by my given name. Even my parents had caved. I followed him into a highly-decorated room off the opulent two-story foyer. A den. Or maybe he called it a sitting room or parlor or conservatory. What did I know about mansions? I lived in a motel room.

"Can I get you a drink?"

I held up my takeout cup of coffee. "No thanks. I'm good."

"Very well, then." He went to the bar and poured himself an inch of some extravagant gold liquid. It was five o'clock somewhere, just not in this hemisphere. Drink in hand, he lowered himself into a leather club chair and motioned for me to sit in one across from him.

He performed the same ritual every month, although sometimes the color of his slacks varied.

"How have you been?" He sipped his drink and made a little lip-smacking noise.

"Fine. You?"

"Can't complain." He leaned forward, smirked. "Actually, I could, but it wouldn't do any good."

"How's Aunt Vera?"

"Wonderful. She's visiting her sister in San Diego."

"Nice." It seemed Aunt Vera was always visiting one of her five sisters. I guessed if I were married to Phil, I'd find an excuse to get away, too, every chance I could.

Now came the awkward pause. Happened every time. Those few quiet moments after the small talk ended and before we started arguing about the motel.

I smiled at Uncle Phil, waiting him out. Finally, he burst, like always.

"I saw the numbers, and they're worse than last month. That's eight poor months in a row. What are you doing to that place, son? Have you no respect for what your father built?" His face darkened.

"We've had decent occupancy rates. But you know how the business goes, up and down."

"I've been waiting for the up. Ever since your father left, in fact."

"The up will come, Uncle Phil. There have always been cycles in this business." I paused, solely for effect. "Even when my father was in charge."

When my parents set out for parts unknown, they entrusted the motel to me. I made the mistake of thinking that meant I was in charge. Somehow, Uncle Phil got in my father's ear—they'd always been very close—and persuaded my father to dictate that we meet monthly, so Phil could provide his invaluable guidance. His support. His essential impartial oversight.

The only thing these meetings gave me was indigestion. Even from five thousand miles away, my father was trying to run my life. Or *ruin* my life, to be more exact.

"I had a long conversation with Cesar the other day."

"And?" Cesar was in the unenviable position of being stuck in the middle, between the old guard and the new regime. He'd always been fiercely loyal to my father, and by extension, to Uncle Phil, but he also was smart enough to know who was running the show now. The motel owner is dead, long live the motel owner.

"And I got the impression that we are heavily discounting many rooms.

Many, many rooms."

Credit Cesar for not telling Phil that heavily discounting meant completely comping. "Not all of our guests can afford the rack rate."

"You can't give rooms away, Benjamin. That's just not good business. Anybody with half a brain knows that. And the types of people you're attracting..." His eyes bored into mine. "I'd hardly call them guests."

My face felt warm. "What types are those? People who need a break? People who've stumbled onto hard times? What happened to your churchgoing attitude I always hear so much about? Helping your fellow man when he's down? Ignoring the plight of the needy doesn't sound so Christian."

Uncle Phil clamped the lips of his starchy mouth together, but I swore I saw a smile in his eyes. He always knew how to press my buttons, and I'm sure he got off on it. I sucked in a deep breath, trying to regain some composure. If I lost it completely, he'd win.

"Look, it's not like I'm turning away people because I've invited a few *guests* to stay with us, gratis." I hit the word *guests* extra hard. "So we're not losing any revenue. And the cost of cleaning the rooms is really negligible."

"Those costs add up. Speaking of costs, I examined the numbers, and the 'Other Expenses' category is through the roof. But that isn't all. My concerns go beyond the dollars and cents. We have our reputation to think about. We want to attract clientele who can afford to stay with us. Eventually, we can position ourselves as upscale, raise our rates. Became a classy establishment. Think, Benjamin, think." He actually tapped the side of his head as he delivered his chastisement.

All his "we" business rankled me. I knew he thought he played an integral part in the operation, but from where I sat—in the motel's driver's seat—he was merely an annoyance. On the other hand, Uncle Phil could definitely cause trouble if pushed too far.

If I were on better terms with my father—and if I knew how to reach him during his exotic expedition—we could discuss the matter. Although I wasn't sure I wanted to find out whose side he was on—his son's or his brother's.

"I don't think going upscale is the direction we should—"

Uncle Phil interrupted me with a half cough, half snort. "Let's back up a bit. Look at the big picture here."

I nodded, bracing for more of his cockeyed life lectures.

"Do you really enjoy working at the Inn? Is that something you've always wanted to do? Because I remember when you were a teenager and you wanted nothing at all to do with it. You didn't want to work there during the summers or during school breaks. You didn't want to pitch in on the weekends. In fact, I often heard you mocking your father's hard work. And now?"

"That was a long time ago." Then why did I feel like a teenager again?

"You know, your parents wanted you to major in business. Get a degree. Go on to grad school." He gave his head a wistful shake. "Even after you decided to get a psychology degree, they tried to steer you toward med school. Become a psychiatrist. That's both a worthwhile and lucrative profession."

At the time, I honestly considered their wishes. After all, I always had the desire to help those less fortunate. But I didn't want to sit in a fancy leather chair in a well-appointed office, and I wanted to do something more concrete. Something immediate. And I wanted to help those in my community who were truly desperate. Opening up my motel to those who really needed a temporary sanctuary seemed like the perfect solution. If only I could get Uncle Phil off my back.

Uncle Phil barreled on. "Maybe it's time you carved out your own place in this world. Pursue one of your passions." He tilted his head sideways at me. "You do have some passions, don't you?"

I had plenty of passions. One of them was helping others less fortunate, something foreign to my uncle, it seemed.

"One of these days, you're going to have to stop living off your parents. You're thirty years old, for chrissakes."

"Actually, I'm thirty-one."

He glared at me but didn't interrupt his lecture. "When I was your age, I'd already forged a career for myself. Gotten married. Settled down. I wasn't playing Mr. Charity with homeless people. Benjamin, you need to grow up, and soon."

I felt like *throwing* up. But it was time to give up before I gave out. Sometimes you had to go along to get along. "Uncle Phil, how about this?

I'll pay more attention to who I give rooms to. And I'll try to keep a better handle on expenses. You're right. If I'm going to run the motel, I should do it properly."

Uncle Phil allowed his entire face to grin, now that I'd capitulated. Of course, words were cheap, and I could spew empty promises with the best of them. I'd had good role models growing up.

"Now you're talking some sense." He savored a long sip from his drink. "I'd hate to have to pull rank and step in for you. I wouldn't want to explain that to your father, but you know, he did tell me to keep an eye on things. That's all I'm trying to do, you know, ensure that what my brother built—from scratch, mind you—doesn't go down the tubes. I'm sure you realize that, Benjamin."

"Yes, I do, Uncle Phil. Yes, I do." I realized a lot of things, you old gasbag.

* * *

I drove back to the motel, chugging along in my dumpy old Corolla. I bought it from a friend for a pittance a few months ago after I'd bashed up my last beater. It was within spitting distance of 200,000 miles, and it looked much older. The seats were ripped. The ceiling was cracked. The armrests had gouges big enough to lose change in. The entire clunker smelled like a Popeye's Cajun Feast. But it did a decent job of getting me where I wanted to go—most of the time. Truth was, I didn't have enough disposable cash to buy anything better. And the way I treated my cars, it wouldn't have been wise even if I had the money.

I pulled into the lot and parked in front of my room. Killed the engine. The Fairfax Manor Inn was built before security concerns all but dictated interior hallways, but I thought it fit in with the original intent of a motel. A *motor hotel*, where you could drive right up to the front door of your room, park the car, tote your bags ten yards, and step right inside. No bell boys, no elevators, no long hallways.

Something quaint about that efficiency, I thought.

A few other cars were in the lot, but some of the people staying with us didn't own a vehicle. We were on a major bus route, and many of my invited guests just walked—or stumbled—right in.

I hopped out, scanning up and down the walkway that fronted the row of rooms.

All quiet, which wasn't unusual for a Thursday mid-morning. I finally spotted life, way down at the other end of the motel, where Kevin sat at a picnic table Cesar had set out last year as part of a refurbishment and beautification project.

Like a strand of pearls around a baboon's neck.

I strolled down the walkway, bending to pick up a few windblown snack food wrappers. When I passed Griff's room, I caught part of a guitar solo from an old Yardbirds song. Griff might have been deficient in many things—probably most things—but his taste in music was top-notch, if a bit dated.

As I approached, Kevin glanced up from his phone and squinted into the sunlight. If he recognized me, he didn't let on. When I reached him, he stayed hunched over, eyes glued to his screen. On the table next to him was a balled-up paper bag and a cup of soda from Hole Lotta Love.

"Good morning. Sleep well?"

"'K."

I debated returning to my room and leaving Kevin alone to occupy himself with whatever was so fascinating on his phone. But I sat down across from him. "Did you and your mom get something to eat?"

His thumbs were busy, but he nodded at the bag on the picnic table. "Yep. Bagel sandwiches."

"Good. I hope you told Sandy that I sent you."

No response.

I observed him for a moment. Past puberty, but not quite grown into a man. Awkward movements, as if he hadn't quite gotten used to his bigger body. A patch of fine wispy hair on the chin, some darker hair forming sketchy sideburns. Most evident: an overall teenage slacker attitude. I recognized the phase because I'd gone through it. Agonizing, as I recalled, and something every kid endures, yet thinks he or she is the only one experiencing it. A pang of sympathy hit me in the gut.

"How old are you, Kevin?"

A little tune rose from his phone, he smiled, then put the phone down and gave me his attention. I guessed he'd won whatever game he'd been playing.

"Huh?"

"I asked how old you were."

He licked his lips. "Eighteen."

If Kevin was eighteen, I was a grapefruit. Fifteen was more like it. "So, you're in high school?"

An indeterminate shrug.

"That would make you, what, a senior?"

"School's out for the summer."

It was only May, but I didn't argue. "Where's your mom?"

Another lick of the lips. "She had something to do. Said she'd be back later today."

I nodded. "You're going through a tough time, huh?"

He eyed me, shrugged again. I wondered if his shoulders got sore from all the shrugging.

"Where are you guys from?"

"I don't know. Different places."

"Moved around, huh?" I spoke softly, as if Kevin were a wild animal that might get spooked if startled or confronted.

He nodded his head. Sort of.

"You know, sometimes people need someone to talk to. Someone who will listen without getting all judgy or preachy. Is there somebody like that you can unload on?"

Kevin stared off into the distance. I was pretty sure he'd heard me; I saw the faint hint of a smirk when I used the word judgy. He didn't answer me, though, which struck me as a normal reaction of a kid who felt hounded—and misunderstood—by adults. Time to move on; I'd done enough wisdom-dispensing for the time being. You had to pace yourself on these types of things.

"Okay, then." I pointed over my shoulder toward my room. "I've got a ton of stuff waiting for me. Is there anything I can do for you or your mom before

I get busy? I know a lot of people in the area who can provide help—with whatever you need."

He shrugged again and picked up his phone. *Dismissed.*

I couldn't wait to have children of my own.

Chapter Three

The Registration Office was Cesar's domain; I worked out of my own office, Room Fourteen. It adjoined my room, and while I tried to keep all my personal stuff in Room Thirteen and all my business stuff in the office, it was a losing battle. Tough to shoehorn thirty-one years of accumulated junk in a single motel room. As it was, I stowed a bunch of boxes in my parents' summer house, in my sister's house, and in a storage unit I rented a couple miles away.

I really did try to keep my office halfway presentable, in case I had to conduct a business meeting of some sort. That didn't happen too often. Most of the established suppliers and advertising sales guys conducted their business over the phone, while the new ones usually pestered Cesar in his office. But every once-in-a-while, I'd meet with somebody from the Chamber of Commerce or some local service organization who'd want to pitch me on something—something that allowed me to display the enormous civic pride the Fairfax Manor Inn exhibited for the City of Fairfax. Of course, that something always cost more money than it was worth, by a significant margin.

The Room Fourteen office was about as fancy as the rest of the place, but it had the distinction of being my creation—it post-dated my father's involvement. I'd set up an old cherry desk toward the back of the room, surrounded by a few of what an old boss used to call "visitor" chairs. Closer to the door, I'd arranged an informal seating area: two loveseats—matching—and a coffee table topped with three stacks of glossy magazines.

Off to one side I'd squeezed in a huge old-fashioned novelty gumball machine that took half dollars. Next to that, a hot/cold water dispenser. On the walls, I hung a few business-y things: A commendation from the city for participating in a July 4th Parade. A picture of a Little League team we'd sponsored years ago—when business was much better. An official proclamation we'd gotten for assisting Fairfax's finest in some kind of Neighborhood Watch thing—I never did know what that meant exactly but the framed certificate looked impressive, so I hung it up with the rest.

Now, Lia Katsaros, a reporter from a local paper called the Fairfax Observer, sat in one of my visitor's chairs. I pegged her for mid-twenties, and a big tousle of curly black hair framed a friendly face. Two huge brown eyes drew me in. A moon-shaped scar decorated one side of her chin, and I wondered how she got it. If I had a chance to slide that question into the interview, I would.

I wasn't sure why, but I'd felt a connection with Lia the moment she glided through the door.

She'd called last week eager to do a feature story on some of the City's long-time businesses, and she found our motel to be charming. From her comment, I could only assume she'd never actually been *inside* any of the rooms.

Until now.

"Thanks for agreeing to this, uh, Mess," she said. "Are you sure that's what you'd like to be called in the article?"

"Sure." I got some variation of that question all the time. At first, I used to feign offense, but that got old quickly. Now I just said *sure*.

Lia pulled out her phone and placed it on the desk between us. "I was planning to record the interview. You don't mind, do you?"

"Not at all. I'll try not to say anything controversial that might come back to ruin my chance at an elected government position."

She smiled, showing off two rows of perfect white teeth, and for a second, I forgot all about the interview.

"Ready?"

"Uh, sure."

She referred to a printout she'd placed on the desk in front of her. "Okay, first question. This motel was built back in the forties, right? When did your family take over?"

"My father bought it in the nineties, and he—and my mother—ran it themselves for about fifteen years. Then he acquired a few more motels in the area, and a couple of car washes, and a few other local businesses along the way, most of which he subsequently sold. So we've always owned it, but in the later years, he wasn't always around. He brought in a first-rate manager, Cesar Ruiz, to take over the day-to-day operations. He's still here, by the way, if you'd like to talk to him, too."

"Thanks, that's a good idea. Get another perspective." She shifted in her chair while consulting her list of questions. "Next. How long have you, personally, been associated with the motel?"

"Well, I kinda grew up here. My mom would bring me here after school and I'd do homework in the office. Sometimes I'd watch TV or read in one of the unoccupied rooms. I did a bunch of chores, too. Hauling trash. Making sure all the rooms had bibles and that the TVs worked. You know, stuff like that. Looking back, I guess it's unusual for a kid to hang around a motel, but I didn't know any different. When I was older—and certainly after I got my driver's license—I wasn't around here very much."

"And now you're back. The prodigal son."

She looked at me expectantly, but I wasn't sure how to respond. It wasn't exactly a question, and me saying simply, "Yep," seemed dismissive. I cleared my throat.

"Yes, I'm back, and..." I paused. I couldn't very well tell her I ran a haven for people in trouble trying to escape from bad situations—not without jeopardizing the whole enchilada. It wasn't the kind of thing I wanted reported in the press, not when so many of my guests wanted to fly under the radar. "... And it's sorta like I never left."

Lia nodded slowly. "In what respects?"

"Well, Cesar still works here, for one. And...I don't know. Maybe it's just a familiar feeling I get."

"Okay. Moving on. What's the biggest change over the years?"

"Beside me actually living here?"

"You live here?"

I jerked my head to the side. "Right next door. I have a very short commute to work."

"Lucky. About the commute, I mean. I'm not sure I could live in a motel, myself."

"Why not?"

"Oh, I just..." She shook her head, and something sparked in her eyes. "Nope. I'm interviewing you. How about the general area? What are the biggest changes you've seen with regard to the community?"

I answered this question—more people, more business, more traffic—and the next question and the next twenty questions. In every answer I tried to be as forthcoming as I could without divulging what really drove me to work here, and what truly inspired me to keep this place afloat.

After about forty-five minutes, she exhaled deeply and turned the recorder app off. "That's it for the questions. Now, if I could just get a few pictures."

"Uh, sure." I smoothed my hair and sat up straight.

"Not of you," she said. "Sorry. Pictures of the motel. And the old mini-golf course next door. That belongs to you, too, right?"

"Yes. Yes it does. Come on, I'll show you around."

I showed Lia around the motel, stopping here and there to let her take some pictures. Of the front façade, of the old-style neon sign, of the distinctive Registration Office. When we were finished with the motel, we headed to the mini-golf course in the adjacent lot.

My father had bought it a year after he got the motel, from an aging owner eager to sell. We'd kept it going for years, but eventually it cost more to maintain than we were earning, and my father made the difficult decision to shut the place down. Although it now was a definite eyesore after years of neglect, it sat on top of some pretty valuable real estate, so my family was determined to hang on to it until they sold the whole parcel of land.

The entire course was enclosed with a chain-link fence but there was a gate around the back. When we got there, I removed the padlock—it wasn't actually locked, I kept forgetting the combination—and swung the door open.

"Nice security," Lia said.

"Believe me, if someone wants to steal something from here, they're welcome to it." We walked onto the course, and Lia pulled out her phone. I held my arms out. "This is it, straight out of the past. Take all the pictures your heart desires, and if you want a live model, just holler."

"Thanks, but I think I'm good." She flashed a quick smile, then drifted off, phone outstretched as she started taking photos.

I leaned against the side of the starter's hut and gazed out over the familiar course. It had been built in the sixties, and, like most mini-golf courses worth a darn, hewed to a theme. Ours featured landmarks from around the world and came with its own tagline: *See the World in 18 Holes!*

Large fiberglass figures, whose bases were affixed directly into the course's concrete foundation, attracted customers and gave the course its international character. Looking back on it now, I realized how cheesy it had really been. But for kids, and for families with kids, it was kitschy entertainment at its most suburban.

A six-foot Eiffel Tower overlooked the first hole. An African lion guarded the fourth. The Statue of Liberty welcomed visitors to hole nine, and a family of kangaroos frolicked alongside the twelfth hole. A large Dutch windmill dominated the fourteenth. Now, the out-of-scale figures seemed tired and lifeless, their bright colors faded by the years, along with my memories.

One thing hadn't changed—the amount of trash that seemed to collect there. While I cleaned up the motel grounds frequently, I wasn't as diligent with the mini-golf course, lucky to get to it once a month, although I didn't remember doing it in April.

Or in March.

Or in February.

Past due.

When I was nine or ten years old, during the course's good years, cleaning up the place had been my main chore. A few times a day, I'd scour the grounds for litter—cups and napkins, old scorecards, miscellaneous stuff people would be too lazy to throw into the trashcans. I felt a sense of pride after I finished when I'd look around and not see any trash anywhere. I guessed the bar was set low for ten-year-olds.

Lia circled the course taking pictures, and every once in a while, I could catch a glimpse of her or hear her laugh out loud. Finally, she met me back at the hut. "What a great course! It must have been really cool to be a kid and have your family own this place, huh?"

"I guess. Not sure I thought that then, though." I shrugged.

She looked at me for a moment, as if I were about to say something really profound. When I didn't, she just smiled. "Well, thanks so much for the local history lesson, Mess. That was great. I never knew so much about this area."

"Not from around here?"

She shook her head. "Grew up outside of Boston. Moved here after college."

"You don't have a New England accent."

"I kinda used to have a wicked strong one." She said it with a very pronounced accent, then laughed. As she did, her moon-shaped scar smiled at me, practically begging me to ask its origination story.

I obliged. "Not trying to get personal, and I realize this might come across as unprofessional, but how did you get that scar on your chin?"

She stared at me, and I realized I'd crossed some sort of line. I hit the backspace key, hard. "Hey, I'm sorry. Please, forget I asked, okay? It was so nice of you to take the time to interview me, and here I am just intruding on your—"

She held up a hand. "Relax. I take no offense."

The scar kept smiling at me. "Look, how about letting me thank you for the interview. If you don't have anywhere to be right now, how about drinks?"

"Well ... sure. Why not? And I can tell you the entire, harrowing story of how I got my scar." She laughed, and the scar danced. "If you think you're strong enough."

I thought I was, but I wasn't always right about stuff like that.

* * *

Early drinks segued into an early dinner at a seafood dive, the Krab Shack, down Route 50. Good crabs and killer cornbread, and the rolls of butcher paper covering the tables gave the place a beachy flavor.

After a few minutes of conversation, I learned that Lia's scar was the result of a childhood accident: a pick-up hockey game on a frozen pond, a pile-up, and a sharp skate blade. The harrowing part consisted of a lot of blood, which actually didn't bother me, but Lia got queasy at the sight of it, so even as she was retelling the story, a wave of dizziness passed over her.

I held her hand until the feeling passed. Least I could do. It had been a while since I'd felt an attraction like the one forming in my gut, and I was a little nervous I'd screw this one up, too. My mind kept whispering, *go slow.* I took a deep breath and tried not to hyperventilate.

We enjoyed our food and chatted until about nine o'clock when she said she needed her beauty sleep—and had to get up for an early morning appointment. I drove her back to the motel so she could pick up her car. We said goodbye and I pecked her on the cheek and promised to call her.

I had an unfortunate tendency to forget many of the promises I made, but this was one I fully intended to keep.

Back in my office, I caught up on emails for about an hour, reviewed a proposal from Cesar about installing new shower rods and curtains, then I moved into my room to watch SportsCenter. At about 11:15, I went outside to stretch my legs. I walked around the motel, picking up trash—the wind always seemed to be blowing flotsam and jetsam onto the property where it would accumulate—thinking about how nice the dinner conversation had been with Lia.

As I came around the back corner of the building, I bumped into one of our guests.

Chapter Four

Kevin was enveloped in a dark hoodie, and he leaned against the wall, one foot up against the bricks, tough-guy style. A security light mounted high on the wall cast weird shadows onto the asphalt, making the tableau seem creepier than it was. When he saw me, he flicked away a cigarette butt and tried to look casual.

"Hey," I said.

"Oh, hey." He raised his eyebrows, feigning surprise.

"What's going on?"

"Nothing."

Technically, he was correct. Absolutely nothing was going on behind the motel. I'd been asking in the larger, more general sense. I pulled out a peppermint I'd gotten after dinner at the Krab Shack and offered it to him. He snatched it off my open palm and unwrapped it.

"Thanks."

"Sure."

He popped the mint into his mouth and let the plastic wrapper float to the ground.

"Yo, guess who has to clean this place up?" I swept my hand toward the litter.

"Oh." Kevin bent over and picked up the trash, then stuffed it—and his hands—into the pockets of his hoodie. He leaned against the wall like someone who's had a lot of practice killing time leaning against walls.

"Where's your mom?"

He shrugged and rattled the mint around in his mouth.

"I was hoping to talk to her." Not getting that chance earlier was really my fault, having gone out for drinks and dinner, then catching up on a few things rather than seeking her out. "Can you tell her I'd like to speak with her tomorrow morning?"

Kevin seemed to consider my request. "We in trouble?"

"That's what I'm trying to find out."

He met my eyes for a moment, probably to gauge my level of interest, then glanced away into the shadows.

"You're not in trouble with me, if that's what you're worried about." I softened my tone. "Are you in trouble otherwise, Kevin? You and your mom?"

"I guess you'll have to ask her." His demeanor changed, as if something had just sunk in. And I noticed a hitch in his voice, too.

"I want to help you. That's why Vell brought you here. To get away from whatever bad situation you were in and to get you going in a more positive direction. But I can only help if you let me."

He licked his lips a couple of times, and I thought for a second he was going to say something, confide in me what terror they were running from, but he shifted back into teenage default mode and didn't answer. Why were some people so resistant to asking for a hand?

"Sometimes it helps if you talk about things."

He nodded, a thin film over his eyes.

It wasn't that long ago when I was Kevin's age—at least not so long that I didn't remember what it was like to be a confused teenager, dealing with hormones and unfamiliar emotions, with societal expectations and peer pressure. When I went through it, however, there was a huge difference: I wasn't on the run, hiding out in motels, fearful for my life. Wondering what the future held. I had a complete support system behind me to offer comfort, perspective, and advice.

Not that I listened to any of the advice or actively sought out the comfort.

"Okay, then. I'll let you get to sleep. If you or your mom need anything, I'm in Room Thirteen. Come interrupt me anytime. And remember to tell your mom I'd like to talk with her, okay?"

With a final nod, he flipped the hood over his head and slouched away, baggy jeans disappearing from sight as he rounded the corner.

* * *

Banging on my door woke me up. As I jumped out of bed, I took note of the time: 2:14 a.m. "Who is it?"

"Kevin. It's Kevin."

I opened the door, and he rushed right in, hands on his head. "She hasn't come back. She said she would, then she called, then she didn't answer any of my texts." Kevin stood in the middle of my room, breathing heavily. After a moment, he began pacing in little circles. The anxiety poured off him in sheets.

"Okay. Relax." I crossed the room and dragged a chair across the carpet. "Here. Have a seat."

Kevin looked around, eyes darting but not really landing anywhere. This was an entirely different kid than I'd seen before. Or more precisely, it was the same kid without his faux-tough shell.

"Sit down."

I took him by the upper arm and gently helped him into the chair. "Okay?"

Kevin nodded numbly.

"Now take a deep breath."

Kevin complied, sucking in a lungful of air.

"And another."

He took another deep breath and his eyes seemed to focus on me.

"Now tell me what happened. Who didn't come back?" Of course, I figured he was talking about his mother, but I wanted to get him talking so I could hear the whole story.

"My mom. She hasn't come back. She said she would."

"How about if you start at the beginning?"

"My mother. She left yesterday morning and told me she'd be back before bedtime, but she called a little while ago and said she wouldn't be coming back." He dropped his head into his hands and practically folded in half over his knees.

"Ever?"

"She didn't say, but I'm afraid ..." Kevin remained doubled over.

"Of what?"

He didn't answer.

"Kevin?"

I got up and retrieved a bottle of water from the dorm-sized fridge I kept in the room. Returned to my seat on the bed and touched it to the back of his hand. "Here. Drink some of this."

Kevin unfolded and accepted the water. Waited for him to take a nice, long sip.

"What are you afraid of?"

"I'm afraid she went back to him."

Shit. It was an oft-repeated pattern for victims of abuse. And it never worked out in the long run. "What makes you think that?"

"I know my mom. She sounded scared and when she gets scared, she runs back to him." He let out a low moan.

"Let's back up. Where did your mother say she was going when she left?" I put my hand on his shoulder and gave it a little squeeze.

"She said she had a lead on an apartment. In Philly. Or maybe it was Pittsburgh. I don't know. Pennsylvania someplace."

"How did she get there?"

"Borrowed a friend's car, I think."

"Okay. What did she say when she called you?"

He took a deep breath. "She said her 'plans' had changed, and she needed to check some other things out, and she wanted me to ask you if it was okay if I stayed here for a while longer."

"Hmm." I parsed a few scenarios in my head. Nicole didn't seem the type to just abandon her kid. "Let's call her and see what's going on, okay?"

I picked up my phone from the nightstand.

"She said she was getting rid of her phone."

"What?"

"That's what she said, and when I tried texting and calling her back, she didn't answer."

Why would she call her kid, then get rid of her phone? Didn't make any sense to me. "Humor me. What's her number?"

Kevin recited the number and I dialed. After a few rings, it rolled into voicemail. I left a message for her to call me. "Maybe if you told me why you had to leave your home we can come up with some ideas of what's going on."

Kevin ran a hand through his thick hair. "I don't know. Mom said to keep my mouth shut."

"I can understand your mother wanting to keep your family business private. Absolutely. But in this case... " I paused, letting Kevin add whatever reason he wanted. No matter how tough this kid wanted to be, no matter how tough he acted, he was still a kid. And at the moment, he was all alone.

A few tears dribbled down Kevin's cheek. He nodded, more to himself than to me. Then he sat up a little straighter and cleared his throat. "My stepdad kicked the crap out of Mom on a regular basis. Finally, she couldn't take it anymore, so when he went to work yesterday, we took off. That's the short version."

I nodded. If I had to bet the title to the motel on one single explanation, that would have been it. Domestic abuser. I'd seen it a hundred times, which, of course, was one hundred times too many. Unfortunately, this problem was right in my wheelhouse. "Believe me, Kevin, when I say I can help you. I've helped dozens of people like you and your mom. It's not easy breaking free and starting fresh, but you two have taken the most important first steps. You've recognized the problem and removed yourselves from the situation."

I only prayed Nicole hadn't gone back to her husband to try to make things right. "Do you have any idea where she might have gone?"

"Nope. Not a clue. She just said she had some more things to do, but she didn't say what or where. Sorry."

"Okay. Why don't we come at this from another angle?" I smiled, knowing this could go downhill very quickly. "Tell me a little about your stepdad."

Kevin pressed his lips together and breathed through his nose. I couldn't get a read on his emotions, beyond the fact they weren't happy ones. "What do you want to know about him?" he said, in a slow, measured way.

"What does he do for a living?"

"Works in a warehouse. He drives a forklift."

"Where?"

Kevin shrugged. "He's moved around in the last year or two. Someplace in Falls Church, I think. He was talking about quitting and getting a job in construction. He doesn't really tell me much."

"Okay." I scratched my chin, buying a moment to think. It would be nice if I didn't feel compelled to know much about the past of people I put up at the motel. I didn't want any prejudices, biases, or pre-conceived notions to interfere with giving people a fresh start. But as idealistic as that all sounded, I often had to dredge the dark past in order to illuminate the future.

"Where did you and your mom live?"

Kevin cocked his head, obviously debating whether to answer the question. Just as I didn't want to saddle people with my assumptions about their past, people in trouble often didn't want to look backward either. Too painful, most of the time. After all, they'd uprooted their entire lives to escape it.

"We live in an apartment in Annandale. A dump, really."

I knew it would take a while before he referred to his former residence in the past tense. "Address?"

He told me exactly where he lived, and I jotted it down on the back of a pizza delivery menu I found on the nightstand. "Does she have any friends or family she might have crashed with?"

It took a few painful minutes of teeth-pulling, but I was able to compile a list of Nicole's friends, along with a half dozen relatives. Kevin scrolled through his phone, and we attached a few phone numbers to the names.

"One more question," I asked. "How old are you really?"

He looked into his lap and mumbled, "Almost fifteen."

After I was done with the interrogation, Kevin still looked agitated, but I think we'd retreated from Defcon 5. I'm sure he felt some measure of relief now that he'd shared his problem with someone.

I glanced at the clock and since it was still the middle of the night, I had more sack time ahead of me. But I had a scared teenager in my room.

"This is what we're going to do." I stood, hoping Kevin would take the hint. "In the morning, if your mom hasn't returned yet, we'll make some calls."

"If she went back to him... " His breathing quickened.

I didn't want him spinning out again. I gripped him on the shoulder. "Kevin. The best thing to do right now is get some sleep. Things will look brighter in the morning, they always do. Come on, I'll walk you back to your room."

Kevin's eyes dilated and his feet stayed glued to their spot on the carpet.

"Have you had any sleep tonight?"

He shook his head.

"You must be exhausted, huh?"

A small nod.

"Then off to bed." I smiled and tried to lead him along by the arm. The more I pulled, the more he resisted.

I sighed. "How about if you take the other bed and sleep here, in my room?"

Another small nod.

"Okay then."

I gathered up three armfuls of dirty clothes from my second bed, walked next door to my office, and dumped them on the couch. When I returned, Kevin was already in bed.

"Goodnight, Kevin."

"Goodnight," he murmured.

Three minutes later, he was snoring soundly.

"Don't worry, Kevin," I said to my sleeping bunkmate. "I'll see what I can do about locating your mother tomorrow."

Chapter Five

I managed to get a few more hours of fitful sleep, and when I rolled out of bed, Kevin was still zonked out. He lay on his back, face devoid of emotion. If I didn't know better, I'd say he was at peace with the world, and hopefully in his dreams, he was.

I decided to let him sleep. If I remembered my teenage habits, he might very well sleep all day long. Maybe I'd have located his mother before he got up.

I dressed quietly, then left a note on my pillow for Kevin to call me, along with my cell number. I slipped out and called Vell on my way across the parking lot toward Sandy's place. He answered, full of pep, and I told him I needed to talk to him, ASAP, but didn't say what about. He didn't ask, but agreed to meet me for breakfast as long as I was buying.

Why should this morning be any different?

When I got to the bagel place, Sandy was behind the counter attending to a line of other customers, so I just waved hello as I took my usual booth. The morning was her busy time, and while I waited, I used my phone to catch up on the news or send a few emails or play a few games to get my mind revved up. If I was especially hungry, I'd go back into the little kitchen and fix my own meal.

If Sandy or Crystal ever minded, they never said so.

Sandy Beech—her parents had a sense of humor, evidently—had eclipsed the seventy mark a few years ago, but she acted like someone thirty years younger. She'd been a cook in the Navy, served in Vietnam, and had never gotten slinging hash out of her system. She'd adopted a daughter when she'd gotten back to the States, and now her adult daughter worked in the restaurant, too. Although they billed it as a bagel café, it served a wider variety of breakfast and lunch items.

I didn't think Sandy cared as much about the food as she did about her customers. Everyone in the area knew Sandy and how big her heart was.

This morning, though, I started calling Nicole's family members. I didn't want to alarm anyone until I heard more, so I told them I was calling from Kevin's school about a missing field trip permission slip and that I'd gotten their number from the emergency contact sheet. No one had seen her lately, so all my clever subterfuge went to waste.

Fifteen minutes later, Vell bounded through the doors and headed directly to my table.

"Order yet?"

"Good morning to you, too," I said. "Nope."

"I'm famished."

Sandy had been busy serving others since I'd gotten there, but the minute Vell arrived, she came rushing over, yielding the counter to Crystal. "Hello, Marvelous."

"Hello, Beautiful."

Sandy was the only person I knew who could mispronounce Vell's given name, on purpose, without getting a swift correction. I thought about pointing it out to Vell, but it was an innocent ritual they had, so who was I to get in the middle of their little lovefest? Of course, if I called him Marvelous, he'd slug me in the gut.

"You boys want the usual?"

Both Vell and I nodded. Peanut butter on a whole wheat bagel and a banana for me; Scrambled eggs, a double order of bacon, and a stack of pancakes for Vell. When you found something that worked, you stayed with it.

"Okay." She turned her head and yelled at her daughter in the back. "Same old, same old." Then she slid into the booth next to me. "The food'll be right out. As you can see, the morning rush has subsided."

Hole Lotta Love was now a whole lotta empty.

"So what's been going on? I feel like we haven't talked in ages."

"I was in here the day before yesterday," I said.

"That's an eternity to me, honey." Sandy's gravelly voice was probably a vestige of a pack-a-day habit in the service.

"I think you met our newest guests. Mother and son."

"Teenage boy. Real quiet. Dark hoodie?"

"That doesn't narrow it down much, does it?" Vell said.

"That's him. Was the mother with him?" I said.

"Not that I saw. Ordered a couple of bagel sandwiches though, if I recall. Said to put it on your tab." She elbowed me. "So I did. Gave myself a pretty good tip, too. Thanks."

Whatever it was, it wasn't enough. "Mother didn't come back."

Vell leaned forward. "What do you mean?"

I gave them the bare-bones version, omitting Kevin's after-hours freak-out.

A little while later, Crystal delivered our food. "Here ya go, guys."

"Thanks. Looks delicious."

Sandy held out her arms, and Crystal helped her out of the booth. "Okay, gents. I'll leave you to it. Good luck finding her, and if there's anything I can do, let me know."

"We'll probably need sustenance to complete our mission," Vell said. "Extra vittles, too."

Sandy smiled as she and Crystal walked away.

"Vittles? What are we, cats?" I asked Vell.

He pointed his fork, loaded with scrambled eggs, at me. "Nicole's gone? That ain't good. We have to find her. Mama will kill me if something happens."

"That's why we're here. To come up with a strategy."

"I knew there was a good reason you were the brains of this outfit."

"First of all, there's no outfit. Second of all, you're right about the brains."

Vell snorted and shoveled another forkful of food into his face.

"As you can imagine, Kevin is terrified that Nicole went back to his stepdad."

"What do you think?"

"I don't really know her well enough to say, and many women do return to a bad situation, but they just left him and that took a whole lot of guts. I would think she'd stick it out a little longer."

"So where is she?" Vell asked.

"That's the question. And we need to find the answer, or the kid's going to melt down. He gave me the names of some friends and family. I've already called those who I have numbers for, no luck." I ate a bite of my bagel, chewed slowly, thinking.

Across from me, Vell inhaled his food as if it would disappear in ninety seconds.

"What do you know about their situation?"

Vell halted his food destruction to answer. "I figure the old man is whipping on her. She finally got up enough nerve to make a break for it. No one came out and told me that, but I'm pretty good at overhearing stuff and piecing little clues together. Like Sherwood Holmes."

"I think you mean Sherlock Holmes."

"No, I don't. Sherwood Holmes was a guy in my third-grade class. Smart SOB, always coming up with the right answers. Probably a professor by now."

I doubted that. Vell was only twenty-three years old. "I was thinking I'd swing by her place—her old place—and see what's what. Although I sure hope I don't find her there."

"Amen, brother," Vell said, mouth full.

"Assuming she's not there, I'll go check out Nicole's place of employment. Maybe they have some idea where she might have gone."

Vell put his fork down long enough to catch his breath. "What do you want me to do?"

"You're tougher than me, so why don't you dig into the stepdad? See if he knows something. Kevin wasn't exactly sure where he worked, some warehouse in Falls Church. I figure with your connections, you should be able to find him, Sherwood."

"So, you're the brains *and* the comic relief of this outfit. It's always the

White guy, isn't it?"

I stuffed the remainder of my bagel into my mouth and grabbed the banana for later. "Don't worry, I got the check." I rose to leave.

Vell looked up from his pancakes. "In that case, I think I'll order some vittles to go. Never know if I'll have time to get lunch, hunting down the stepdad and all."

I hollered goodbye to Sandy on my way out.

* * *

When I got back to the motel parking lot, my car was gone. Most people might panic, but this happened to me on a fairly regular basis. I had a standing "open car-door policy." In other words, if one of my invited guests needed to borrow my wheels, they could.

I left the keys under the driver's floor mat. All I asked was that they sign it out in the Registration Office. Which was exactly where I went. I stepped inside, and the over-the-door bell rang. A moment later, Cesar appeared, smile on his face. When he saw it was me, the smile faded.

"Oh. Morning, Mess."

"Hey Cesar. How are things today?"

"Fine. No issues." He arched one eyebrow. "Looking for your car, perhaps?"

"As a matter of fact... "

"The young ladies in Room Three borrowed it. Said it was for a job interview. Said they mentioned it to you."

"They mentioned the interview, just didn't say they needed my car. I hope it goes well. After so much bad luck, a job would really help them out."

"Making money is a good thing, that's for sure," Cesar said, more pointedly than he had to.

"I still need a car, though."

Cesar stared at me, waiting for me to ask to borrow the motel's courtesy vehicle. I owned the place—more or less—so I didn't really have to ask, but since Cesar ran the place, I felt I owed him that respect.

"Could I please borrow the limo?"

Our limo was a five-year-old Accord with a magnetic sign that stuck to the side reading The Fairfax Manor Inn.

Without a word, he reached under the counter and produced the keys. "Could you wash it when you're done? And don't mess up the inside, okay? You never know when we'll have to drive a guest someplace—a real live paying guest."

I saluted. "You got it."

Before I left, Abraham Lincoln Ruiz, Cesar and Diego's nine-year-old, emerged from the back. "Hi, Uncle Mess."

"Hey, Abie. How's it going, big guy?"

"Good."

"Shouldn't you be in school?"

Abie made a face. "Dentist appointment."

I made a face back. "Bummer."

"Did you know that even though the wolverine is the University of Michigan's mascot, they almost never see wolverines in that state?"

"No, I didn't know that."

"Did you know that a badger is related to a wolverine and that their homes are called setts?"

"What are you studying in school, weasels and friends?"

"Weasels are part of that family, too. Along with polecats and ferrets, and—"

Once Abie got on a roll, he was hard to derail. "Hey, did *you* know I saw a weird-looking animal behind the motel, near the dumpsters yesterday? I could have sworn it looked like a hippopotamus."

Abie laughed. "There aren't any hippopotami around here! That's the word for more than one hippopotamus. Hippopotami."

"I know. I said it was *like* a hippo. It had two horns on its head—I think it's called a *horn*opotamus." I put my index fingers alongside my head and made snorting noises while I stamped my feet.

After a moment, I looked up to find Cesar staring at me, unamused. Abie stood next to his father, sporting the same flat-line expression.

"Maybe it was just a stray cat, after all," I said. "But a real big one."

Chapter Six

The motel's Accord was a much better vehicle than my dilapidated Civic in all respects—newer, cleaner, peppier, more features, no lingering odor of food or trash piled up in the back seat. I didn't drive it much, but I had to admit that it came in handy. Uncle Phil had pushed for its purchase right after my father gave up control of the motel, thinking we could compete with some of the higher-end places in the area if we offered to pick up guests from the Metro or even from Dulles Airport. Never mind that there were sixty better hotels—legitimately—closer to the airport.

I'd once suggested to Cesar that I drive the car exclusively; I reasoned that driving around with the motel name affixed to the side would be great marketing, but he'd simply shaken his head. I'd gotten the message.

I supposed it was the right call, considering my track record with cars.

I took Route 50 east inside the Beltway, then turned off onto a side street. A few miles winding through neighborhoods, a couple of U-turns, and I found the apartment building where Nicole and Kevin lived.

I pulled up to the curb across the street and turned off the engine.

From the outside, the building looked like a dump. Four stories tall, the white brick façade was crumbling in places, and parts of it had turned black, unevenly, as if someone had forgotten a corncob on a grill. The frame of a bicycle—no wheels—sat in a small grassy patch that served as the building's front lawn. A few battered cars were parked in a tiny lot off to one side.

Unfortunately, the apartment building fit in perfectly with the surrounding area. On my side of the street, a stand-alone business of some sort had been boarded up. Graffiti filled one brick wall and about ten busted shopping carts had gathered in a corner of the sloped parking lot.

Half a block up the street, two overturned trashcans spilled their contents onto the sidewalk; traces of the escaping garbage could be seen forty yards in every direction.

I sat in my car for a few minutes, observing. People came and went on foot and in cars, none wore smiles.

I climbed out, locked the car behind me, and crossed the street. The lock on the building was busted—no surprise. I went in, and since Kevin said they lived in apartment 202, I found the staircase, pushed open the fire door, walked upstairs and down the corridor to the opposite end.

At the apartment door, I hesitated, listening for sounds from within.

All quiet.

I rapped on the door with my knuckles, not quite sure what I'd say if Todd, Kevin's stepdad, answered.

I didn't have to worry because nobody answered the door. After about three minutes, I gave up and moved on to 204. This time, my knocking got a response.

"Hello," a voice said from inside the apartment. "Who is it?"

"My name's Mess," I said. "A friend of Nicole's. I was wondering if you'd seen her?"

"Hang on."

After some fumbling around with the locks and latches, the door swung open. Maybe the oldest person I'd ever seen stood there. I tried not to breathe too heavily, afraid she might blow over.

"Friend of Nicole's?" she asked.

"Yes. And Kevin, too."

Her eyes narrowed. "Todd?"

"No ma'am. Never met him."

"Best if you kept it that way. He's a bastard, he is." She shuffled aside. "Care to come in? I can't stand too long. I got nothing of value, so if you're thinking about stealing something, you've come to the wrong place."

I followed her in and she plopped down into a Queen Anne chair facing a TV about four feet away. I stood, leaning against the ancient pressed-wood entertainment center.

"Have you seen Nicole?" I asked.

"What did you say your name was? Les?"

"Actually, it's Mess."

"Mess with an M? What kind of name is that?"

"It's a nickname, actually. Had it since I was a kid."

A game show was on the television, and her eyes keep flitting from it to me and back again. "I'm Betsy."

"Pleased to meet you." I smiled and told myself to go slow. Vell was always harping at me to do a better job of exercising patience. Which was ironic, coming from him.

"How do you know Nicole?"

"Friend of a friend, I guess you'd say. Have you seen her lately?"

Betsy put a finger to her chin. Thought. "I saw her a few days ago. But I heard her—and that bastard husband of hers—day before yesterday, I think." She shook her head. "Terrible, all that constant carrying on over there. Pity her, and the boy. They didn't deserve what they got."

"What's that?"

She kept shaking her head but didn't answer right away. After a prolonged silence, she said, "Once I had to call the cops. But... " She reverted back into head-shaking mode.

"Seen him around since then?"

"Matter of fact, no. Ain't seen nobody since their last argument. Terrible, just terrible."

"What's terrible?"

Betsy kept her eyes fixed on the screen. Out of the corner of my eye, I could see some lady jumping up and down as if she'd just won a car.

"I'm trying to help Nicole and Kevin. It would help me if I knew what kind of situation they're in here."

She shifted her gaze in my direction. "He treats them awful bad. Physically, you know, and other ways. *Every* way, really. I've been telling her for years she should... " More head shaking.

"Well, I think she's finally taken your suggestion. She and Kevin have come to me for help. But I need to talk to her, real bad. Do you have any idea where she might be now?"

"She's safe? And the boy, too? Praise the lord." She closed her eyes and mouthed a silent prayer.

"Betsy?"

Eyes sprang open.

"Any idea where she might be?"

"I think she has a sister. In California. And I know she's got a few friends from around here, but... I'm afraid I don't know their names."

"She go to church? Play bridge? Shop at a certain store?"

"I wish I could help you, I really do. But I don't know much about what she does." Betsy scowled. "Ask me about that bastard, I could tell you some things."

I perked up. "Okay. I'm all ears."

"I saw him in the hallway last week, and I tried to ignore him, but he comes up to me, all friendly-like, laughing and making small talk. I think he believes that if he's nice to me, I won't call the cops on him." She pointed a bony finger my way. "That's a crock, I can assure you."

I didn't doubt her for a second. "What did you talk about?"

"He talked. I listened, only for as long as it took me to get inside my apartment."

"What did he say?"

"Said he got a new job with Benton's Furniture. Warehouse supervisor. Seemed proud of it. I don't care if he's the Prince of Wales—if he beats his wife, he should be locked up."

No argument there. "What's he look like?"

"Big. Strong. Like a football player or a lumberjack. Slicked back black greasy hair. Permanent sour puss. Big nose. Wears boots all the time, too. Always the strong ones like to pick on the small ones. He's a coward, that's what I say. If I was twenty years younger... " She gritted her teeth—or maybe it was her dentures—and made a fist. I wouldn't mess with her at any age, that's for sure.

"Do you think he's at work now?"

"Don't know. Haven't seen or heard him in a couple of days. If we're lucky, he had a heart attack and is lying on his floor, right now, dead and cold as a mackerel." She crossed herself and raised her eyes toward the ceiling. "Forgive me, Jesus, but you know I'm right."

* * *

I called Vell from the car. "Nobody's home at Nicole's apartment."

"No shock there, compadre."

"I talked to a neighbor, and she confirmed the stepdad is, in her words, a bastard. She told me he works at the Benton Furniture warehouse. Know where that is?"

"Not off the top of my head, but they have this great new invention, the Internet, where you can find practically anything."

"Can you find your sense of humor there?"

"I'll Google it."

"Have you found out anything else about the stepdad?" I asked. "Or do you expect me to do all your work for you?"

"You get what you pay for."

"I owe you a quarter. Now tell me what you know about him."

"Know his name is Todd Payton. Know he's ex-Army. Know he places bets with Jimmy the Raisin. Know he hangs out at that scuzzy joint Gerry's and gets into a lot of bar fights and wins most of them. Know the names of a couple guys he runs with. Also know that Nicole is his second wife, and they've only been married a couple years. Know that he's a mean SOB."

"Find all that on this Internet thing?"

"I got my own personal Internet, on the streets. People see me coming, they're dying to tell me stuff. Think of me like Vellipedia."

Vell had a point; whenever we went anywhere, he always bumped into people he knew. "Must be nice to be so popular."

"With great power comes great responsibility. Where are you going next?"

"Nicole's place of business. You?"

"Now that I know where Payton works, I think I'll pay him a visit. As it happens, I'm in the market for a new chiffarobe."

I clicked off.

* * *

Nicole worked as a receptionist for a Ford dealership. I entered the showroom and was immediately accosted by an eager sales guy. "Good afternoon." He checked a fancy watch on his wrist. "Yep, just barely afternoon. You picked a good day to buy a car."

"Well, I'm not— "

"You'd look awesome in a new Mustang." He held out one arm so I couldn't get by him, and with the other, he tried to guide me over to check out a gleaming Mustang.

"I would, but I just got out of prison and I don't have a job," I said.

His smile evaporated. "Service department is around the corner."

"Actually, I'm looking for Nicole Payton."

"Who?"

"Receptionist. Nicole?"

He shook his head, as if I'd asked him to calculate the cube root of seventy-four. "Sorry. I don't know all their names."

"Maybe if you point me to the receptionist's desk I can take it from there."

"Sure." He jerked his thumb over one shoulder across the showroom floor. "Over yonder. And if you ever need a car, don't forget, my name's Kyle. You really would look great behind the wheel of a Mustang."

I made it to the receptionist area without being harassed by any other salesperson. The receptionists sat behind a huge semi-circular counter that jutted out into the cavernous showroom. Several workstations had been strategically placed around the perimeter of the counter so that between them, the receptionists could survey the entire sales floor. Presumably, they could then point out any unattended customers and alert the nearest vulturific salesperson.

At the moment, two of the three workstations were occupied, so I moseyed up to the closest one. "Hello. I'm looking for Nicole Payton."

The lady, a striking brunette with ruby red lips, flashed a 500-watt smile. "I'm sorry, Nicole isn't here today. I'd be happy to help you."

"Thanks, but I'm a friend of hers and... " I smiled back, but I'm sure mine was a good deal dimmer. "Do you know when she's scheduled to work again?"

"Just a minute." She switched her attention to the computer screen on her left, clicked the mouse a few times. Behind her, another woman at the copy machine glanced in my direction, then looked away quickly. Too quickly.

The receptionist turned toward me. "Well, she was scheduled for today. Called in sick, I guess."

"Did she leave a number where she can be reached? It's important I get in touch with her."

The lady kept smiling—a well-trained receptionist, no doubt—but shook her head. "I'm sorry, even if I had that information, I couldn't give it to you. To protect her privacy, of course."

"Of course. Thanks."

I stepped away, then turned back, looking for the woman at the copy machine. She'd left the reception area and was heading for a row of glass-walled offices that lined the back of the showroom. I drifted in that direction, picking up a truck brochure—Ford Tested Tough—along the way, and I pretended to read it as I followed her.

She ducked into the second office from the left and immediately picked up the desk phone before her butt even hit the chair.

I strolled by her office and read the nameplate: Angela Damone, Support Staff Supervisor. I kept strolling and circled back around until I found a spot on the showroom floor where I could keep an eye on her, as I leaned against an SUV.

Ten seconds later, a different sales guy came up to me, lupine grin on his face. I cut him off with a "just-looking-if-I'm-serious-I'll-let-you-know-thanks" and waved him off.

He shrugged and peeled off to practice his powers of persuasion on some actual customer.

I picked up Angela again through her office window. She spoke into the phone, and the way her lips moved without pausing made me think she was leaving a message. She pressed a few numbers, then spoke into the phone again. A few moments passed, and then she left what seemed like another message. She repeated this routine twice more, although she stopped between the third and fourth call to consult her cell phone.

After she hung up the final time, she shook her head, and I didn't have to be a mind reader to know she was clearly agitated. Angela sat there, just staring into space.

Were her phone calls related to me asking about Nicole? Hard to know, but it sure seemed likely. I contemplated my next move. I could make up some excuse to talk to her, but buying a car just to get some information was a bit extreme. Apply for a job here? Follow her home?

Or, I could just fall back on the truth.

I started toward her office when my phone rang. I didn't recognize the number, but I answered anyway, readying my "please take me off your list" reply.

"Hello."

"This is Kevin."

"Oh, hey, I see—"

"Did you find my mom yet?"

"Working on it. How are you doing?" It was only early afternoon. I figured with all he'd been through, the kid would have slept until dinnertime. He was giving teenagers a bad name.

"I'm okay, I guess."

"Did you get something to eat?"

"Not yet." A pause. "Where are you, anyway?"

I could tell he was still wound up, but he sounded a lot calmer than he did last night. Or, rather early this morning. "I'm at the Ford dealership now."

"Where my mom works?"

I started to hit him with a snappy comeback, purely out of reflex, but held my tongue. He deserved kindness, not sarcasm. "That's the one. Hey, do you someone named Angela who works here?"

"That's Angie. Her boss."

"They get along?"

"I guess so. We went to some holiday party at her house last year."

"Are they close?"

"Close?"

"You know, do they hang out together?"

"I don't know." A long pause. "Are you coming back soon?"

I figured I'd need to meet with Vell to see what progress he'd made. We could do it at the motel as easily as any other place. "Sure. On my way back now. See you soon."

Kevin hung up, and I shoved the phone back into my pocket. Across the showroom, two other people entered Angie's office and spread out some papers. Looked like a meeting was about to begin.

I swung by the receptionist counter and snagged a business card so I could call Angie later. As I headed for the exit, I waved to Kyle who was standing by himself next to a racy car with a shiny metallic finish.

I had to agree with him. I really would look awesome behind the wheel of a Mustang.

Chapter Seven

Back at the motel, I parked the courtesy car behind the office and went in to return the keys to Cesar.

"Good afternoon, Mess."

"Afternoon." I slapped the keys on the counter. "Thanks."

"Did you fill it up?"

Crap. "I forgot. Sorry. Want me to do it later?"

Cesar shook his head and let out one of his too-common exasperated sighs. "No, thanks. I'll take care of it."

"Did Avia return my car yet?"

"Not that I'm aware."

I made a mental note to check in with them to see how the interviews were going. "Okay. Thanks." I turned to leave.

"Is now a good time for our meeting?" Cesar asked.

I spun around slowly. "Meeting?"

"The one you postponed from Wednesday. Which you'd postponed from the previous Friday. Which you postponed from the previous Tuesday. Our weekly meeting that we haven't had for a month."

"Oh. That meeting." I was more of a big-picture guy than a details guy. "What was it about again?"

Cesar looked at me the way a father would look at his son who was trying to concoct a story to explain missing curfew. "We need to go over last month's numbers. We need to discuss the proposal for the shower rods. We need to discuss the agenda for the upcoming Chamber of Commerce meeting. We need to talk about repairing one of the vending machines. And whatever you'd like to discuss, too, of course." He ticked the action items off on his fingers as he recited them.

"Sounds like a long meeting. And I'd like to give it the time it deserves. But today... " I held out my hands, palms up. "Today I'm swamped. Let's do it tomorrow. Say 2 p.m.?"

"There's something else, too."

My heart sank. The way he said it sounded serious, and all kinds of tragic scenarios sprang to mind, Cesar leaving among them. If he quit, I'd have to step in and run this place day-to-day. And I could think of no faster way to have Uncle Phil bigfoot his way in, after my inevitable crash. On the other hand, Cesar was known to exaggerate and blow things out of proportion, and he was always telling me about the time he had played Captain Hook in a community theater production of Peter Pan, as if that explained something. It might have, but I never had a clue what.

"Yes?" I held my breath, bracing for the worst.

"It's a matter I think we need to discuss at length, sitting down, relaxed, when we both can concentrate." He tipped his chin up and all but huffed. "And obviously you have more important things to take care of right now."

I had a distraught teenager in my room whose mother had gone AWOL. Whatever drama Cesar had brewing could wait. "I'm sorry, I really am. But I'm trying to locate this kid's missing mother. You know how it is, right?"

"I do indeed," he said. "I do indeed."

* * *

As soon as I got back to my room, I sent Kevin over to Sandy's to get some lunch—he'd had a late breakfast—and waited for Vell in my office. He got there a few minutes later and promptly dumped all the clothes covering my couch on the floor so he could have a place to perch. Then he stretched out, his usual pose. "You should keep this place neater. How do you think you'll ever sucker some poor girl into becoming your wife if she sees what a slob you are?"

"I was hoping my natural charm would overcome any of my other short-comings."

"Ain't that much charm in the universe. I were you, I'd try to be neater."

"Uh huh. Did you locate Todd Payton?"

Vell smiled. "I confirmed that he does work at the furniture warehouse, but he wasn't scheduled to come in today."

"Did you buy a chiffarobe?"

"No. Shoddy construction. After that, I went to his apartment, too, and asked a couple of delinquents loitering around if they knew what he drove. They were pretty sure he drove a black SUV."

"That's great! There are probably only 50,000 of those in the area. We'll have him in no time."

Vell nodded. "Yeah. You're probably right. But do you think they all have a giant skull-and-crossbones decal in the back window and funky rims?"

"You could have led with that."

"And spoil your feeble attempt to humiliate me? I don't think so." Vell interlaced his hands behind his head. "I put the word out to let me know if anyone sees his ride."

"Good." I wasn't sure how Vell did it, but he had a street army willing—and eager—to work for him. Hopefully, it would just be a matter of time until someone spotted Payton's SUV and let us know.

"How about you? Any progress?"

I told him more details about my conversation with Betsy, and I told him about Angie, at the Ford place.

"You think she called Nicole? Tell her you were asking about her?"

"Could be. Or maybe she just remembered she forgot to feed her cat and was trying to reach a neighbor. I'll follow up with her, see if maybe she knows where Nicole is. Or at least how to reach her."

"Worth a try."

"Mama give you any insight into this? What their situation is, more explicitly? What their plan is? I'm sure they don't expect to stay here permanently."

"'Course not. Who lives in a motel?" Vell gave me a deadpan look.

"I work here, too."

"Sure, sure." Vell nodded in super slo-mo. "Mama just told me they needed some serious help. And not to screw up. We'd better find her cuz I don't want to face Mama's wrath. She can holler with the best of them. And when she's done hollerin'... " Vell punched his fist into his palm.

Having been on the receiving end of a few tirades, Vell was understating things. "We'll find her."

"Sure. Where's the kid, by the way?"

"At Sandy's. Stuffing his face, I imagine."

"How's he doing?"

"How would you be doing if your mother was AWOL?"

A huge grin materialized on Vell's face.

"Speaking in general terms, not in your particular case." I picked a pen off my desk and chucked it at him. It sailed over his head and bounced off a picture of the motel taken back when my father bought the place. Back when the paint was fresh, the parking lot wasn't cracked, and the mini-golf course next door was thriving. "He's scared, mostly. Heck, he'd be plenty scared if his mom was standing here, right next to him, and not who knows where. Lot of turmoil to get his head around."

"You got that right." Vell rose from the couch. "I'm going to check out a few of Payton's favorite spots, including Gerry's. I'll let you know if I find him."

"Don't approach him if you find him. Better if we do that together."

"What? You don't think I'm tough enough?"

"You're plenty tough, Vell. I just hope you're not stupid enough. By now, Payton's probably figured out his wife and kid ran out on him and he's liable to be pretty mad. No telling what he might do."

"I'll keep you posted," Vell said. Then he left.

* * *

I pulled out my phone and the business card I got at the Ford dealership.

Punched in the number and asked for Angie Damone. I got transferred and ended up on hold for about five minutes. I hung up, hit redial, and got the same person who answered before. Probably the one I talked to in person, the one with the megawatt smile and bright red lipstick.

"I'm trying to reach Angela Damone. I just called and got stuck on hold."

"Oh. Can you hold again?"

"I'd rather not."

"Then may I take a message for her?"

"I really need to speak with her directly."

"And what is this regarding?"

I took a quick breath, telling myself I'd have a better chance of getting what I wanted if I played nicely. "It's a personal matter, and it is pretty important. I'd be very grateful if you could locate her for me."

I thought I heard a sigh, then, "How about this? I'll transfer you back again. If she doesn't answer, you can leave a message. When I see her, I'll make sure to tell her you called and left a message." She lowered her voice. "It's possible she's just out back on a smoke break. If so, she'll be back in ten minutes, okay?"

"Sure, thank you very much."

"My pleasure. Hang on while I transfer you and have a nice day."

Angie didn't pick up, so I left a semi-cryptic message with my phone number. I put the odds at 60-40 against that she'd call me back.

Next, I called Sandy. "Hey, good looking."

"Hey yourself. That kid you sent over is going to eat all my food."

"I'm sure he'd get sick before it was all gone."

"I'm not sure how to take that," Sandy said.

"That's okay, I'm not sure how I meant it. How's he doing?"

"Hard to tell. Every time I try to talk to him, his mouth is full. The only time he comes up for air is to ask for something else to eat."

"That's fine. Just keep track and put it on my tab."

"No."

"What do you mean, *no*?"

"This is one of your humanitarian projects, right?"

"I wouldn't put it that way, exactly, but yeah, he and his mom are in need of a little TLC."

"Then it's on the house."

"Thanks, but I can't—"

"Shut your face. I'll decide who I give food to, not you. At least for today. You worry about finding the kid's mother, okay? I'll worry about making sure he's well fed."

"Thanks, Sandy. You're all right."

"Don't get carried away. After today, it goes back on your tab." She winked at me. "You want me to continue keeping an eye on him?"

"If you don't mind."

"I don't mind. I'll get him to clean the bathrooms or something."

"About time someone cleaned them."

"Goodbye, Mess."

I got up to stretch my legs. In one corner of my office, a Nerf basketball hoop hung over a closet door, so after taking a few minutes to locate the orange foam ball—under the couch next to a dust bunny about the same size—I shot a few hoops. Mostly trick shots, banking the ball off the back wall with just the right spin with a few 360-degree spinning slam dunks thrown in the mix.

On a real basketball court, Vell could destroy me, even if he played on his knees. Here, with my deft skill and hours of practice working the angles and the trick shots, the playing field was leveled, so to speak. On a good day, I could hold my own against him in a game of H-O-R-S-E.

But today wasn't an especially good day. I tossed the Nerf ball onto the floor, flopped into my chair, and wondered about Nicole and Kevin's situation.

What must it be like to live under threat of getting beaten in your own home, by your husband? What must it be like to watch your stepfather brutalize your mother? Wouldn't it create some tremendous internal pressure to have two people in your family always fighting? And not just squabbling but going at it physically.

Of course, it wasn't even close to being a fair fight. Payton outweighed Nicole by a hundred pounds or more.

Whatever Todd Payton had been doing to Nicole had most likely been happening for a long time. I didn't think Todd just woke up one day with violence on his mind—and in his fists. What had transpired to cause Nicole to act now? An especially bad beating? A threat of something even more heinous? Some imminent danger to Kevin? I figured there were a lot of mothers who might put up with certain things when it came to themselves, but had an entirely different measuring stick when it came to their children.

I thought back to when I was Kevin's age. Like most other kids, I just *knew* my parents were stupid, strict, judgmental, anal, out-of-touch. It wasn't until I turned twenty-one or twenty-two before I realized I'd been the one out-of-touch—they were still controlling, all right, but not nearly as bad as I'd believed. Regardless of how I felt as a teenager, I still knew, on some level, that if I was in a desperate situation, my parents would always be there—to support me, to root for me, to love me.

They had my back, whether they showed it or not.

I couldn't imagine what Kevin was going through, not knowing those things.

I felt my pulse quicken and my anger rise. At Todd. At Nicole. At fate.

I closed my eyes and took a couple of slow, deep breaths. Whenever I worked with people in dire, often hopeless, situations, I had a tendency to get caught up in their emotional maelstrom. And I usually found that to be counterproductive to helping them solve their problems. There was a place for compassion, certainly. Maybe even a place for a *lot* of compassion. But as soon as my emotions began to cloud my thinking, to push me toward *tilt*, it was time to step back and concentrate on actionable items. Move down the checklist. Kevin and Nicole didn't need someone else wallowing in despair.

They needed a solution.

And right now, Nicole was missing, and Kevin was in rough shape.

I picked up the phone to make a call, but it rang before I had a chance. "Hello?"

"This is Angela Damone from Fairfax Ford. May I please speak with Mr. Hopkins?"

"This is Mess."

"I'm sorry I missed your call earlier. What can I do for you?"

Truth or not truth? In this case, maybe half-truth. "I was calling about one of your employees, Nicole Payton."

A pause. "Yes? Is there a problem?"

"Well, I came into the dealership, and... " So far, true. "This was last week, and she was going to hook me up with the best salesperson and we got to talking and she mentioned her son, Kevin." So much for sticking to the truth.

Another pause. "All our salespeople are excellent. Why don't I transfer you to our sales depart— "

"No, no, that's okay. During our conversation, Nicole mentioned that her son was interested in a basketball camp. I have some information about one I think Kevin might be interested in, and I was hoping to give it to Nicole."

This time, there was silence.

"Hello?"

"Kevin plays soccer."

Busted.

"You were in here earlier today, asking for Nicole, weren't you?"

Busted again. "You're her friend, right? I'm trying to help her, but I need to talk to her."

"How do I know that?"

"I guess you don't."

"No, I don't. And what do you get out of it? What's your interest?"

"I don't have an interest," I said, about to add that I "just like helping people." I didn't, knowing how that might sound like a total crock, even if it were mostly true.

"Sure. A do-gooder." Angie paused, and I waited for her to say something, anything, else, but there was just silence.

Kevin had given me his mom's phone number, and I'd left a bunch of messages for her. Maybe she'd respond to her friend. Or her boss. "Look, I know you're trying to protect her, but if you know how to reach her, please tell her to contact her son. He's worried, and rightly so."

"What do you mean?" she asked.

"He hasn't seen her for a day, and she hasn't answered his texts."

More silence, and I pictured Angie scratching her chin as she decided how to play this.

"Are you saying that you know where Kevin is, but you don't know where Nicole is?"

"That's exactly what I'm saying."

"Is Kevin with his father?"

I thought I detected a note of worry in her voice. "No. Nicole dropped him off with me."

An audible sigh of relief. "May I speak with him?"

"He's eating lunch now. And dinner, too, I think," I said.

"That sounds like Kevin."

"Don't worry, he's safe."

"Okay. I'll see what I can do, but I haven't been able to reach her either," she said.

"Thanks." I gave her my number, along with the motel's office number, and asked her to let me know if Nicole responded.

"One last thing. Kevin's relationship with his stepfather is complicated, so please don't let him go back home right now. That wouldn't be good for anybody," she said.

"Got it."

I hung up, and although Angie said she'd keep trying, I wasn't hopeful. Nicole had gone incommunicado for a reason. I mean, if you're not going to answer your own kid's texts...

I couldn't shake the feeling that something bad—really bad—had happened to Nicole.

I picked up my phone and punched in a number. A nasal voice answered, "Hey, Mess."

"What's up, Detective?"

"Chasing bad guys. The usual. What's up with you? Harboring the homeless? Nurturing the needy? Mending the marginalized?"

I'd known Eric Ostervale since we were both goof-offs in Mr. Payne's tenth-grade history class. He went on to be a cop and was recently promoted to detective. A good guy, despite his undying love of old-time country music.

"Something like that."

"How can I help?" he asked.

"I'm trying to locate somebody. A woman."

"Some things never change."

I faked a laugh. "Funny. But no. She and her son came to stay with me at the motel yesterday morning. She took off and we haven't seen or heard from her. She's not returning texts or phone calls—even from her kid."

"I'm assuming she's one of your rescuees?"

"She needs a little help at this point in her life, is all. And I was hoping you could help me help her. Off the record, of course."

"Of course. Isn't that your middle name, 'Off-the-Record'?"

"Please? It's important."

"Isn't it always? Give me the details. I'll do a little digging. You can owe me one. Or maybe two, depending on how much digging I do. By the way, you still owe me for the last three favors. And fifty bucks, too."

"You know me; I'm good for it."

"That's what they all say."

I gave him Nicole's vitals and briefed him on the situation as I knew it. After I was done with the call, I put my head down on my desk and grabbed a ten-minute cat nap.

Chapter Eight

Knocking on my door startled me awake. A line of drool trailed across some unpaid invoices on my desk. For a moment, I thought the banging might just be in my head, but it started up again. "Just a second."

I got up and answered the door. Kevin stood there, holding a cup from Hole Lotta Love.

"Come in."

He came in and went straight for the couch, sitting in the same spot all my visitors chose.

"Hear from your mom?" I asked.

"Nope. You?"

"Nope. I talked to Angie. She said she'd try to reach your mom, too, and ask her to text you. On the bright side, I found no evidence she went back to your stepfather."

Kevin nodded. "She's not coming back, is she?"

"Why do you say that?"

"She couldn't take living with my stepdad, and she couldn't stand living with me, and she just took off." Kevin's words themselves were bad enough, but the deadpan, matter-of-fact way he delivered them was chilling. And it was a complete reversal of the emotional state he displayed last night. Times like this I wished I had a psychologist on speed dial.

"I don't think that's true at all. She loves you and didn't just 'take off.'" I hoped I was right. I wanted to be right. But I didn't really know anything about Nicole that would add weight to my pronouncement. And I sensed Kevin knew I was a leaky fountain spouting wishful thinking.

Kevin shrugged. "If she loved me, she wouldn't have dumped me here and run away."

"What do you want to bet she comes walking through that door later today?"

"Face it. She's gone. I bet she's never coming back. Just like my real dad. Couldn't stand raising me, so he split. Left my mom holding the bag. Now she got smart and did the same. She doesn't need me dragging her down. I mean, who needs that? Don't worry, I'm used to being neglected. I'll deal. I always do."

Time to change the subject. "You get enough to eat at Sandy's?"

"Uh huh." He held up his cup. "My second milkshake. Maybe it won't be so bad living here the rest of my life. At least I'll be well fed."

I needed to find Nicole, and fast. For Kevin's sake and for my wallet's sake.

* * *

About an hour later, Vell called. "Hey Mess. The man himself just walked right through the front door. Mr. Todd Payton."

"Where are you?"

"Gerry's. I promised you he'd show up. Man is a creature of habits."

I didn't remember any ironclad promises, but I didn't call him on it. "I'll be right there. Don't approach him. Just keep an eye on him."

"Might have to order a burger to hold my place here. You buying?"

"Sure. You can even order extra fries."

My car was still being used by a guest—this time for a doctor's appointment—which meant I needed to borrow the motel's courtesy car. When I went in to get the keys from Cesar, he was on the phone, so I didn't have to come up with any excuses for why I had neglected to deliver whatever it was I was late delivering to him.

Traffic was sluggish on Route 50—nothing unusual about that—and it took me about twenty minutes to get to Gerry's. I found a parking space in the second row, hopped out, and headed in, passing Payton's truck in the front row.

Happy Hour had just started, and the place was pretty crowded. I found Vell at a two-top tucked near the restrooms. He was about halfway through a burger, mouth still full when he greeted me with a muffled, "Hey."

I sat, and when I put my elbows on the table, the table wobbled causing Vell's soda to slosh and the ice to rattle.

"Easy, now," he said. "I don't want to be wearing my Coke."

"Sorry." I leaned in. "Where is he?"

"Ugly dude in the corner over there. Slicked back hair. Tattered shirt." He still held his burger in both hands, but he pointed with one pinky to a booth in the back, just beyond a pool table. Some burger grease dripped down his fingers. "Him and all his buddies, backslapping and grab-assing and falling all over themselves. Immature, if you ask me."

About six guys were crammed into a booth. Most wore t-shirts. Most had scruffy beards. Three pitchers stood on the table, and there was a lot of laughing and yelling and general boisterousness. After a few minutes of observation, and from across the room, Vell's assessment seemed pretty accurate. Hard to tell, but Payton appeared to be the ringleader.

"We need to talk to him."

"Can I finish my food first?" Vell asked.

"Just be quick."

Vell inhaled the rest of his burger and, with a little help from me, his mountain of fries disappeared quickly. I left fifteen bucks on the table and scooted my chair out.

"How we going to do this?" Vell asked.

If we simply walked up to his table, our chance of success seemed slim, and we'd likely come away with a few bruises. We needed some way to separate Payton from his pack of hyenas. "Hang on a second."

I went outside and took a picture of Payton's license plate number. Then I came back in and told the bartender a truck—with a skull-and-crossbones decal in the rear window—had its lights on. I motioned Vell over and we watched as the bartender went over and gave Payton the message.

"Come on," I said to Vell.

We ducked out the front and waited off to one side for Payton to emerge. A moment later, he came bursting through the door, on a beeline to his truck. Vell and I fell in behind him and when he saw his lights weren't on, he pulled up short and spun around. If I had to guess, he'd been duped like this before.

I stepped forward and smiled, trying to put him at ease. "You Todd Payton?"

"Yeah. Who are you?"

"We're looking for Nicole."

At the mention of his wife, his nostrils flared. I also noticed his hands ball into fists at his sides. Evidently, Vell saw it too because he took two steps farther to my right. "What do you want with Nicole?"

"She didn't show up for work today and... " I held my palms up, as if that explained everything.

Payton examined me, then shifted his attention to Vell. He blinked several times and I figured he was plotting his next moves. Were we enemies or were we neutral parties? Him considering us friends was out of the question.

"She's out of town," Payton said. "Now, unless you want trouble, you'd better tell me what you want with her."

"We don't want any trouble. Heck, trouble's the last thing we want," Vell said. "We just want to know if you've spoken to her recently."

Payton squinted at Vell. "You don't work at the car place, do you?"

"No," I said. Maybe if Vell and I alternated speaking, Payton's neck would get sore, and he'd capitulate and tell us where Nicole might be. "All we want to do is talk to Nicole. Do you know where she might be? Maybe visiting a friend?"

"Why all the fuss about Nicole? She do something wrong?" Payton flexed his fists, and his breathing became faster. "She say something about me? About us?"

"No." Vell had caught on to the alternate-speaking routine.

"Why do I get the sense you ain't telling me something?"

"I don't know."

Payton stepped closer, scowled.

"Okay. You deserve to know what's going on," I said.

Vell looked at me. "Are you sure... ?"

"I'm sure. Todd here deserves to know. Nicole is a finalist for a grant from the City of Fairfax Developmental Department of Intra-Agency Community Affairs."

Next to me, Vell coughed a few times, the same move I used when I didn't want to laugh in church during the sermon.

"A grant? How much?" Payton asked.

"Well, it depends on a few things, of course. Nicole needs to fill out some paperwork and the deadline is fast approaching." I looked around and lowered my voice. "I wasn't supposed to tell anyone but Nicole about this, so if you'll just keep this to yourself, I'd appreciate it."

Payton stared at me, then at Vell, trying to noodle things through. But his fists unclenched and for the first time in a while, I took an easy breath. "Sure. Who am I going to tell, anyway?"

"Thanks."

There was a long pause, and Payton nodded to some question only he could hear. "Coach sent you, didn't he? We had a deal. And I plan to live up to it. He'll get his money tomorrow, like we agreed to."

"Who are you talking about?"

Payton squinted at me, reassessed the situation. "Coach didn't send you, did he?"

"We just need to talk to Nicole. I'll give you my number in case you hear from her," I said.

"You know, I just might have an idea where she is. Hold on." He pulled his phone out and punched in a number, then a moment later spoke into it. "Hey, there. So, I'm in Gerry's parking lot and I was wondering if maybe you could meet me here. As soon as possible would be good."

He ended the call and stuffed his phone into his pocket. "Won't be long."

"Nicole's coming?" Vell asked.

"Something like that," Payton said, grin spreading. The hair on my forearms bristled.

"Come on, Vell, I think we need to be going. Right now." I moved to my left, and Payton countered by shifting to his right. He held his arms out, as if he were a bouncer trying to control a surging crowd. His eyes shifted to something behind us, and I turned around. Through Gerry's glass windows, I could see Payton's posse weaving their way through the bar, heading for the door.

"Run," I called out to Vell. I juked inside then spun around to Payton's right, while Vell sprinted in the other direction. Payton was a big lug, all right, but slow, and he'd fallen for my feint, so I had a slight lead on him. I raced for the car, then stopped abruptly, turned, and put my shoulder down, bracing for the impact.

As Payton collided with me, I rammed my shoulder into his gut, giving it a little extra juice, and finished it off with an arm bar to the chin, old-school linebacker-style. He teetered back, dazed, then lost his balance and sprawled over the hood of a parked SUV.

When I got to the courtesy car, Vell was already in the passenger seat and had opened the driver's door. I dove in, started her up, and roared off, just as Payton's buddies had managed to get him to his feet. In the rearview mirror, five middle fingers saluted our getaway.

"Whew, that was close," Vell said. "Nice hit on Payton, by the way. You play football?"

"You bet." I didn't mention I got cut three days into the high school freshmen team tryouts, after being so sore I couldn't lift my arms over my head.

"I would have liked to nail him like that." Vell pounded his fist into his hand.

"Maybe you'll still get the chance." I had a feeling we'd be seeing more of Todd Payton, and next time, he would probably be even less hospitable.

I also wondered who the heck Coach was. And exactly what kind of trouble Payton was in. I wondered if Nicole was mixed up in it, too.

Chapter Nine

We'd decided to leave Vell's car in Gerry's parking lot, rather than risk going back for it right now. He said he'd get a friend to take him to retrieve the car later, so I dropped him off at his place and headed back to the motel.

Before I'd left to confront Payton, Kevin had been pretty down, and I'd tried talking to him about it, but he shut me out like a typical teenager. I'd left him in his room watching TV, telling him I'd be back to get him for dinner.

I figured seeing a happy, well-mannered family interacting while eating a delicious, nutritious home-cooked meal might boost his spirits, but because that was a ridiculous pipe dream, I picked him up and drove him out to my sister's place in McLean.

I rang the bell and when Izzy opened the door and saw it was me, she smiled, then frowned, then leaned in to kiss my cheek. But instead of kissing me, she punched me in the shoulder. "Damnit, Mess. Why didn't you call?"

"Two for dinner?" I said.

"What?"

Kevin had retreated to the side of the porch, so I gently pulled his sleeve to bring him into view. "I brought a guest. This is Kevin."

"Oh, hi, Kevin! Nice to meet you. I'm Mess's sister, Izzy." She ran a hand through her curly black hair. Then to me, "You *really* should have called." She appeared flustered for a moment—Izzy almost never seemed flustered—then gathered herself. "Please come in and join us. We're just sitting down to eat."

"It would be rude not to." I followed her in, and Kevin trailed, three steps behind.

As soon as I entered the dining nook, my twin nieces erupted. "Uncle Mess! Hi Uncle Mess!" They scrambled out of their chairs and glommed onto me, each with a deathgrip on one of my legs. I stuck my hands out in front of me and pretended to be a zombie, walking stiff-legged around the table. "Brains! Feed me brains! I want braaaaains!" The girls giggled as only seven-year-old girls can while they hung on for dear life.

I glanced at Kevin and saw a hint of a smile, the very first I'd seen from him.

After two laps around the table, I ended my death shuffle. "Okay. Last stop. Everybody off the zombie train."

Emma and Olivia, still giggling, let me out of their clutches and hopped back into their seats.

While I'd been entertaining my nieces, Izzy had been setting two more places at the table. "Okay, here we go." She gestured for me and Kevin to sit.

I pointed to the empty seat at the head of the table. "Where's Russell?"

"Stuck in traffic. He'll be here any minute."

My brother-in-law was a high-powered lobbyist who was always stuck in traffic, on his way to or from the airport, or in some very important meeting, with very important people. Who was I to judge? His hard work paid for this very, very nice house and my nieces' private school education.

I settled in. Next to me, Kevin sat stiffly, hands clasped in his lap. I wondered when the last time he ate dinner in a setting like this was.

"Girls, this is Kevin."

"Hi," they said in unison.

A couple of baking dishes sat on trivets in the middle of the table. One held lasagna, the other garlic breadsticks. The lasagna was huge, but since Kevin had already gorged himself at Sandy's, I figured there might be enough for everyone, if I limited myself to a small portion.

"Go ahead, dig in everybody." Izzy sat and wiped her forehead with the back of her hand, as if she'd just cooked for a dinner party of eighty.

"Looks delicious." I grabbed the serving utensils and doled out some lasagna to each of my nieces, then gave a bigger piece to Izzy and an even bigger piece to Kevin. He'd been silent since we'd arrived, and I wondered what my nieces thought of him. Probably nothing special. That was one of the great things about being seven. Unadulterated innocence. If only they could hang on to that for another twenty years, the world would be a less cynical place.

"So, Mess, what's going on?" Izzy had been busy getting us set up and hadn't yet had a chance to pepper me with the inevitable questions. Although I saw her every week or so—and not much new happened in my life—she always seemed to be expecting life-shattering news from me. Living vicariously?

"The usual."

Izzy smiled. Extracting information was a game to her, a challenge, and she was a ferocious competitor who hated to lose. "How are things at the Inn? Cesar?"

"Good and good." As much as she enjoyed the questioning, I enjoyed making it difficult. Couldn't make it too easy. I mean, where was the fun in that?

I forked a bite of lasagna into my mouth and forced it down. Unfortunately, Izzy had learned to cook from my mom. Despite making a healthy dent in Sandy's inventory, Kevin didn't seem to have any problem devouring the mediocre lasagna. He'd almost finished his hearty slab before I'd taken my second bite.

I reached over, grabbed Russell's empty plate, and served him a piece of lasagna, just in case Kevin kept chowing down. Izzy glanced at Kevin and smiled at me, then went back to her own dinner.

"Kevin, if you'd like more, just help yourself."

"Thanks."

Izzy put her fork down. "Any new women in your life?"

"Nope." No matter what my relationship situation was, it hadn't taken me long to realize that answering anything else but "nope" opened me up for a long—and painful—interrogation.

"You're just a chatterbox tonight, aren't you?"

"Sorry." I swallowed some lasagna. "Hey, here's something cool. A reporter is doing an article on the motel. How it fits into the city's history."

Izzy's face lit up. "Seriously? Wow. You'll have to show me when it comes out."

"I will. She took some photos of the mini-golf course, too."

Her face got even brighter. "Do you remember the windmill?"

"Of course." The windmill hole was found on about ninety percent of miniature golf courses, and ours was no exception.

"And how we would crawl up inside that big foundation and hide? Then you would poke everyone's golf ball with a stick as it came through the tunnel? Those people had no idea what was happening. Every time I think about that, I still laugh." Izzy giggled, much as she did back then. I missed her infectious laugh.

"We had some good times there." Inside the windmill was the perfect hiding place, unobserved from the outside, cool in the shade. To this day, I wondered what some of our customers must have thought about all the giggling coming out of the windmill.

It was my favorite hole to play, too. One day, I spent the better part of an afternoon there, working out the exact timing necessary to make sure my ball didn't hit the rotating vanes. I still remembered the sequence: When a vane was pointing straight up, I'd start counting One Mississippi, and when I got to the second "i-s-s" in the second Mississippi, I'd give the ball a firm stroke, aiming two inches from the left side of the tunnel. The ball would just miss the swooping vane, curve to the right and carom off the right sideboard, then bounce off the back wall and drop into the cup. I figured I got a hole-in-one there about eighty percent of the time.

Funny. Now the windmill could be a metaphor for my life. Spinning in circles. Moving, but not getting anywhere.

"Mess? You okay?"

"Huh? Sorry. Spaced out for a moment." We *did* have some good times back then.

She gave me an odd look, then turned to Kevin. "So, how do you know Mess?"

Kevin stopped eating, stared at Izzy. Opened his mouth and shut it. Repeated that move a couple of times, then opted for a shrug.

"Ah, a disciple of the great communicator Mess Hopkins," Izzy said with mock disgust. My sister was my closest relative, and I loved her dearly. I wasn't annoyed with her probing questions but amused. And I think my amusement annoyed her. Her annoyance amused me, too. She turned to Kevin. "Did Mess tell you how he got his name? I gave it to him."

"No," Kevin said.

"I'm sure Kevin doesn't care." Just because she nicknamed me didn't mean she had to tell everyone who entered my life about it.

Izzy stuck out her lower lip at me, pouting.

"Okay. Fine." I turned to Kevin. "When I was about five, I got sent to my room and threw a tantrum. Made a giant mess. Hence the name. Thanks to my dear old sis."

"You're welcome," Izzy said, beaming.

The dinner conversation shifted to the twins' activities, and we got a rundown of Girl Scouts and pee-wee soccer and Dee Hartline's recent birthday party. After we'd finished, the girls ran off to play.

"Traffic must be terrible," I said. Russell's piece of lasagna looked lonely on the white plate. Cold, too.

"Must be." She forced a smile. "Seriously, Mess. Nothing new?"

"Not really. I thought Kevin might appreciate a home-cooked meal."

"If you'd called ahead, I would have made something a little more..."

"Edible?"

She laughed. "It wasn't that bad, was it? Kevin had seconds."

Kevin had thirds. "Just teasing. People have different strengths. You're a great mom, and that's what really counts."

"And you're a great uncle. You'd make a great father, too, but first you need to find a great girl. Don't worry, it will happen."

"I'm not worried. Are you? Because you do sound kind of concerned."

She blanched. "Not at all."

The muffled rumble of a garage door broke our moment. "There he is now."

A door opened and closed, then another opened and closed, then Russell walked into the dining area. "Hello, Mess. To what do we owe this pleasure?"

He said it as if he'd just swallowed a lemon. There was no love lost between me and Russell, and although I thought I kept my true feelings in check, he didn't care who knew he despised me. "Just visiting my sister and darling nieces."

"Uh huh." He went to the sink and washed his hands, then came back and sat at his place.

"Let me heat that up for you." Izzy grabbed his plate and whisked it to the microwave.

"Who's your friend?"

"Kevin. And, Kevin, this is Russell."

"Hello," Russell said, plenty of starch in his voice.

"Hello," Kevin replied, then set to work moving some invisible lasagna scraps around on his plate.

I once brought a homeless vet to one of the nieces' recitals and Russell never let me hear the end of it. On one hand, I understood the fierce protectiveness of his family. But did he really think I'd do anything to endanger them? I took his attitude to be a scathing indictment of his feelings about me.

Izzy returned to the table with Russell's dinner. Instead of digging in, though, he turned to Kevin. "Did you know that Mess here is always looking for people he can help? He's a real asset to the community."

"Russell, please," Izzy whispered.

He glared at her. "What? I'm complimenting your brother on his humanitarianism. A real do-gooder. I wish more people could be like him."

"I think Mess already knows what you think of his humanitarianism."

I gritted my teeth and turned to Kevin. "If you need to use the rest room, it's right through there, second door on the right."

Kevin hesitated, and I nodded to encourage him. He got the message and scooted his chair out. "Uh, excuse me."

I glared at Russell until I heard the bathroom door close in the hallway. "Look, if you've got something to say to me, now's a good time."

Russell's eyes dilated and a predatory grin appeared, and he reminded me of Todd Payton before he squared off against me and Vell. "This is my home. Where my family *lives*. My two little girls. And you bring this...this... delinquent here? Now he knows where I live and the layout of this place. Hell, he's probably casing the joint right now."

Izzy interjected. "Now, Russell, I don't think—"

Russell held his hand up. "Your brother asked me if I had something to say. I do. And I'm not quite finished."

I started to say something, too, and was met with the same hand. "If you want to save souls, that's fine with me. On some level, it's even commendable. But do not bring them around here. What did this lost kitten do? Knock over a 7-Eleven? Assault and battery? Grand theft auto? Dealing drugs to third graders?"

"Kevin hasn't done a thing, except get a terrible domestic situation thrust upon him. You can't choose your relatives, you know." Not even your in-laws, unfortunately.

"I sympathize, but..." Russell shrugged and pointed his fork at me. "Are we clear? No more down-and-outs in my house or around my family, please. If I wanted a stray, I'd go down to the pound and pick up a dog."

I rose abruptly, and my chair went screeching across the floor. "Yeah. We're clear. And you're clearly an asshole." I looked up to see Kevin standing in the doorway, face flushed. "There you are. Time to go."

Izzy sat, dumbfounded, so I bent over to kiss her cheek. "Thanks for dinner. Say goodbye to the girls for me, okay."

She mumbled something and gazed at an indeterminate spot on the far wall, away from me, away from Russell, away from the ugly scene.

"Thank you for dinner," Kevin said, face still red, not quite sure where to direct his thanks.

"You're welcome, Kevin," Izzy said, still staring in the other direction. "I hope you got enough to eat."

"I got plenty," he said.

As Kevin and I filed out of the dining area, I glanced Russell's way. He was studiously eating his lasagna, but the tomato sauce at the sides of his mouth couldn't hide his hateful smirk.

Chapter Ten

I kept my blood-boiling rage in check until we'd left McLean and gotten onto the Beltway. Then I took a few deep breaths before assessing the damage. "So, how long had you been standing there, in the doorway?"

Out of the corner of my eye, I saw Kevin shrug.

"Long enough, huh?"

"I guess."

We drove in silence for a few more minutes, while I waited for some inspirational words to come dropping out of the sky and fall into my mouth. No such luck, I was on my own. "Sorry you had to hear that. Russell can be kind of a jerk sometimes."

Kevin shifted in his seat to face me. "No, Mr. Hopkins, I'm the one who's sorry. This is my fault. If I hadn't been with you, you'd still be there. Probably having dessert right now."

"Please, call me Mess." I smiled, doing my best to lighten the mood. "You have nothing to apologize for. What Russell said was inappropriate, inexcusable, and flat out wrong. He's somewhat detached from the real world, and he thinks if he buries his head in the sand, he won't have to deal with anything he doesn't want to."

"If I had a family, I'd want to protect them, too."

"Being a human being and protecting your family are not mutually exclusive things."

"I never did any of those things, by the way. Stealing or whatever."

"I know." If this was what being a parent was like, maybe I wasn't ready. "Try to put it out of your mind, okay?"

Kevin shifted in his seat again, this time to stare out the window.

When we got back to the motel, it was almost nine o'clock. Considering the situation, I didn't see how I could send Kevin back to his room alone. I thought about calling Vell to come over and help babysit, but I was a little afraid of what kind of values Vell might imprint onto an impressionable—and vulnerable—teenager.

"You want to watch a movie or something?"

Kevin shrugged, natch, but I could tell he was pleased, but even more so, relieved.

In my room, we kicked off our shoes and settled in. I reclined in my bed, and Kevin made himself comfortable in the second bed, the one he'd slept in last night. He fussed with the covers and folded and re-folded and arranged the pillows, just so.

Looked like I had a roommate for the foreseeable future.

I let Kevin choose the movie, and he picked one about a secret agent whose only mission, it seemed, was to destroy luxury automobiles and carve up deserted warehouses with semi-automatic weapons.

I half-watched while checking my phone. Four messages from Cesar, four things I didn't want to be bothered with. I wasn't sure if he really wanted my input or if he just wanted to keep me in the loop to make me feel an integral part of the motel management. I sent him an email telling him to go with his gut, and hoped nothing came back to bite me in the ass.

Vell had left me a couple of messages, both saying he hadn't had any luck finding anyone who knew where Nicole might have run off to.

Lia also had sent me an email. She had a few questions about our interview and wanted to follow up with me. Interesting that she didn't just leave the questions in the email.

After a crazy—and extra-long—scene where the hero vanquished what seemed like an entire army of bad guys in a blaze of bullets and explosions, the movie ended.

I turned the TV off with the remote. "So what did you think of the movie?"

"Pretty cool."

"Tired?"

He looked at me, and I detected a flash of panic as he thought I might kick him out.

"Why don't you bunk here again?"

"Yeah?"

"Sure. It'll be just like summer camp."

"I never went to summer camp."

"You didn't miss much. Unless you like mosquitos and crappy food. Go ahead, you can use the bathroom first."

I turned the lights out fifteen minutes later. "Goodnight, Kevin."

"Goodnight, Mr. Hopkins."

"Look, Kevin, you're making me feel old. Please, call me Mess."

"Uh, okay. Goodnight, Mess."

* * *

I was awakened shortly after 3 a.m. by shouting in the parking lot. I threw on some clothes and told a groggy Kevin to stay put. Then I grabbed a baseball bat I kept in the closet and went out to see what the hell was going on.

Six doors down, a hulking figure stood silhouetted by the light of the Fairfax Manor Inn sign. He was waving a gun in his hand, and not your ordinary handgun, but some kind of cross between a pistol and a bazooka. No ordinary firearm would do for Griff.

I called out before approaching, not wanting to discover how itchy his trigger finger might be. "Hey Griff! It's me, Mess. What's going on?"

He didn't move for a moment, then he lumbered my way, six feet nine inches—and 360 pounds—of tightly wound muscle. Unlike Vell, Griff never played college basketball. As far as I knew, Griff never even went to college. "Heard something next door. Three guys in ski masks. Roared off in a dark SUV before I could grab them." He brandished his weapon again. "Or before I could introduce them to Roger here."

"Why don't you go put Roger back in a safe place?"

He grunted but headed for his room. I followed. From time to time, we'd have some sort of trouble at the motel. Mostly vandalism, but occasionally a fight would break out. With Griff around, the fights only lasted until he showed up. Rarely did we end up having to bother the cops.

I waited outside Griff's room while he stowed Roger. About three months ago, I'd made the mistake of entering his room. Because of his size, he wasn't comfortable on a standard bed—even two pushed together—so he'd moved the beds out. In their place, he'd created a sleeping area on the floor, all bedsheets and blankets and pillows, like some kind of rodent's nest. The rest of the room wasn't much better, and the entire effect gave a new meaning to man caves.

A minute later, Griff met me outside his room. "Have any idea what they wanted?" I asked him.

"Something in Room Eight, I'd say."

"Oh?"

"That's where the commotion came from."

"Did you check it out?"

"Not yet. They slammed the door on their way out, and I was too busy chasing them."

"All right, let's take a look." I pulled out my master keycard and got ready to stick it in the slot. We'd still used old-fashioned keys until a few years ago, but Cesar had finally convinced my parents to splurge for the electronic locks—only about fifteen or twenty years after everyone else had. Progress moved slowly at the Fairfax Manor Inn.

Behind me, I could sense the immense bulk of Griff. I bet he was hoping an intruder was still hiding in there, so his evening wouldn't be a total loss. Beating up on one guy wasn't as good as knocking heads with three, but it was something.

I gripped my bat tighter as I went to insert the card key. But the door swung open before I had the chance. The intruders must have kicked the door in and messed up the latching mechanism. I put the card key back in my pocket and slowly pushed the door in.

No one sprang out at us. The room was empty. At least I think it was, tough to tell amid all the destruction.

The intruders had left the lights on, but that's about all they'd left alone.

The entire room had been upended. They'd taken a knife to the mattresses and stuffing poked from the angry gashes. Empty dresser drawers had been tossed on the floor, and all of Nicole's and Kevin's clothes had been ripped to shreds and scattered everywhere. The TV had been smashed, as had the bedside lamp.

"Holy crap," Griff said.

A man of understatement.

I walked farther into the room, each step crunching something. The bathroom had been similarly trashed. Bottles of shampoo and lotion and tubes of toothpaste had been emptied and smeared on every surface imaginable.

On the mirror, in red lipstick—presumably taken from Nicole's toiletries—was a message: *We want the money. And we'll be back for it.*

Not a very original way to deliver a message; I'd seen it done that way dozens of times in movies. But it was effective nonetheless. My insides had turned to runny goo.

Griff peered into the bathroom. "That's not good."

"No, it isn't."

"Gonna call the cops?" he asked.

"Not sure yet. What do you think?"

"Well, I didn't get a very good look at them, or what they drove, beyond a dark SUV. So I wouldn't be of much help. And they were wearing gloves, so probably no fingerprints. And it would probably be bad for business if potential customers found out about this. So...it's up to you, boss. Cops or no cops, I'll be keeping a closer eye on things, that's for sure."

"You have some good points" I could tell Griff was taking this personally. We let him live here and paid some of his expenses, in exchange for providing security. I had no doubt this episode would make him more vigilant.

I didn't know much about Griff's background—I'd never asked, and he'd never told—but I had the feeling he'd spent part of it on the wrong side of the law. People's pasts didn't bother me much, as long as they'd turned things around. I was more a believer in the *now* and the *future.*

As far as I could remember, in those few instances when the police had been called, Griff wasn't to be found.

"Let me check with Cesar. If we decide to call the cops, I'll let you know if we'll need you."

Griff nodded tentatively.

"But like you said, you didn't really see much, so... we probably won't need you."

He exhaled. "Okay. Want me to clean this place up?"

"Naw. I'll take care of it."

I left Griff and headed across the parking lot to the registration office. I was pretty sure Fareed, the college kid who worked some of our night shifts, was on the desk, studying for finals, but I peeked through the window just to make sure. He had his nose in a textbook and earbuds in his ears, oblivious to the world around him, so I didn't think he knew about the break-in. Which was good by me, the last thing I wanted was for him to snap a picture of the trashed room and plaster it all over Twitter and Instagram.

I walked over to Cesar's unit. His two-bedroom suite had a separate back entrance that opened up onto the side of the parking lot, as well as an entrance that led out to the front office. I didn't want to wake up Abie, so instead of knocking on the door, I called Cesar and told him I needed to talk to him. He said he'd be out in a minute.

It was clear from the message on the mirror that someone wanted to collect "their" money. So I had to assume that either they knew Nicole and Kevin were staying here, or they'd made a grievous mistake and had gotten the wrong room. I'd have to check the registration information, but off the top of my head, I couldn't think of any current guests who would seem to be likely targets.

Thinking someone—this "Coach" character—had sent us, Payton had asked for more time before repaying a debt. So it was clear he owed someone money. But how did that involve Nicole? Had whoever done this thought Payton was here with Nicole? Is the debt why she ran? Was Todd Payton after her? Had Nicole stolen their nest egg on her way out?

So many questions.

An image flashed through my mind, and my stomach lurched. When Vell and I fled Gerry's, Payton could have seen the motel's sign on the side of the courtesy car. And they could have been watching when Kevin went back to his room to get some of his things before bunking in with me.

Three big guys in a dark SUV could easily have been Payton and a couple of his buddies from Gerry's. And they would have had enough muscle power to kick in the door, too, without even breaking a sweat.

Had I screwed up, big-time?

Cesar emerged from his room wrapped in a silk kimono and fancy embroidered slippers. Not a hair on his head was out of place. "What's the problem, Mess?"

"Vandals broke in and completely trashed Room Eight." I took a minute and explained, in more detail, what had happened, leaving out the message on the mirror, for now.

Cesar examined my face. "I see. Was anyone hurt?"

"No. Luckily, the room was unoccupied."

"Where are the guests?"

"The mother is still 'whereabouts unknown.' Kevin's sleeping in my room. He wasn't there when they broke in."

"Good, good. Does Fareed know what happened?"

"Nope."

Cesar made a show of looking over my shoulder into the parking lot. "Have you called the police?"

"Nope."

"Shall I do that now?"

"Well..." Until I talked to Nicole and found out what was going on, I was reluctant to get the cops involved. I didn't want to make her problems—and by extension, Kevin's—irreversible, which getting arrested had a tendency to do.

"So you think the guests might be the specific targets?"

I was about to say, "Mirror messages don't lie, pardner," but I just kept my mouth shut.

Cesar nodded, a knowing expression on his face. He'd seen me grow up through my teenage years, and he probably knew me as well as my parents, if not better. "I can understand you wanting to protect the mother and her boy by not having the police involved, although I think they might actually help the situation. But it's my responsibility—and yours, I might respectfully point out—to protect *all* the guests, present and future—of the Inn."

I didn't want to get into a pissing contest with Cesar—I never seemed to win those—especially when he was right. "Okay. How about this? We call the cops, but we inadvertently leave out a few details, like guests' names."

"And when they see the clothes and other personal belongings in the room?"

"Yeah, well, maybe we could clean up a bit first."

"And by 'we' you mean me?"

"You've seen how well I clean, right?"

"Uh huh. Why don't we do it together, then? Maybe you'll learn something."

"Sure. You go change, and I'll meet you there in a few minutes," I said.

I washed the mirror before Cesar got to the room.

When I finished in the bathroom, I returned to the main part of the unit. Kevin stood there, calmly, surveying the damage. I rushed over to him. "Come on, back to bed. There's nothing you can do about this now."

He brushed me aside and spun in a slow, three-hundred-and-sixty-degree turn. No words escaped his mouth, but I could see the terror in his eyes as he must have been thinking what would have happened if he'd been in the room, sleeping, when the goons had broken in.

I shivered at the thought, too. I wondered if Payton would have done this if Kevin and Nicole had been in the room. Or would he have done something worse?

I shivered again.

I put my arm around Kevin's shoulders. "Let's go. I'll clean this up and try to salvage what I can. Remember, this is just stuff. The important thing is no one got hurt. Don't forget that, okay? You can always get new stuff."

He nodded, still in shock, as I led him back to my room. I got him settled into bed and made him promise not to leave. The sadness in his eyes ate at me. What must it be like to know how much your stepfather hated you and your mother?

I met Cesar back in Room Eight. He'd changed into crisp jeans and an ironed t-shirt, which for him, were his down-and-dirty clothes. We were on a mission, and Cesar and I took to the task like champs.

First, we collected all of Nicole's and Kevin's clothing, sorting out the few intact items, which, all told, barely filled a plastic grocery bag. We tossed all the destroyed stuff into the trash.

After all traces of Nicole and Kevin had been removed, we wiped the place clean, making sure there were no traces of shampoo or lotion anywhere.

"We're on a roll. Might as well keep going, huh?" I said.

Cesar shook his head, smiled. "Sure, why not?"

We continued clearing the demolition debris, and we got Griff to lend us some brawn as we hauled the destroyed mattresses, lamps, busted TV, and other wrecked furnishings out to the dumpster behind the motel, then replaced it with surplus inventory from the storage unit. An hour and a half later, we'd put the room pretty much back together.

Cesar, Griff, and I stood in the room admiring our work.

"Not bad, guys," I said. "Thanks for your help."

"Good as new," Griff said.

"Just about," I said. All we had left to do was replace the TV and repair the lock mechanism. "In fact, it hardly looks like anyone broke in here at all. Be a shame to bother the cops, when there are so many more important things they could be doing. Catching dangerous criminals, and all."

Cesar slowly shook his head. "I'll call someone to take care of the door in the morning, and I'll order what we need to replenish our inventory."

"Sounds like a plan."

"Goodnight, Griff. Goodnight, Mess." Cesar left the room without looking back.

Chapter Eleven

I returned to my room and tried to go back to sleep, but I mostly tossed and turned. Judging by the steady breathing coming from the other bed, Kevin had no such problems.

I finally ended up falling asleep at about five and slept late, until about 9:30. Kevin was still asleep, so I went next door to my office for a while, catching up on emails.

When he woke up, he didn't even ask about what happened last night, as if a terrible thing in the middle of the night was a routine occurrence. Most likely, he just wanted the memory to fade, like an awful nightmare. Unfortunately for him, I had a few questions. Of course, things might go smoother on a full stomach.

"Let's get some breakfast," I said.

We both got dressed and walked across the quiet parking lot to Sandy's place. Took my usual booth and I watched as Kevin read every entry on the menu. I remembered when I could eat like a glutton without putting on weight. Those days were in my rear-view mirror, emphasis on the *rear*.

"Okay. I know what I want." He put the menu down.

"I thought you pretty much sampled everything they had yesterday."

He relinquished a small smile. "It was all good."

Sandy wasn't in yet, so Crystal arrived with some water for Kevin and coffee for me, then took our orders. After jotting them down, she practically ran off, without any small talk beyond a quick *howyadoin* and *backinajiffy*. Sandy was a world-class chatterbox, but Crystal hadn't inherited that gene. Which was okay with me, especially this morning. I had a few questions to fly by Kevin, then Vell and I had some people to visit.

"How'd you sleep?"

"Okay, I guess." His eyes didn't meet mine.

"Do you remember waking up in the middle of the night?"

"Yeah."

"Pretty scary, huh?"

He shrugged as if getting your room vandalized in the middle of the night happened every other day. His ho-hum reactions to horrible events upset me. A lot. "Well, it scared the crap out of me."

"I guess." He peeled the paper off his straw and stuck it into his glass, but his hands shook as he did it. He slurped a big gulp of water, taking an extra-long time, trying to avoid the unavoidable ensuing conversation. I'd seen lots of kids and their false bravado, and while it might provide a temporary coping mechanism, in the long run, I thought it was better to face things head on, embrace the issue, and forge ahead. I saw no reason not to try that now.

I leaned back and put my arm across the back of the vinyl seat. "I have a question."

Kevin set his glass down.

"Do you have any idea why someone would want to break into your motel room and trash it like they did?" I tried to ask the question in as even a tone as I could muster.

He stared at me for a moment, then shook his head. Earnestly. "No, I don't. Maybe it was a mistake."

"Possible." But unlikely. "Is there anyone out to get your mom?"

"Besides my stepdad?" His stare had turned into a glare.

"Do you think he could have done this?"

"Yes."

"Do you think he did it?"

Kevin shrugged.

"Why?"

"Because he hates to lose. At anything. And if he can't have Mom, then..."

"Then he'd try to harm her?"

He nodded. "Yeah. Exactly."

I considered that. A scathing—and chilling—indictment of a man. Living with someone like that, day-to-day, must have been terrifying. But what about the note on the mirror? "Do you know anything about any money your mom might have received lately? Bonus check from work? Inheritance? Anything like that?"

Kevin half-closed one eye, like I'd seen him do before when I'd asked him a question. I didn't know if he was aware of it and had adopted it as some kind of teenage affectation, or whether it was some kind of natural by-product of thinking about his answer. The more I hung around Kevin, the more I realized I had a lot to learn about teenagers. And about raising them. I'd gleaned how to interact with little girls from playing with my nieces, but teenagers were practically another species altogether.

"No. I don't remember Mom talking about any money or anything. If she had, maybe we wouldn't have had to come here, you know?"

An excellent point. "Okay. If you think of something..."

"Why do you want to know?"

"Just trying to locate your mom. You never know what bit of information will help."

"She's not coming back, is she?"

"She'll be back, Kevin. As soon as she takes care of whatever it is she's taking care of. There's no way she'd leave you behind."

Crystal brought our food, and we ate in silence. Toward the end of the meal, Kevin's phone buzzed, he looked at it, then put it aside, but his features tightened.

"Who was that?"

"Nobody." He ate another bite of waffle. Chewed. Swallowed. "Did you try talking to my stepdad? Maybe he knows where my mom is."

"Is that who just texted you? Your stepdad?"

"What? No." His gaze flitted over my shoulder. "It was just a friend. Don't worry, I didn't tell him where I am."

"Okay." I pushed my empty plate aside. "Do you know if your stepfather owns a gun?"

Kevin stared at me for a moment, then nodded his head a fraction of an inch. I wasn't surprised by his answer; in fact, I'd be surprised if a guy like Payton didn't own one. Or more. Nice to know for sure, though.

"You have a key to your old apartment, right?"

"Yeah."

I held out my hand. "Mind if I borrow it?"

* * *

My car was still on loan—to whom, I wasn't exactly sure—so I headed back to the registration office to get the keys to the courtesy car. About a month ago, I'd told Cesar I thought it would be more convenient if I just kept the keys on my own keyring, rather than having to bother him every time I needed the car. He'd thought otherwise, and after he bored a hole into my head with his steely gaze for about sixty seconds, I'd come around to his way of thinking.

I opened the door and walked into the office, and as soon as I did, Uncle Phil popped out of one of the four chairs in the miniscule area we jokingly referred to as the lobby. He took a few steps forward, making sure he crowded into my personal space, and started haranguing me.

"There you are. What's this about a break-in last night? One of your special guests acting out? We can't have that kind of thing happening here. You're going to kill our business with episodes like that." He punctuated his words with finger jabs into the air. "I demand you fill me in immediately, and we need to come up with an action plan for turning this place around."

I felt as if I'd been sucker-punched, and it took a moment for me to regain my balance. He stared at me, waiting for a response, as I took a few deep breaths.

"Okay, Uncle Phil. Relax and we'll talk about it." I glanced behind the counter, and Cesar was calmly reading the newspaper, pretending not to pay attention to my reaming out. "Let's have a seat."

"I don't want to sit. I want some answers."

I took his elbow, trying to steer him to a chair, but he flapped it like a chicken wing and shook me off. "Benjamin, this has gone too far."

Out of the corner of my eye, I saw Cesar raise his head when Phil called me by my given name, as if he thought I was going to smack the old guy in the face or something. "Uncle Phil, please. Let's have a seat and we can discuss this." I looked around. "What if a customer came in and saw us standing here, arguing like a couple of cranky old men? That would be bad for business." Of course, the odds that a customer would be walking in here on a Saturday morning at nine a.m. were pretty slim, but Phil, living in his fantasy tower, wouldn't know that.

He nodded.

I grabbed his elbow again, and he shook me off again, although not as hard as before. Progress.

We took seats next to each other, knees touching. "How did you find out about last night?"

"I called this morning to ask Cesar about the latest financial report, and his...Diego answered. Wanted to know if I was calling about the incident last night. The *incident*." He shook his head, back and forth, as if we were talking about the tragic deaths of a dozen people rather than the destruction of a couple of mattresses and a flat-screen TV.

"I don't know that I'd call it an *incident*. More like a minor dust-up. And it wasn't any of our guests going on a rampage, by the way."

I glanced behind the counter to gauge Cesar's reaction, but he'd disappeared. Obviously, Cesar had told Diego what happened, and Diego had spilled to Phil. Maybe I should try to impose some kind of gag order when it came to communicating with Phil. Cesar wouldn't like it, but it would sure make my life a lot less stressful.

"Were you ever going to tell me? You know, I promised your father I'd keep an eye on things while he was out of the country, and I take my promises very seriously. You need to keep me apprised, Benjamin. For the good of the business and for your own good, too."

"Okay. I'll try to keep you filled in." Fat chance.

"I'm not kidding around," he said. "I speak to your father on a regular basis, you know."

"Say hi for me."

"Don't be disrespectful, Benjamin. Without this..." Phil held his arms out. "You'd be working in a fast-food restaurant or something. Don't bite the hands that feed you."

I bit my tongue instead.

"Now, about last night. First, what happened to the security system you were supposed to install? We earmarked some funds to do that."

I'd used the money to help a family who'd been evicted move to a new place in Delaware. "Yeah, we need to get on that."

"And did you ever fix the parking lot lights? Vandals look for easy opportunity, you know. They like dark, vulnerable places."

That money went to help a family rebuild after a house fire. "It's on our list." I didn't see the need to tell Phil the truth about the intruders. Better he thought it was some kind of random mischief than that one of my *special guests* had been targeted. "Something like this could have happened anywhere. At any motel in the area."

"But it didn't. It happened here. Where was your Griff character, anyway? Don't we pay him to prevent this kind of thing from happening?"

"Griff scared them away. It could have been much, much worse if he hadn't been here. How about if I show you the room so you can see what a minor issue this is?"

"Finally, a good idea."

We checked out Room Eight and, predictably, Phil fixated on the still-broken door lock, rather than on the restored room. "How soon can you get this fixed? Every room not available is a potential loss of revenue."

"Cesar's got someone coming out today or tomorrow, I think."

"Good, good. I hope you know how valuable he is. If we lost him..."

"You're right about that."

"What I'm trying to say is, don't do anything to antagonize him. Whatever you do, make sure he's happy, okay?" Phil pointed his finger at me, and I resisted the urge to swat it away.

Nice to know who mattered more to Phil, Cesar or me. "Sure, Uncle Phil,"

I said. "Sure."

* * *

Vell and I stood in the dirty hallway outside Payton's apartment.

"You sure this is a good idea?" Vell asked.

"Actually, I'm pretty sure this is a bad idea."

I'd gotten Payton's phone number from Kevin, and we'd called it, but no answer.

We'd also called the Benton Furniture warehouse and asked to speak to Payton, to ascertain his whereabouts. The person who answered paged him, but when he didn't answer it, she didn't know if he'd come to work or not. Some people didn't have to work on Saturdays, she said in a tone that led me to believe she wasn't happy she was.

In other words, Payton could be reaching for the doorknob on the other side of the door at this very second.

So we were pressing our luck. At the very least, if Payton was home, it was unlikely he had his army of buddies with him in his apartment. Which meant our two against his one. Which meant we were probably only slight underdogs if things devolved into a fight. And based on how things went yesterday at Gerry's, I'd say it was a strong possibility.

I knocked on the door, three quick raps. Listened for footsteps. Nothing.

Waited a minute and tried again. Still nothing.

"Guess he's not here," Vell said. "Oh well. We can come back another time."

"Okay, we're going in," I said. "All set?"

"Not a chance. But go ahead."

I stuck the key in the lock and slowly turned the knob, tensed and ready for whatever may happen.

I wasn't ready for what I saw.

Chapter Twelve

The entire place had been tossed, just like Nicole's motel room. Except because there was more stuff, there was more destruction. By a factor of ten. And here, the broken pieces of furniture, appliances, and electronics had been mounded in the center of the main room to create a foundation of sorts. Everything else in the apartment—food, dishes, glasses, clothing, shoes, books, posters, plants, even the toilet paper—had been dumped on top to form a gigantic mountain of trash.

Whoever had done this wasn't right in the head.

"Jay-zus," Vell kept repeating under his breath.

We checked out the other rooms in the apartment. Whatever could have been moved to the main dumping area had been, and those items that were too large and heavy had been destroyed in place. The vandals had brought tools with them; it appeared that crowbars and hatchets and who knew what else had helped in their demolition.

I went to the master bathroom and checked the mirror. Another missive in lipstick. *Money Money Money. Where's our money?*

The vandals were consistent about both their method of communication and the message.

Vell hadn't said much as we assessed the damage, just kept muttering under his breath. I'd seen some truly disturbing things in my life, but this ranked among the worst.

"What is Nicole mixed up in?" Vell asked.

"Something nasty, that's for sure." I picked up an errant shoe that must have rolled off Mount Debris. A blue Nike. Someone had cut the tongue off, and I hoped it wasn't a sick metaphor for something yet to come.

Questions abounded. What role did Nicole play in this? Victim? Or something else? Where the hell was Payton, anyway? Could he have trashed his own place? For insurance? To get back at Nicole for leaving him?

I examined the junk pile a little more closely to see if any of Payton's stuff had been wrecked. Hard to tell, but I'd say everybody's belongings were ruined.

Too many questions, not enough answers.

"Anything in there worth salvaging?" Vell asked as I continued to root through the debris.

"Nah. I'm assuming Nicole and Kevin took their most important stuff with them, so there's probably nothing in here they care about. As for the rest..." I shrugged. One man's trash is another man's treasure, but I didn't think anyone could find treasure in this jumble. "Pretty hard to do this much damage without making any noise. Let's go talk to a neighbor."

Vell followed me next door to Betsy's, and she recognized me right off the bat. She let us in, offered us coffee—which we refused—and ushered us into her living room. This time, she turned the TV off so we could talk in relative quiet.

I introduced Vell to Betsy. "What kind of name is Vell? Is it German?"

"No. It's short for D'Marvellus." Vell accentuated the *Vell* very distinctly.

"Of course," Betsy said, as if she knew a dozen D'Marvelluses. "Well, I like it."

"Thank you, ma'am," Vell said.

"Don't ma'am me. Ma'am is my mother."

"Okay, sure." Vell closed his mouth, knowing when to cut his losses.

Betsy turned to me. "Find Nicole?" Hope colored her words.

"Not yet," I said.

"That's what I was afraid of." She wrung her hands in her lap. "Are you here about what happened last night?"

"Maybe. What happened last night?"

"Oh my. It was terrible, simply terrible. All that noise. And the banging shook my apartment. I should have called the police, I know. But...last time I did, Mr. Payton came over and talked to me. Scared me, he did. So last night ... I just turned the TV on real loud. No one got hurt, did they? I didn't hear any screaming. If I had, I would have called 9-1-1, for sure."

"No one got hurt, Betsy. Just some stuff got damaged. And you can always replace stuff, right?"

"Yes. Thank God." She seemed to relax a hair. "Thank God."

"About what time was it?"

"A little past eleven. I was watching the news."

"I don't suppose you saw who did it?"

She shook her head.

"Any idea how many there were?"

"Not really. At first, I thought maybe it was just Mr. Payton having a tantrum. You know, if his wife had left him. But after it went on for a while, I wasn't so sure. Thinking back, it could have been a few people. Probably was, in fact." A change seemed to come over her. She stuck her hand down between the arm of the chair and the cushion and when she removed it, she held a gun.

"Whoa, now." Vell held up his hands. "No need for that."

I held up a hand, too, and spoke in a low, smooth voice, as if I were talking to an angry mutt. "Easy, Betsy."

"If they had knocked on my door last night, I would have protected myself. I know how to use this thing, you know." She struggled to hold the gun steady, her frail hands shaking with the weight. "Living in this place, you have to know how to protect yourself. And protect others who may not be able to fend for themselves. There are children who live in this building. On this floor, even. They bothered one of those kids, I would have shot them bastards, sure as I'm sitting here."

"I'm sure you would have. But could you put the gun down now?"

She held the gun out and looked at it like she'd never seen it before. Then she slowly lowered it. "I'm sorry. I didn't mean to...It's just that..." She blinked back some tears as she stuffed the gun back under the chair cushion.

"It's okay, we understand."

Vell blew out his breath and the tension in the room eased. In one very important way, Betsy reminded me of Vell's mama. Half the physical size maybe, and without such a colorful vocabulary, and with a much softer voice and a few more years in the bank, but both ladies had huge hearts and cared about other people's welfare more than their own.

"Do you think they'll be back?" Betsy asked.

"I don't think so. I think they accomplished their mission last night."

"If they do, maybe you ought to call the cops, let them take care of things." Vell still seemed a bit rattled. Not that I blamed him. My pulse was chugging along pretty good, too.

Betsy eyed him. "We'll see."

When I was a kid and my parents said, "We'll see," it meant no. I hoped Betsy didn't operate the same way. Despite what she thought, the children in this building didn't need a near-sighted ninety-year-old with a trembling trigger finger playing vigilante. "I think Vell has a point. You should call the police. Let them handle things."

"I heard him." She crossed her arms and lifted her chin slightly.

Stubbornness, another quality she shared with Vell's mama.

I rose and Vell followed suit. "Before we go, is there anything else you can tell us about what happened?"

She screwed her face up and patted the chair cushion. A small cloud of dust wafted into the air. "I'll tell you that if they show up here again, they'll wish they hadn't."

We pondered that on our way out.

* * *

I dropped Vell off at his place, then drove back to the motel, going over the facts, trying to piece everything together. Nicole and Kevin had fled, escaping the abusive Todd Payton. Nicole had gone missing the next day. Nicole hadn't shown up for work, and none of her friends knew where she was. According to Kevin, she'd left of her own accord. But could she have been abducted somewhere along the way?

No evidence of that, but then why would she just up and go, leaving her kid behind? I could understand why she might not respond to my calls, those of a meddling outsider, but why wouldn't she respond to her son's texts and calls? Didn't sound very motherly to me.

We'd talked to Payton, and he was as advertised, a total asshole. Quick to violence, I had no trouble believing he abused his wife. And I had no trouble believing he and his friends had come after Nicole, in search of retribution or whatever.

But where did the message about the money fit? That put a wrinkle into things.

And then seeing Payton's place trashed, too? That threw more wrinkles into my working theory that Payton trashed Nicole's motel room. Unless Payton destroyed his own place. Which was entirely possible. I could think of several reasons he'd do that—he could have wanted a fresh start, he could have wanted to destroy any trace of Nicole from his life in a vindictive rage, or he could have just gone off in a drunken frenzy.

Which led me to this: We'd lost track of both of Kevin's parents, all of the Paytons' possessions had been destroyed, and someone—someone violent—was after some money.

No matter how you looked at it, things were worse now than when I'd first met Nicole and Kevin, with one very notable, and very important, exception: Payton was no longer beating on them.

I'd left Kevin with Cesar. I thought having him help Cesar with the mundane chores required to run the motel would help the kid feel more normal, while taking his mind off the hell his life had become. If nothing else, maybe Cesar would teach the kid how to answer verbally rather than shrug.

I found them in Room Four. The furniture had been moved to the center of the room, and white drop cloths had been draped over everything. Kevin held a paint roller in his hand and little flecks of white paint speckled his hair and clothing.

Next to him, Cesar seemed unmarked.

"Well, well, well. If it isn't Picasso and his able assistant Sancho," I said, entering the room, careful not to rub up against a wall.

"Don't let him distract you," Cesar said to Kevin. "You're doing great. Just remember to wipe off any excess paint and use v-shaped strokes."

"Copy that," Kevin said.

"Good. I'm going to step out for a minute and talk to Mess. If you have any questions, please ask. Better to take a moment to ask, rather than make a mistake you can't fix. Especially when we're painting."

"Okay," Kevin said, then dipped his roller into the tray and wiped it against the side to remove the excess.

Cesar and I went outside. "How's it going?" I asked.

"Fine. Better than fine, in fact. Kid doesn't mind hard work." He tilted his head at me. "More than I can say for some people."

"Maybe we can hire him on, then. Odd jobs and such."

"Maybe so." Cesar moved away from the doorway to the room, farther out of earshot. "Any luck locating his mother?"

"Not really. I don't suppose he opened up any. Mentioned something that might help us find her?"

"Not that I could determine. What's the plan here, Mess? As much as I could use a hard-working assistant, he can't stay here forever. Besides, he's got a life. School, sports, friends. He's what, fifteen?"

"Not quite. And right now, I don't think he has much of a life. But your point is well-taken. He can't stay here long-term. For now, though, we're the best he's got. So take advantage of the captive labor. Maybe spruce up the landscaping?"

"Indentured servitude isn't a thing anymore."

"So we'll pay him. Ten bucks an hour. A win-win. And I need you to watch him for a while longer, too."

"How much longer? I've got some things I need to do. You know, things that need to get done so this place will keep running."

"Not too much longer, I hope. Couple hours? I've got a meeting with that reporter who's writing a feature on us. She had a few follow-up questions."

"Oh, no problem, Mess. Maybe Kevin can watch the front desk and check in customers. Or maybe he could do laundry for all our guests. Or maybe he could overhaul our website. Or maybe he could teach Abie about the birds and the bees."

I ignored the sarcasm. "I'm sure Abie would learn a lot from Kevin. Then it would be a win-win-*win* and everybody would be happy."

Cesar sighed. "Whatever. Go. I'll watch him. You're the boss."

I wished people would stop saying that.

Chapter Thirteen

This time, Lia and I skipped the "interview in the office" part of our meeting and met right at The Krab Shack. She had arrived first and gotten a table and was already sipping a glass of wine when I plopped down in the seat across from her.

"Hi, Mess," she said, and the day's stress eased a bit.

"Hello, Lia. Sorry I was late. Day got away from me, as usual."

"Ten minutes is hardly late. And from a guy named Mess, I'd say ten minutes late was on time." She smiled, and I wasn't sure if she was somehow mocking me.

"Well, I try to be punctual—and tidy—despite my name."

"How'd you get your nickname, anyway?" Lia asked.

"From my big sister. When I was about five. I was pretty sloppy, and she thought calling me Mess was hilarious."

"Well, you clean up pretty good," she said.

"Thanks." I hadn't changed much, mess-wise, in the years since, but I had spent some extra time getting ready this evening. I flagged down our server and ordered a Coke.

"You're making me drink alone?"

"Sorry, but I think I've got a tiring night ahead of me."

She stiffened. "Thanks a lot."

"Oh, no, not you. I've got this...you know that mother and son I mentioned the other day?

"Yeah?"

"Mother still hasn't resurfaced."

"I hope she's okay."

"Me too." If something happened to Nicole, I had no idea what would happen to Kevin, but a dozen terrible scenarios flitted through my mind. Foster homes, life on the street. Things even worse.

"Have you spoken to the police?"

"I did, but it was off the record. I need to follow up on that. Maybe officially fill out a form or something." Everything I knew about filing missing persons reports I'd learned from *Law & Order*.

"Poor kid. Must be scared."

The server returned with my soda, and we ordered our meals, same as last time. They were delicious, so why take a chance on something else?

After the server left, I sat up straighter. "So, you probably have a lot of contacts in the community, huh?"

She eyed me as if I was about to ask her to borrow some money. I had some familiarity with those looks. "I guess so."

"And you probably know someone at the paper who covers the crime beat?"

She laughed. "The crime beat? This isn't the 1940s. We call it the crime desk. Guy's name is Will Stokes. Everybody calls him Shotgun."

"Tough guy?"

"Hardly. I think he got his name from a childhood incident involving a shotgun, a squirrel, and a wobbly bird feeder. I'm not sure; the story changes every time he tells it. He's a character, but he seems to know what's going on in Fairfax's seedy underbelly."

"Think I might ask him a few questions?"

"Why not? Maybe you'll get the real story behind his nickname. You know, from one memorable nickname to another. Is there a secret club for people with interesting nicknames?"

"You're funny."

"I try." Her scar wiggled and seemed to beckon me.

Our dinners came and we chatted about whatever, a meandering tour of our histories, our hobbies, our favorite flavors of ice cream. After the food had been consumed and the plates had been cleared, Lia pulled out her phone and glanced at the time. "How about right now?"

"Sure," I said. "But what are you talking about?"

"Shotgun Stokes, the crime guy. He's probably finishing up tomorrow's article right now. And he's old school, so he always goes into the newsroom to do his thing. Come on, let's go talk to him."

I paid the check, and we drove to the newspaper building.

Lia's paper occupied the first floor of an office building in the City of Fairfax's Old Town section, across the street from the Old Town Hall. Although much of the infrastructure of the Old Town area was referred to by the Old Town adjective, the demographics of this part of Fairfax were actually pretty young, influenced heavily by George Mason University, which abutted the area.

We parked next door in a public garage and entered the building through a side door, ten steps across the lobby from The Fairfax Observer offices. We went in and even though Lia worked there, the night receptionist had me sign in on the official visitor's log, which sat on her desk next to a stack of newspapers. The current issue, I assumed, with the headline *Sponsors Line Up for Spring Festival.* In the background, about a dozen people sat at cubicles, either talking on the phone or pounding the keys of their computers.

"This way" She led me through the cubicle farm to a small, windowed office that overlooked an alley. A skinny bald guy at a messy desk hunched over his keyboard. When he noticed us standing in his doorway, he barely grunted, then went back to his typing. About a minute later, he nodded to himself, looked up, and flashed us a crooked grin, although it seemed to be more directed toward Lia. "Sorry, Lia. Just putting the finishing touches on something. What can I do for you?"

"Do you have a few minutes? We don't want to interrupt anything," Lia said.

"For you, I've got all the time in the world. Come on in." He gestured at a couple of straight-back chairs pushed up against a wall. "Pull up a seat."

Lia and I dragged our chairs in front of the desk, and Lia handled the introductions. "Mess Hopkins, this is Will Stokes."

"Please, call me Shotgun."

"Uh, okay, Shotgun." I felt silly calling a grown man Shotgun, but if a guy named Shotgun wanted me to call him that, I would.

"Shotgun's our crime expert. Been at it a while, too," Lia said.

"Not that long." He smiled at her. "So, what do you need, Lia?"

"Actually, Mess is the one with the questions. He runs the Fairfax Manor Inn."

He turned to me and wiped the smile from his face. "I know the place. Very...distinctive. What do you want to know?"

I cleared my throat. "Do you happen to know a guy named Todd Payton?"

Stokes picked up a pen and began tapping it against his chin. "Heard of him. Big guy. Angry. Dumb as a bag of walnuts."

"That's the one."

"What'd he do?"

I explained, briefly, about Nicole ditching out on him, and about our altercation with him at Gerry's.

"Like I said, a peach of a guy."

"He implied that he owes some serious money to a guy named Coach. That ring a bell?"

"Coach? Like a sports team coach?" Shotgun frowned.

"I assume so."

Stokes made some *chukking* noises with his mouth. "Coach, coach. I'll have to look into that. Payton could owe anyone, of course, but if this coach guy is a big player, someone who's new on the scene, that would be interesting."

I guessed a crime reporter had a different idea of what was interesting. "Ever hear about a gang—or whatever—leaving messages on mirrors?"

Stokes cocked his head at a weird angle. "Say more."

I told him what happened at the motel and at Payton's apartment.

"Interesting. I'll have to look into that, too. This could be the basis for a very nice article. Maybe even a series of articles."

Glad to help. "I don't suppose you've heard anything about Nicole? She's sort of missing."

"Sort of missing?"

"Well, I just don't know where she is."

Stokes laughed. "I think that qualifies as missing. And, no, I haven't heard a thing about any missing woman."

"I'd really like to locate her, so if you hear anything—"

"You'll be the first to know." He glanced at Lia. "Actually, you'll be the second. I'll tell Lia, and she'll tell you."

"Thanks."

Stokes took the pen he'd been playing with and pointed it at me. "You got it, sport." He swung back around to his keyboard. "So, if there's nothing else..." He began typing without even waiting for a response from us.

Dismissed.

We got up and put the chairs back against the wall. On our way out of the office, Lia stopped and turned back. "Thanks, Shotgun."

Now he paused and glanced up from his computer, grin wide. "Anything for you, babe."

Back in the car, Lia put her hand on my forearm, just as I was starting the car. "Hang on a minute."

"Okay."

She pulled a thumb drive from her bag and handed it to me. "These are the pictures I took the other day. Motel and mini-golf. Thought you might like them."

"Thanks." I stuck it in my pocket.

"And here's a draft of the article. Well, your portion of the article." She pulled a sheaf of papers out of her bag. "Would you mind giving it a quick read? A fact check, more or less?"

"I'll put it at the top of my to-do list." I folded the papers and opened the console compartment to stuff them in, but she put her hand on my arm again. A guy could get used to that.

"How about now? There's still time before deadline, but I don't like waiting until the last minute."

"Okay, sure." I unfolded the papers, turned on the overhead light, and began reading. Her writing style was crisp and engaging, and she made the history of the motel—and its place in the larger history of the city—actually seem halfway interesting. When I got to the bottom of the last page, a sentence had been highlighted in yellow. *Charm exuded from Mess Hopkins, the handsome and witty proprietor.*

I looked up, straight into Lia's smiling eyes.

"Handsome and witty, huh?" I asked.

"I highlight the things in yellow that are completely false, so my editor has something easy to cut out."

"I see."

"Keep going. There's one more sentence."

The last sentence had been highlighted in blue. *And he's an excellent kisser.*

"What's the blue highlight mean?"

"Oh. That just indicates something I need to conduct more research on."

I had very suddenly become a big, big fan of research.

Chapter Fourteen

Lia invited me to her place, but she wasn't sure if her roommates might be around, and the last thing I wanted to do was meet new people and engage in polite conversation. So we went back to the motel and tried to make ourselves comfortable, despite the obvious challenge, namely that it's a motel room.

It's hard not to be thinking about sex, sex, sex when the most prominent furniture in the room is the bed. Of course, that's what I often thought about during dates, bed or no bed.

I supposed we could have gone into my office, but the couch in there was covered with all the stuff I'd cleaned up to make room for Kevin.

Lia started to perch on my bed, then got up and stood between the two beds. "You have a roommate?"

"What makes you say that?"

"Both beds looked slept in. And that duffel bag with clothes on the floor there is kind of a giveaway."

"Yeah, well, it's just temporary. He's occupied at the moment." At least I hoped he was. I asked Cesar to keep track of Kevin until I came and fetched him.

"This is kind of weird, Mess." She was cute—cuter—when nervous.

"Not really. Although I can see why you might think that."

"You living in a motel. With a roommate. Seems kinda like freshman year in the dorms, you know?" One of her eyebrows arched.

I sighed. "Yeah, you're right. Maybe we should go to your place."

"You'll be nice to my roommates?"

"Of course. I exude charm, remember?" I tilted my head sideways like I'd seen George Clooney do once when he was trying to be charming.

She rolled her eyes. "Okay, let's go."

I opened the door to leave and came face-to-face with Kevin and Cesar. "Hello, Mess," Cesar said.

"Hello." The four of us stood there, not speaking for a moment. I could imagine what was running through each person's mind. Kevin had probably been hoping to flop down in bed and watch TV, getting a break from Cesar. Seeing Lia put that in jeopardy.

Cesar undoubtedly wanted to divest himself from babysitting, and seeing Lia put that in jeopardy.

Lia had been hoping to research my kissing ability, but seeing Kevin put that in jeopardy.

I knew what was running through my mind and I had a feeling it matched Lia's thoughts.

I think I'd had enough practice being a parent.

Cesar broke the silence. "Hello, I'm Cesar. I run this Inn."

"I'm Lia. I'm the reporter working on a story about the Inn's history. Mess might have mentioned me?"

Cesar bowed his head. "He did, he did. But he failed to say how lovely you are."

"Thanks." Lia giggled, and it was my turn to roll my eyes.

"This is Kevin," I said, jumping in before someone got nauseated from all the saccharine.

Kevin mumbled something.

"I hate to do this to you, Mess, but Diego and I have plans. A sitter's with Abe, and Fareed is watching the desk." He waved his arms in the air and bent over, in some kind of elaborate bow. "It was nice meeting you, Lia. I look forward to reading your article. Goodnight, all." He left without even giving me a chance to beg him to take Kevin along with him and Diego, wherever they were going.

Now the three of us stared at each other. "Have a good day with Cesar?"

Kevin nodded. "Sure." He tried to get by me and enter the room, but I stood my ground.

I turned to Lia. "Kevin's my roomie for a few days. While his mom is..."

"I bet Mess snores, doesn't he?" Lia asked Kevin.

The sides of his mouth curled up for a second, and I knew that meant Lia had scored.

"Mess and I were just going to my place to watch a movie. Want to come?" Lia asked.

Kevin glanced at me then back at her. "Sure. Why not?"

I could think of a reason or two, but I kept my mouth shut.

* * *

Kevin and I got back to my room around midnight, and unfortunately Lia never had the chance to conduct her research. She did give me a raincheck, which I gladly accepted. On the ride back, I'd asked Kevin a few questions about his day, and about his mom, and about his stepfather. All I got were grunts, mumbles, and shrugs. Which was better than the emotional torrent he'd unleashed the first night when his mother hadn't returned.

In fact, after that episode, Kevin hadn't seemed emotionally distraught at all. Concerned at times, but not really invested. I wondered if he'd already come to grips with the long-term prospect of living without his mother around. If so, I thought that was very sad, indeed. Kevin was way too young to have such a hardened heart.

It took me a while to get to sleep.

* * *

The next morning, before Kevin and I had even made it over to Sandy's to get some breakfast, Vell called. Said Mama wanted to see me. Whenever it was convenient, he said.

Which meant right away.

I left Kevin with Cesar again—despite the numerous non-verbal clues Cesar was emitting—and Vell picked me up a few minutes later.

"Did she say what she wanted?" I asked, trying to prepare the best I could. I once talked with Mama unprepared, and I still shuddered when I thought about it.

"I asked, believe me." Sunday morning traffic was light, and Vell negotiated Route 50, without needing to use any of the customary DC-drivers' lane changing tricks and one-finger salutes. "But she wasn't talking."

"Crap."

"You got that right."

Fifteen minutes later, we pushed through Mama's door, Vell in front to deflect any incoming rounds.

"Hey, baby," Mama said, enveloping Vell in a bear hug. She was a tall woman, and stout, and it wasn't hard to see where Vell had come from, even removed a generation. Although Vell called her Mama, she was really his mother's mother. Both of Vell's parents had been killed in an auto accident when he was six. "I missed you yesterday."

Vell wormed out of her clutches. "Busy, busy."

"Come now, you're never too busy to visit me." She laughed, and it sounded like a thunderstorm was rolling in.

Then it was my turn. "Come here, Mess."

I got my very own bear hug. "I could ask you the same question. How come you don't come around more often?" She released me, and I swallowed a big gulp of air.

"Sorry, sorry. I need to be better about that."

"Yes, you do. Now come on in and let's get comfy."

We entered the townhouse. It wasn't large, but it was clean and tidy. In the main hallway, Mama displayed a wall of pictures arranged chronologically, and almost every one showed Vell, usually with a big grin. Some of the grins were missing teeth. With every step down the hall, Vell—the one in the pictures—got older and older, and the hairstyles and clothing fads changed. I'd seen the pictures before, many times, but they never failed to bring a smile to my face.

She led us into her living room, which doubled as her place of business. A computer workstation occupied one corner of the room, and behind it was something akin to a miniature movie set. There was a fake window, dressed in a dozen, multicolor gauzy curtains. An antique table stood next to an ancient bookcase, and both held all sorts of mystical tchotchkes—a crystal ball, a lava lamp, some voodoo dolls, a few animal skulls, candles, and a bunch of things I couldn't identify. Nor did I want to try.

For twenty-three years, Mama had been a devoted nurse, working long hours and crazy shifts to provide for her and Vell, but a balky back and aching knees made it more and more difficult. According to Vell, about eight years ago, looking ahead to Vell's college tuition, she'd started telling fortunes to augment her income. Palmistry. Tarot cards. Numerology. Dream interpretation. Reading candle wax drippings. You name it, she'd read it, as Vell once told me.

He'd shrugged the whole thing off as just a hobby.

At least until she started offering a Read-By-Skype service. The thing had gone viral, business boomed, and she was able to retire from nursing. She said she makes more now telling fortunes than she ever did as a nurse, even if you counted all the extra-pay overtime shifts. She was now even contemplating training a couple other fortune-tellers to expand her empire.

Vell and I sat on the couch, while Mama rolled her computer chair across the floor so she could face us.

"How's business?" I asked.

She closed her eyes and placed her fingers on her temples. "I see a bright future." She cracked her eyes open and delivered another guttural laugh.

"Give it a rest, Mama," Vell said.

"You may not be a believer, son, but my talents are putting food on the table and keeping a roof over my head. You have an open mind, don't you, Mess?"

"Absolutely." I wasn't sure I believed in anything Mama was peddling, but I considered myself to be open-minded, in general.

Vell shook his head. "Mama, he's just sucking up to you. Don't be trying to clown my friends, okay?"

Mama feigned offense. "Sorry, son. I wouldn't want to embarrass you."

Vell didn't bite. "Why did you want to talk with Mess anyway?"

"All business today, huh? Well, okay, I understand. You're a busy, busy boy." She glared at him.

Vell glared back. I had a feeling that if I didn't say something, the authorities would find them, in these same positions, in a week. "Mama, you said you wanted to tell me something?"

Slowly, Mama turned toward me, and her sneer morphed into a smile. "Yes. I do." She threw a glance at Vell with a curl of the lip, then focused on me again. "A client told me his brother was involved in some shady dealings, and he was real worried about him. We got to talking some more, and this man's brother broke into an apartment recently and vandalized it."

An alarm bell went off in my head. "Nicole's?"

"That's right."

Vell leaned forward and asked the obvious question, "Who is this guy?"

"As I said, a client's brother."

I opened my mouth to ask my own question, but Vell spoke instead. "I thought your interactions with clients were confidential."

"Honey, I'm a fortune teller, not a doctor or a lawyer."

"Then who was it?" Vell asked. Evidently, I'd been cut out of my own conversation.

"I may not be a doctor, but I'm not a fool, either. Telling you the man's name wouldn't be good for business, if it got out I was blabbin'."

"There must be something more you can tell us," Vell said.

"There is. Eat your vegetables, stay out of trouble, and visit Mama more often."

"That's it?" Vell asked.

"That's all I can *tell* you. Now, I'm going to get myself a glass of water. While I'm gone, whatever you do, don't be nosing around on my desk, looking for a piece of paper with a man's name on it, you hear? Oh, the dude's address might be on there, too." Mama got up and as she left the room, she reared her head back, and the booming sound of thunder shook the house.

Vell beat me to the desk by two seconds. He snatched up the paper and read the name. "I heard of this guy. Think he'd be in the mood for visitors?"

"I hope so, because I'm in the mood for visiting."

Chapter Fifteen

The dude's name was Billy Lane, and Vell recounted what he'd heard about him as we drove to the address Mama had left for us. "A loser. Had his hands in all kinds of minor crap. B & E, joyriding, even swiping packages off little old ladies' doorsteps. Don't think he's ever been inside, but that's probably because 5-0 decided he wasn't worth their time. Probably figured he'd self-destruct on his own somehow."

We parked around the corner from his house, in a run-down section on the border between the City of Fairfax and Annandale. The homes there were squat and ugly, and the yards had suffered from years of neglect. It wasn't too far from NOVA, the community college, so the area served a basic purpose—providing cheap housing for students who most likely had their hands full working while going to school, maybe even starting a family.

Based on his petty crime history, I had the feeling Lane did none of those things.

"What's our play here?" Vell walked next to me, both of us in the street because there were no sidewalks.

"Let's knock on the door, see what happens. He's probably out kicking kittens or participating in some other charity work. Making the world a better place. Just let me do the talking."

"How come you get all the fun?"

"Didn't Mama teach you to respect your elders?" I said.

"And you're what, fifty?"

Lane's house was like the other houses on the block. Unfortunately for him. An old SUV was parked in the carport, wedged between five or six dented aluminum trash cans.

Was that the black SUV Griff had seen peeling away from the motel?

The presence of the vehicle made it more likely someone was home.

As we walked up the path to the door, I kept an eye on the front windows for any movement, but all was still.

I rapped on the door frame and stepped back, motioning Vell over to the other side of the door, out of sight. Vell did as I suggested, flattening himself against the wall. Lane would be more apt to open the door if he didn't feel outnumbered from the get-go. And face it, my just-under-six-foot frame was less imposing than Vell's six-three.

There was no answer, so I thought about ringing the bell, but returned to the *rap-rap-rap* on the door. Seemed more insistent. More like something from the TV show *Cops*.

I increased the intensity and the frequency of the knocking, until I was sure the neighbors were going to answer their doors. Finally, I heard someone shouting loud, over my racket, "Shut up, dammit, I'm coming."

The door opened and a burly guy stepped forward out of the dark interior and squinted through the screen door into the bright sunlight. Shirtless and hirsute, he looked like a bear emerging from his hibernation. An angry bear. "What the hell do you want?"

"Congratulations. You've just won some Nationals tickets as part of a promotion." I moved to my left and took a few steps backward so that he needed to open the screen door to keep his eyes on me.

"What are you talking about?" His anger seemed to have dimmed. The promise of free stuff had a tendency to do that, I guessed. "I won baseball tickets?"

"You sure did." I continued moving backward, and began checking my pockets, pretending to look for the imaginary tickets. Lane tracked my progress, inching farther and farther out of the doorway.

I kept going backward until I was off the porch and onto the grass. Then I fake-tripped on something and fell down.

Propelled by the lure of free tickets, Lane ventured from his cave to help me up. I popped to my feet before Lane reached me, and Vell came up behind him.

"What..." Lane spun around, evidently sensing Vell. "What's going on? Don't think I won't kick your asses." He moved his weight forward to the balls of his feet and crouched, ready for action.

I held up my hands, a gesture of goodwill. "We just want to ask you some questions."

Lane looked at me and then at Vell, and he kept alternating, back and forth to prevent getting ambushed. "About what?"

"A recent demolition job you were on."

His brow furrowed. "I haven't done any construction work in a while."

"More like domestic destruction. You and a few buddies trashed an apartment on Hartwell Street."

His brow unfurrowed. "I ain't saying I had anything to do with that. But what are your questions?"

"Why'd you do it?"

"Why do you care?"

"We're friends of the residents of that apartment."

Something lit up in Lane's eyes. "Oh really?"

"Yeah, really."

"So?" He opened and closed his fists.

"So just tell us why you trashed it and we'll be gone. Won't bother you anymore, won't go to the cops. We'll be out of your hair for good," Vell said, breaking his silence.

"Who sent you to ask me?"

"I told you, we're friends of the residents."

"Uh huh. Where are they?"

I shrugged. "Don't know exactly where they are? Do you?"

Lane's eyes narrowed to slits. "How about this? When you find them, why don't you tell them my employer would like to talk to them? Then you can butt out of this and let the pros handle things."

Lane took a couple of steps to the side, away from where I stood, and picked up a small tree branch that had fallen. "Now, get the hell out of here, unless you want me to beat you to a pulp. And if you don't think I can handle you two chumps by myself, you're dumber than you look." He brandished the branch, and I thought I heard him growl.

Vell and I exchanged glances again. We definitely weren't dumber than we looked. We slowly backed away as Lane returned to his cave.

He didn't even ask for his free Nats tickets.

Back at the car, Vell spoke first. "You have any idea what's going on here?"

"Wish I did. It's obvious that Lane broke into Payton's apartment following someone else's orders. And it's also obvious whoever is behind the break-ins hasn't yet found Payton."

"Or the money?" Vell asked.

"Right. It's always about the money," I said, stating the obvious. "And, if we can believe lipstick mirror messages, someone wants his money back. Any ideas?"

Vell snorted. "Could be anybody. Loanshark? Bookie? Drug dealer? Somebody Payton ripped off? The Pope?"

"I doubt if the Pope lent Payton money."

"Okay, probably not the Pope. At least we can eliminate somebody," Vell said.

"You said Payton has a gambling problem so it could be a bookie. Anything else come to mind?"

"Didn't seem like the junkie type. But hell, a man could borrow money for any of a million other reasons."

"Okay, let's say Payton owes some serious money to someone, and that someone wants it back. Would explain why he's in the wind."

"Yeah, but he was out in public, at Gerry's." Vell exhaled loudly, probably remembering our little altercation there.

"But he told us he had another day to pay off, and he didn't seem worried. Like he already had the money and was ready to give it back."

"If that's true, what happened to it?"

I put the key in the ignition. "That, my friend, is a damn good question."

"And how does Nicole figure into this? If it's Payton's debt, and this guy

Coach—or whoever—is after *him*, why would *she* take off?"

I shrugged. "Dunno. Maybe she's afraid she'd be judged guilty by association. Hell, that could be the reason she decided to leave Payton *now*. Or it could be something totally unrelated."

"Or could be she didn't take off at all. Could be she got abducted. Could she have been taken as ransom? You know, pay us back or you'll never see her alive again?"

"Lane didn't seem to know where Nicole might be, and he certainly didn't say—or even hint—anything about Nicole being abducted."

"Keeping it close to the vest?" Vell suggested.

"Nah, I doubt an asshole like him could keep a secret that big without giving something away. Plus Nicole ran away from Payton. You think he would fork over serious money to get her back, just so she'd run again? He didn't strike me as that kind of guy."

"Something just don't add up." Vell's turn to state the obvious.

"That's for sure. Let's go, I want to make a stop before we go back to the motel."

* * *

We swung by the Ford dealership. I left Vell to check out the latest models and harass the sales guys while I went to see Angie. I found her in her office, talking on the phone. When she spotted me in her doorway, she ended her call with an "I need to go, I'll call you back."

To me, she said, "Please come in. And close the door."

I lowered myself into a molded plastic chair at the side of her desk, probably the same place where her employees sat when she instructed them about how to make each customer feel special. I didn't feel very special right now.

"Have you located Nicole?" she asked.

"Still looking."

She took off her glasses, pinched her nose. Held the glasses in her hand while she spoke. "This is very upsetting. It's not like Nicole to just vanish."

"I'm surprised, too. She hasn't tried to contact you? Let you know she wouldn't be coming to work?"

"You're trying to help Nicole, right?"

"Yes." The last time I'd spoken with her, she hadn't quite believed me when I'd told her that. What had happened that she now believed me?

"What I'm about to say isn't for public knowledge."

"I don't work for CNN. Your information is safe."

She eyed me. "No need for sarcasm."

"Sorry." Not everyone was bowled over by my charming wit.

"Uh huh. Nicole wasn't going to work here anymore. She didn't want her husband to be able to track her down."

"Really?" I'd been wondering about this, but Nicole disappeared before I'd had a chance to discuss her future plans with her.

"Best for everybody's safety. Wherever she relocated, I was going to put in a good word with the local dealership. She's a good worker; she won't have any trouble getting a similar job elsewhere."

"Where was she thinking of going?"

Angie smiled, patronizing me. "I guess you'll have to ask her."

I smiled back. "I will when I see her."

"I hope that's soon."

"Me too." I nodded. "Why do I get the impression you know more than you're telling me?"

"What? Why would I withhold information?" Her smile dried up.

"Because you know where Nicole is."

"I assure you that I—"

I held up my hand. "Please. I know something's off here. It's a gift I have, a finely-tuned bullshit detector. And it's beeping loudly."

She gave me a stone face.

"Look. Today, you consider me to be a friend of Nicole's, telling me she's no longer working here. Last time we talked, you didn't tell me anything, not sure whose side I was on. And I don't blame you for that; I just as easily could have been sent by Payton to find out where Nicole had run off to. But something happened in between."

"And what was that?"

"I think you've spoken to her."

Angie's stone face cracked, just a hair.

"And I'm guessing you know where she is."

More splintering of her veneer.

I rose. "Please do me a favor. Ask her to call me, okay?"

She didn't respond.

I left her office and went to collect Vell who was making race car noises as he sat in the driver's seat of a souped-up Mustang. Before leaving the showroom floor, I glanced back at Angie's office, and she was on the phone. My bet? She was informing Nicole about my visit.

Chapter Sixteen

I called Cesar from Vell's car as we drove back to the motel and asked him if he'd give his teenage assistant a break so he could meet me at Sandy's.

"Sure. He's a good kid. Works hard. Catches on quick. Kinda quiet, though."

"Typical teenager."

"Somehow, I can't picture Abe being quiet."

"Just wait. Adolescence changes everyone." I tried to keep the doom and gloom out of my voice.

"Thanks for the warning. I'll have Kevin meet you there."

Vell dropped me off at Sandy's and Kevin was sitting at what was now our usual table, playing with his phone.

"Hey." I slid in across from him.

"Hey," he said without looking up.

"How's it going?"

Kevin grunted, still mesmerized by whatever was on his screen.

I spent a lot of my time on my phone, too, but I liked to think that when I was with someone else, I paid attention to that person. "I asked how it was going."

"Okay." Head still down.

"Kevin."

His fingers danced across the screen.

"Kevin, could I have your attention for a minute?"

He didn't seem to hear me, so I reached across the table and covered his phone screen with my hand. Now his head shot up. "What?"

"I'd like to have a conversation. Could you please put your phone down?"

He frowned, and I'm sure he still wasn't used to adults—besides his mom and stepfather—giving him orders. With a sigh and a petulant face, he put the phone down on the table.

"Thank you."

He slumped in his seat.

"What were you and Cesar working on this morning?"

"Painting and other stuff." As he spoke, his eyes fell on his phone.

I reached over, took the phone, and placed it screen down in front of me. "What kind of other stuff?"

"Trimmed some bushes. Cleaned out some gross storage room."

"Sounds like fun."

"Yeah, a blast." He glanced at Crystal who was behind the counter, fielding a take-out order on the phone. "I'm hungry. Can we get something to eat?"

"Didn't you and Cesar get lunch?" It was almost three o'clock.

"We did."

Ah, growing teenage boy syndrome. "Sure. When Crystal's done, you can order something from her."

"Cool."

I lobbed a few more questions at Kevin, but he batted them all away with a shrug or a grunt. After a few minutes, he must have gotten bored. "I'm going to the bathroom, then I'm going to order. Do you, uh, want me to get you something?"

Kevin, being considerate? I tried not to let my amazement show. "No thanks."

He slouched off to the bathroom.

I sat in the booth, and that niggling feeling I'd been having, that little voice in the back of my mind that whispers snatches of sometimes indecipherable nuggets, came in loud and clear. I'd been wondering how a caring mother could take off without letting her son know where she was or how she was. I'd been wondering how a mother could leave her child behind without keeping track of how *he* was doing.

Trick question. She wouldn't.

With one eye on the hall to the restrooms, I picked up Kevin's phone and checked his recent texts. At least a dozen were from *Mom*.

Gotcha, kid.

I stuck the phone in my pocket, got up, and waited by the café door. When Kevin emerged from the back and headed to the counter to place his order, I called out to him, "Hey, something urgent's come up. After you're done eating, catch up with Cesar, okay?" Then I pushed through the door and jogged to my car, which, thankfully, had been returned.

I left quickly so Kevin wouldn't have a chance to run me down once he realized I'd taken his phone. I parked in a grocery store lot a few blocks away so I could read the text exchanges between mother and son.

When I was a kid, we used to play a game of keep-away, where two guys tossed a ball back and forth while a third guy tried to intercept it. We called it monkey-in-the-middle.

I felt like the monkey-in-the-middle involved in a game of information keep-away Nicole and Kevin were playing. From what I could tell from the texts, Kevin knew his mother was safe and sound, and she had instructed him to pretend like he didn't know what had happened to her, and to pretend that he was worried. I recalled Kevin saying, word-for-word, what Nicole's text had told him to tell me, when he sat on the couch in my office.

I bet she's never coming back.

She couldn't stand living with me, and she just took off.

If she loved me, she wouldn't have dumped me here and run away.

I thought about going back to Sandy's, busting Kevin, and getting him to tell Nicole that I was onto their ruse. But I'd be hard pressed to believe the charade had been Kevin's idea. I called up Nicole's most recent text—from about an hour ago—and typed in a response: *I need to see you.*

A couple moments later, she responded. *Something happen? U ok?*

Fine.

We talked about this. For ur safety, we can't let mess know.

I paused, trying to word my request like a fifteen-year-old. *It's real important. Can u meet me? In the parking lot of the Fairfax Heights Church? I'll be alone.*

When?

The church wasn't far, and I could be there in under five minutes, but I tried to guess how long it might take a kid to walk there from the motel. *15 minutes?*

I can be there in 30. K?

K.

I was about to hit enter, but I added the same sign-off I'd noticed Kevin use in previous text exchanges. *Luv u, mom.*

Luv u, Kev.

It was the attention to detail that mattered.

* * *

I went straight to the church and parked around the side, out of sight. There were still some cars left over from the morning's service, I guessed, but things were pretty quiet. I walked around the building, scoping out the grounds for the best vantage point, then settled on a spot in a shadowy doorway with views of the front drive and parking lot. Some parts of the puzzle were beginning to clarify, but other parts weren't coming into focus.

Why had Nicole run off and left Kevin with me? Was there something she had to do that could only be done without Kevin? Obviously, she was still in the area. Why couldn't she have stayed in the motel and done whatever it was from there?

Was another man involved? Kevin hadn't mentioned anything, but I supposed if Nicole had been stepping out on Payton, she wouldn't have told her son. But if that was the case, why come to me and the motel? Why not move in with the other man?

Maybe the other man was married, and she *couldn't* move in with him.

And I kept coming back to the money. If Nicole had taken it, and it was a big enough sum to have muscle involved, why come to the motel? Why not book first class tickets to Bermuda?

Other crazy scenarios sprang to mind, but I didn't really think space aliens were involved.

I leaned against the church wall and called Cesar. "Hey man. Kevin with you?"

"Yes. He's a bit agitated about his phone. Says he left it on the table at Sandy's, went to the restroom, and when he got back, it was missing. Thinks you might have taken it."

"Yeah, about that..."

"Seriously? Separating a teen from his phone is practically a felony."

"I'll explain later. Tell him I accidentally put it in my pocket, and I'll return it when I see him."

"I'll tell him you have it, but I'm not going to lie for you."

"Fair enough." I hated lying, but sometimes you had to do what you had to do. "Tell him I'm sorry, too. Because I am."

A sigh. "You're always sorry about something, aren't you?"

"Thanks." I hung up. Cesar had a point; I always seemed to be apologizing for one thing or another. Or both things.

A car turned off the street and curled down the church driveway. A woman drove, slowing as she circled the parking lot. Nicole searching for Kevin. She made two laps around the large lot, looking between the parked cars and scanning the adjacent lawn.

She pulled into a slot but didn't get out of her car. I stayed hidden in my little alcove.

In my pocket, Kevin's phone vibrated. I pulled it out and read the text. *I'm here. Where r u?*

The grounds were well-landscaped, so there were dozens of places Kevin could conceivably be waiting. A thick hedge separated the back lawn from the parking lot. I responded. *On a bench. On the back lawn.*

B right there.

Nicole got out and rushed across the asphalt toward an opening in the hedge. After she'd disappeared behind the greenery, I left my spot and followed her, in no big rush. She'd have to double back to get to her car.

She was about twenty yards ahead of me, ducking her head into every nook and cranny of the back lawn, checking behind every tree and bush, searching for her son. I closed the gap to about fifteen feet when she must have heard me. She whirled around, expecting to see Kevin, and when she saw me, her eyes went wide for a moment.

Then her shoulders slumped, and she just stood there, staring at her feet.

I approached slowly. While I didn't think she'd do anything rash, I didn't know Nicole very well, and I'd heard stories about mothers protecting children, at all costs. Since I didn't know what this was all about, I decided to err on the side of caution. For all I knew, she carried a piece in her purse.

"Fancy meeting you here," I said. "Come to commune with nature and embrace the word of the Lord?"

Chapter Seventeen

Nicole picked her head up, appearing unamused. "Where's Kevin?"

"Back at the motel. He's helping Cesar spruce up the place. Making a little pocket change, too." I made a mental note to remind Cesar to cut the boy a check for services rendered.

She nodded.

"Why don't we have a seat and talk?"

We alighted on a stone bench next to a flowerbed. Red, yellow, and white flowers bloomed and when the breeze shifted, we got a whiff of their sickly-sweet floral scent.

"What's going on, Nicole?"

She clasped her hands together in her lap so tightly her knuckles were white. "What would you like to know?"

"Why don't you tell me everything?"

Nicole smiled, but it wasn't your typical smile, the kind you might see when you tell a joke or when someone you love does something cute. I recognized hers as the smile of someone who's absolutely terrified, someone who knows an awful thing is headed their way, and there's nothing left to do *except* smile.

"Maybe I can help."

Her smile changed, and now it was one of amusement. "Don't think so."

"Try me. What have you got to lose?"

She licked her lips and stared at the dazzling flowers so long I thought maybe she'd gone to sleep with her eyes open. Finally, she sighed. "Okay.

You're right. What have I got to lose? I've already lost it all."

"Take your time and start at the beginning. I'm a good listener."

"My husband Todd used to be a good man. Caring. Responsible. But over the last year or so, he's changed. Gotten hard. He always drank, you know, blowing off steam with the guys, but it's gotten much worse. And he's gotten meaner, too. I guess that started when he got laid off and couldn't find a job for months."

"Must have been rough."

"It was. He started taking out his frustrations on those around him." She paused to wipe her eyes. "On me. Physically."

"How long has that been going on?"

"The violence itself? Nine months. A year." Nicole looked around the yard, at the flowers, at a birdbath, at a bench across the way. Everywhere but at me.

I didn't know what to say, and although it had taken a while to learn from my experiences, I kept quiet, realizing that there's nothing I *could* say to make things better. It's the *listening* that's most helpful.

"I thought about leaving many times. Thought about Kevin *all* the time, especially when Todd was..." She finally looked at me, fire in her eyes. "He never touched Keven. Never. If he had..."

I took her hand, and she averted her eyes again.

"Finally, I couldn't take it anymore. I talked to a friend, and we planned our escape. Got in touch with Mama and she led us to you." She let go of my hand. "I don't know if I did the right thing. I..." She choked up.

"You're scared, is all. When things settle down, you'll realize you did the right thing."

She didn't answer.

She also hadn't explained why she ran out on Kevin.

"Kevin misses his mother," I said.

"Did Kevin tell you?"

"Tell me what?"

"That I... that he..." She shook her head. "Never mind."

"No, Kevin didn't let on that he knew you were okay. He played his part well. But he's only fifteen, and fifteen-year-old boys aren't the best actors."

She flashed a wry smile. "No, I guess not."

"I don't understand why you left."

Nicole rose abruptly but didn't go anywhere. I gently grasped her wrist and pulled her down. She sank onto the bench without any resistance. "For his safety."

"Still don't understand."

"Todd has a gambling problem. A big one. And it got way, way out of hand. He owes some serious money. And ..."

"And?"

"And the people he owes want the debt repaid."

"Do you have any idea who these people are?"

"Not really. I heard Todd mention a guy named Prune or something odd like that."

"Jimmy the Raisin maybe?"

"Yeah, that's it. Raisin, Prune, whatever."

"Does Todd have any money to repay the debt?"

"He says he's been doing some odd jobs. But..." She closed her eyes for a moment. "I don't think they're the kind of jobs you get W-2s for."

"Illegal?"

"And probably immoral. I tried not to ask too many questions, hoping the whole nightmare would just go away. Pretty stupid on my part, huh?"

"Not stupid. You wanted to believe something good would happen. It's natural. Nobody wants to accept that their life has taken a wrong turn. Very hard to do."

"The signs were there. Todd got more and more physical. The drinking. The gambling. My whole world was going down the drain, and I just pretended nothing bad was going on. Pretended it was just a temporary bump in the road." Nicole sniffled.

"Don't be too hard on yourself."

"You don't get it, do you? If it was just me, I could deal with it. My bad choice, my terrible consequences. But Kevin. I screwed up his life because I couldn't do the right thing. I'm a terrible mother. That's why I took off and left him with you? I didn't want Kevin mixed up in it, if they happened to come looking for me." She swallowed, hard. "I could never live with myself if that happened."

"But if you've left Todd, I don't understand why they'd come after you."

"These people like money. They don't always think rationally. For all I know, they could think me leaving Todd was a sham." A few tears dripped down her cheeks. "Kevin told me what happened to our motel room. These people play rough."

"They do. But even rough people act in their best interests. And you have nothing to do with the money, right?"

"Oh, Mess. These are the kinds of people who like to provide incentives to their borrowers. Like, 'we'll break your arms if you don't pay us back. Now.' Those kinds of incentives."

"Have they threatened you before?"

Nicole didn't answer, but the way she didn't answer told me what I wanted to know.

I didn't press for any details. "I spoke to Todd. Couple days ago."

Nicole fixed her attention on me. "And?"

"I got the sense he was planning to pay these guys back. Then something happened, and now Todd's gone underground, and these guys still want their money."

"What happened?"

"I have no idea. Either Todd decided to keep whatever money he'd amassed, or—"

"He wouldn't have done that. He knew what they would do to him. He might be a terrible man in many respects, but he's not a complete fool, at least when it comes to his well-being."

I had a tough time believing anything nice about Payton, based on the stories I'd heard—and my interaction with him—but I recognized that Nicole might still have feelings for him, despite what he did to her. I'd seen the same pattern plenty of times, battered women still in love with their batterers.

"Maybe someone else got their hands on the money." I stared at her face, searching for any sign that *she'd* somehow taken the money.

Not a flinch.

"Any idea who?" she asked.

"Maybe one of his posse?"

Nicole nodded. "Could be. He ran with some dirtbags, that's for sure."

"Billy Lane one of them?"

"He's a piece of work, all right. They had a falling-out a couple of months ago. But... I don't know. Lane seemed..." Nicole trailed off.

"What?"

"Like a wimp. All bluster. But who knows with these guys, right?"

That's the truth. "Know anyone named Coach?"

Nicole looked at me blankly, then shrugged in a way that reminded me an awful lot of Kevin. "No."

"Were you staying with Angie?"

"No. Didn't want to drag her into this either. I holed up in a dumpy motel off the interstate."

"Whose car then?"

"Angie let me borrow it. It's her son's or something." Nicole exhaled. "I begged her not to tell you where I was, to keep it secret for Kevin's sake. I wanted to tell you, I did, but I needed to think about what's best for him."

"You should have told me where you were. Or at least that you were okay. I was worried."

"Sorry, but... I don't really know you that well, and I don't know. I figured if you didn't know where I was, you couldn't accidentally tell someone where I was. When it comes to Kevin, I can't take any chances. And I didn't want to get you mixed up in this, either. For *your* safety, you know?"

I understood why she didn't tell me, sort of. "Why didn't you just get on a Greyhound for parts unknown?"

"I thought about that, too, of course. But these men have long arms and wide connections, and I figured it just might be safer if I stayed around here. At least I have a few friends who can help me out. Like you and Mama."

She gave me some puppy-dog eyes, and for a second, I wondered if I was still being played. "Do you have any idea how much money Todd owes?"

"Who knows exactly? Todd isn't the most forthcoming guy, especially when it comes to gambling debts. Something more than fifty thousand and less than half a million."

Wide range. Not inconsequential whatever the true number. Arm-breaking money, for sure, at the low end. Head-breaking money at the top. "What if we got a message to these people that you're not involved, that you're not living with him anymore, and that you know nothing about any money?"

"I don't know." She put her hands on top of her head, elbows wide. "I don't know anything anymore, and I certainly don't trust my judgment. Honestly, I think I'd be afraid to even talk to them."

"Maybe I could do it."

Nicole turned to me. "You'd do that?"

"Look, you don't owe them anything, right? So why should they be bothering you? I'll paint it all as one big misunderstanding. They leave you alone so they can concentrate on their real target." That last part just came out, and I wasn't sure how she'd feel, thinking about Payton getting kneecapped, or worse.

Nicole winced.

"I didn't mean that—"

"It's okay. I know what you meant. But I don't know, Mess... Talking to them seems like it's just inviting trouble."

"You trust me, don't you?"

"I left my kid with you. Of course, I trust you. In fact, I trust you completely—your reputation for helping people is the reason we turned to you. It's those loan sharks or bookies or whatever you call those scumbags who I don't trust. I'd hate for something bad to happen to you on my account."

"That makes two of us. I'll be careful, I promise." With everything going on, I wondered how a mother could abandon her son. I guessed she really did trust me. Not sure if that was such a good idea. "Come on, let's return Angie's car and then go back to the motel. I'm sure you want to see Kevin. I'll put you in a different room, and we'll ask Griff to round up a few of his friends to help watch the place. You—and Kevin—will be fine, and once I get this thing straightened out, we can concentrate on getting you two set up someplace else, more permanent. You could really use a fresh start."

That all sounded nice and easy and heartwarming, but I had a feeling it was going to be harder than it sounded. Much harder.

* * *

I told Cesar my plan to put Nicole and Kevin in Room Six and have Griff invite a few friends to a sleepover in Room Five. Cesar wasn't happy—understatement of understatements—with these proposed arrangements, but I promised it was just a temporary solution. We discussed and debated and argued until I finally wore him down.

With a sigh, Cesar slid the card keys across the registration counter, and we were in business.

I wasn't really expecting any more trouble; the heavies had already paid a visit, found nothing, and left their message.

I helped Nicole and Kevin get settled in their new room. This time, they had much less stuff to put away. There were a few things we'd salvaged from their original room, but that was it. A quick trip to Walmart tomorrow was probably a good idea.

"Anything else I can do before I turn in?" I asked.

"No, thanks. I think we're good." Nicole still seemed tense, but I guessed that was to be expected. Nothing in her situation had really improved, after all.

Kevin shook his head without looking up from his phone. His usual position. I hadn't spoken to him much since returning with his mother, but not for lack of trying. When I'd given him his phone back—with an apology—he'd snatched it from my hands without comment. Then he'd withdrawn into a corner and had examined it very carefully, as if I'd done something to it.

We'd had some kind of connection, but now that I'd broken his trust, I didn't think I'd ever regain it. I tried to think back to when I was his age and imagine how I would have reacted, and I didn't think it would have been much different. I didn't blame him for feeling like I betrayed him, but given the same circumstances, I would have done what I did one hundred times out of a hundred.

Sometimes a person's welfare trumped a person's privacy, especially when you were talking about a kid. But that was a lesson you learned from experience and the passage of time.

"Okay, then. Remember, Griff is in Room Seven. His friends are in Room Five. They're going to take turns keeping an eye out tonight, so if you hear someone moving around, don't be alarmed. You're safe." I realized my little speech was a virtual repeat of the one I'd given them on their first night, and they really hadn't been safe. Maybe I needed to be a little less optimistic and a little more realistic.

Maybe next time.

* * *

When I awoke the next morning, I felt relieved. No middle-of-the-night yelling. No tires screeching. No doors slamming. No nighttime commotion whatsoever.

I checked in with Fareed at the front desk to get an overnight update, and he confirmed what I'd thought. No trouble. "About an hour ago, those sisters in Room Three stopped in and asked if you were awake yet. I told them I could call you, but they said it wasn't important."

"Know what they wanted?"

"Nope. Seemed to be happy about something. The one who does all the talking was dressed up, if that helps."

Maybe another job interview? One could hope. "Thanks. I'll catch up with them later. And I'll talk to you later, too." I hung up and called Vell, told him we had another drop-in appearance to make. Then I took a shower and got dressed in my best bookie-meeting clothes.

Stopped by Sandy's and got two coffees and a couple of muffins, to go. Sunshine Salutation for me, Decadent Chocolate Chip to satisfy Vell's chocolate craving.

Vell had reached out to a few of his street contacts and secured the address of Jimmy the Raisin. He lived not far from Payton's apartment building in

Falls Church. I'd lent my car to Nicole to go shopping—with Griff along as bag-toter/bodyguard—so Vell drove while I navigated.

"You swiped the kid's phone and duped Nicole into meeting you?"

"Not sure I'd frame it that way exactly."

"Sounds like something I'd do." Vell broke off a piece of muffin and stuffed it into his mouth. Chewed and talked and drove at the same time. "About time I started rubbing off on you. Don't try to fight it. Just sit back and enjoy the transformation."

"Like when Dr. Bruce Banner hulks out?"

"But even more spectacular."

"Right. So here's the deal: We tell this Jimmy guy that Nicole has left Payton, and that she has nothing to do with any gambling debts, and that she doesn't have any money even if she did."

"Seems reasonable to me. Let's just hope Mr. Raisin is a reasonable fellow."

"Let's be clear and firm. Leave no room for ambiguity. Nicole is absolutely not responsible for her husband's debts."

"What does the law say, by the way?"

I had no idea, but now that Vell brought it up, a spouse might legally *be* responsible. "We'll emphasize the part about Nicole having left Payton."

"And the other part about her not having any dough."

"Yeah, that too."

We pulled up in front of Jimmy's house, a small Cape Cod in disrepair. Weeds gone amok, devouring the lawn. Two cars were in the driveway. An old Chevy. And a black SUV, with a skull-and-crossbones decal on the back window.

Chapter Eighteen

"Well, well, well." Vell turned to face me in the seat. "This is an interesting development, huh?"

"Indeed." Looked like we'd found Payton.

"Now what?"

"You got any pressing business this morning?"

"Nah."

"Good. Let's just watch for a while." I drove to the end of the cul-de-sac, turned around, and parked across the street, two houses down, where we had a clear view of Jimmy's house. If Payton was just placing a bet, then his visit shouldn't take very long, but this wasn't Jimmy the Raisin's business storefront; this was more like his home office. So, really, we didn't know how long Payton might be there. Vell and I slumped in our seats to avoid detection and settled in.

We relaxed in stake-out mode, shooting the breeze.

"Whatever happened to that job your cousin offered you?" I asked.

"The drywall thing? Do I look like I'd be good at hanging drywall?"

"I think you'd be an excellent drywall hanger."

"Means I'd have to work with my cousin."

"That a bad thing?"

"Terrible thing. Besides, I'm more into community outreach than home renovation."

"Outreach?"

"You know, moving among the people. Fostering change. Supporting the downtrodden. A champion for the less fortunate."

"Very noble of you."

"I do what I can."

"You just think being a man of the people will get you laid more often, right?"

Vell shrugged. "No matter what line of business I'm in, I attract the ladies. Catnip to the felines. Can't be helped."

With that, we dipped into silence mode, lost in our thoughts. After about an hour, though, Vell spoke. "So what's the deal here?"

"Ready for some community outreach, are you?"

"Ready to get out of this car."

"Okay, then. Let's go knock on the door, see what happens."

We got out, and Vell popped open the truck. Came out with two golf clubs. A wedge and a nine-iron.

"I didn't know you played golf," I said. "What's your handicap?"

"Right now, you." He handed me one. "In case things go south with Payton."

"We can chip him into next week?"

"Something like that."

We crossed the street and walked up to Jimmy's front door. A welcome mat read, "Go Away." I tried peering into one of the adjacent windows, but they were too grimy to see anything. We spread out like we had when we visited Payton's apartment, except this time Vell was the front man. Before he rang the bell, he leaned his golf club against the wall.

Vell poked the doorbell, and it chimed from within. A minute later, the door opened a crack, security chain still engaged.

"Yeah?" A scratchy, high-pitched voice.

From my angle, I couldn't see anything except Vell's face.

"Looking for Jimmy," Vell said.

"What for?"

"Was hoping he'd take some action."

"He don't usually conduct business here," the disembodied voice said through the crack in the door.

"Maybe he could make an exception. I'm a friend of Todd Payton."

"Oh yeah?"

"Yeah. That's his ride, isn't it?" Vell hooked a thumb over his shoulder. "He here?"

"You think I just fell off the pumpkin truck?"

"No sir."

"Don't need to sir me." The door closed.

Vell glanced at me, shrugged.

"Do you think he's going to tell Payton we're here?" I gripped my wedge a little tighter and Vell picked his club up.

"What should we—"

The door opened wide, and an ancient man stood there, about five foot two. His face was so wrinkly his wrinkles had wrinkles. You didn't have to be a genius to realize where Jimmy the Raisin got his nickname.

He addressed Vell. "Who's your buddy?"

"Uh, that's Mess."

"I'll bet." He pointed to the golf club on my shoulder. "If you guys are looking to fill out your foursome, I think you're in the wrong neighborhood. This is more of a bowling crowd."

I lowered my club, and Vell did the same. We didn't have anything to worry about with Jimmy, and if Payton showed his face, we'd have time to react.

"Come on in, Vell. I'm tired of standing here letting my nosy neighbors learn my business."

"You know me?"

"Everyone knows Mama, and I'm guessing the apple don't fall far from her eye. Now, will you stop fooling around and get in here? You can relax, that Payton turd isn't here." He turned on his heels and receded into the darkness, calling out over his shoulder, "Don't touch anything."

We followed, still holding our clubs. You couldn't be too careful, and even if he knew Mama, that didn't mean we knew—or trusted—him. He was a bookie, after all.

The procession stopped in what was once the living room but was now a control center of some kind. TV screens covered the walls, and a small bank of computers covered two tables that had been pushed together. A big leather swivel-recliner dominated the center of the room. Jimmy plopped right down into it.

There was no place for us to sit, so we stood there, two subjects facing the king on his throne.

"What can I do for you? I owe Mama, not for anything she did for me directly, but a few years ago, she provided some excellent advice and guidance to a couple of mopes who needed some excellent advice and guidance. Which benefited me, in the long run. So I feel like I am indebted to her."

Since Jimmy owed Mama, I let Vell do the talking. No need for me to insert myself into the situation.

"We're looking for Payton," Vell said, cutting right to the chase.

"So I gathered. He's not here."

"His car is."

Jimmy laughed and the crevices on his face merged and separated and came back together like some kind of macabre human kaleidoscope. "Not anymore. That's my car now. I think I might put huge monster truck tires on it. Get a big-ass woofer, too. Ride around town blaring my tunes, picking up chicks. Whaddya think?"

The image of Jimmy cruising the streets in a souped-up SUV was utterly ridiculous, but I kept quiet. To each his own.

Jimmy stared at us, then cackled again. "Nah. Gonna sell it. You in the market?"

Vell shook his head. "Did you buy it from him?"

"Why would I want that monstrosity? We negotiated a settlement for the debt he owed me. I wiped the slate clean; he signed over the title to his car."

"Did your negotiations include breaking into his apartment and trashing the place?"

Jimmy recoiled. "What kind of businessman do you think I am? Of course not. I don't negotiate like that. You've got me confused with some of the connected guys, in the District or up in Philly. I run a nice, reputable suburban operation. No strong-arm techniques needed."

I wondered what he declared on his taxes.

"Just to be clear, you got Payton's car and he doesn't owe you anymore?"

Jimmy nodded. "That is correct."

Vell looked at me. "So Payton is debt-free. Wonder if that means this whole thing is over?"

"Hold on there." Jimmy looked as if he'd swallowed a canary. Maybe two.

"What?"

"He doesn't owe me, but I wouldn't call him debt-free."

"Keep talking," Vell said.

"Word on the street is that Payton is into a big fish for eighty large."

Vell whistled.

I couldn't keep quiet any longer. "That would explain a few things. Who does he owe?"

Jimmy looked at me as if I was speaking Russian. Then he turned and spoke to Vell. "That's where I draw the line. Self-preservation, and all that. No names."

"What about Coach?"

Something registered on Jimmy's face, then it was gone like a gnat in the breeze. "I said no names. I like living."

"Okay, no names. How did Payton rack up that kind of debt? I'd think by the time he was twenty thou in the hole, he would have been cut-off."

Now Jimmy spoke directly to me. "Let me explain it to you. Payton borrowed from a lot of people. They were having a tough time collecting, so these creditors sold the debt to a consolidator for a fraction of what he owed. Now that consolidator wants the whole nut."

"So Payton really owed a lot more than eighty thousand dollars?"

"Now you're catching on."

"How come you were able to settle with him?"

Jimmy smiled and it was like looking at a happy raisin. "I'm a nice guy. And persuasive, in my own way."

"We realize that you can't name names, but we really need to get a message to this guy, this big fish. Here's the deal." I went on to explain Nicole's situation.

When I was through, Jimmy pursed his pruny lips. "I sympathize, I do. But I'm sure not going to stick my neck out trying to be some kind of middle-man. Sorry. I have a feeling he wouldn't believe it, even if it were true."

"It is true."

"Yeah, well I believe you, but he's liable to think it's just a bunch of crap, that Payton's only trying to save his family's skin. And listen to me very carefully. This guy doesn't jerk around. He plays hardball, with a capital hard. Now, if you'll excuse me, it's time for my nap." He got up from his chair, ushered us out of the control room and down the hall. Opened the front door and waved his hand at us, as if he were clearing the room of smoke.

From inside, Jimmy got the last words. "Tell Mama that an admirer says hello. And boys? Be real, real careful, okay? The big fish don't like people pissing in his ocean, and he don't play nice."

* * *

On the way back to the motel, I got a call from Detective Ostervale. "Hey, Mess. How's the world treating you?"

"I'm fine." I'd forgotten to tell him that we'd located Nicole. "Listen, I'm sorry I didn't call you yesterday, but we found Nicole Payton. Thanks for looking into it. I owe you one. Dinner at Artie's?" Forgetting to follow up with Ostervale was just another sign I needed to get the little things in my life organized. Unfortunately, a personal assistant wasn't in my budget. Maybe there was a freebie app for my phone that would do the trick.

"Well, that's sort of why I'm calling."

"Huh? About Nicole?"

"Perhaps. The name Billy Lane mean anything to you?"

My breath caught. "Maybe."

"Billy Lane was found this morning, beaten to death. Dumped by the side of the road, down near Lorton."

Chapter Nineteen

These guys do play rough. Really rough. "And how is this related to Nicole?"

"Lane used to run with Todd Payton."

"Ah." I paused, waiting for Ostervale to cough up more inside information. When none came, I said, "So? Nicole has nothing to do with Payton anymore. If he ran with Payton, he probably deserved what he got."

"That's beside the point. Man got killed, I need to investigate. That's my job. I leave the part about judging if people got what they deserved to a higher authority."

"Police Chief?"

"Funny. You have any idea where Payton might be now?"

"You think he killed Lane?" I asked.

"No evidence of that. Right now, he's just a person of interest."

"Well, I know plenty of places where Payton isn't, but I don't know where he is. Sorry."

"Then what good are you?" Ostervale said.

"I've been hearing that question all my life."

"Payton's connection to the dead man is just one lead, and we've got stronger ones, but at some point I may need to talk with Nicole. You say you know where she is now, right?"

"Yeah."

"If you want to ask her a few questions and get back to me if anything interesting comes to light, I'd take your call," he said.

"Sure."

"One more thing. We haven't informed next of kin, so keep this quiet, okay?"

"Who am I going to tell?"

"Thanks. Later." Ostervale hung up.

I turned to see Vell staring at me.

"Would you mind watching the road?"

He faced forward but cut his eyes in my direction. "Someone got killed? Spill, brother, spill. I love a good murder mystery, long as I don't know the victim."

I filled him in, and Vell just kept whistling and shaking his head. What had we stepped in?

* * *

Vell dropped me off at the motel, and I joined Nicole and Kevin at Sandy's for lunch. They'd already started, so I ordered something quick—a chicken salad sandwich with avocado—and sat at their table. "Have a productive outing at Walmart?" I'd given her $150 worth of gift cards out of my emergency stash.

Nicole nibbled on a French fry. "Yes. And we went to Target, too. We're good to go, at least for a while. I can't thank you enough for what you've done for us."

"You're welcome. Maybe someday you can pay it forward."

Kevin devoured his chicken fingers while playing on his phone, studiously avoiding looking in my direction. Still pissed at me for taking his phone and using it to dupe his mom. All I could do was be nice and wait it out. Try to act normal. "Did you get what you needed, too, Kevin?"

He pretended not to hear my question. Nicole rolled her eyes at me. "Griff was very nice. Very accommodating. He's..." She scrunched up her face, thinking. "He's an unusual man, isn't he?"

"Yeah, he is." I've heard Griff described with all sorts of adjectives, and *unusual* wouldn't make the top fifty. "You don't want to get on his bad side."

"Oh, he seems like such a teddy bear."

A grizzly bear might be more accurate. "Got some bad news. Remember us talking about Billy Lane?"

Nicole had a mouthful of food, so she just nodded.

"He's dead."

"Oh my," Nicole put her burger down. "That's terrible."

Kevin glanced up from his phone.

"Yeah. Someone killed him. Left him by the side of the road. Nasty. I don't suppose you have any idea who would kill him?"

She didn't say anything for a moment. Then, "Do you think Todd killed him?"

"Do you?" I asked.

Kevin put his phone down on the table, and his lips parted as he took everything in.

Nicole shook her head. "I don't. But I suppose I wouldn't be totally shocked. There was some bad blood between them."

"Well, the cops want to talk to him. Not as a suspect, but as a person of interest. You have any idea where Todd might be hanging out?"

Nicole's face darkened. "Don't know. Don't care. Why do you? I mean, really Mess, what does all his bad stuff have to do with me and Kev? Can't you just leave us out of all this?"

"You came to me for help. Part of that help is keeping you safe from him. And from anyone else. The more I know about the situation—and that includes where Todd might be—the better I can do that."

A change seemed to come over Nicole, as if she'd just figured out the answer to some burning question. But instead of divulging the magical answer, she took a big bite of her burger. When she finished chewing, she said, "I'm done with all this nonsense. Nothing bad is going to happen to us. Let's talk about something else."

"Something else?"

"Yes. Something more pleasant."

"Listen, Nicole. I'm sorry this conversation isn't pleasant enough for you. But I'm concerned. Things I don't know make me nervous, and I think we need to face reality." I tried not to raise my voice, but I could tell that was going to be a losing battle if we continued on our present course.

"You don't think I'm facing reality?"

I shook my head. "Let's look at the facts. Your room here was broken into, as was your apartment. Correct me if I'm wrong, but Todd seems like the vindictive type. So if you think you're completely, 100 percent safe, you're..." I stopped short of calling her naïve or worse, feeling the heat rise on my cheeks. Why was it that so often the people who needed the most help were the ones blind to reality?

Nicole's eyes were as big as our lunch plates. "You have no idea what you're—"

I held up my hand. "Sorry. But it seems to me that I'm taking this thing a whole lot more serious than you are. This isn't a picnic, you know. People are getting hurt and you—and Kevin—could very well be next."

Nicole put the last bite of her burger on her plate and pushed it into the middle of the table. "Mess, you don't know me very well, but I assure you I'm taking this seriously. Do you have any idea what I've already endured? Do you think it was easy for me to leave my husband? Do you have any idea how difficult a decision that was? Uprooting my life? My son's?" Her face had turned a shade of red you didn't usually see in humans.

Kevin stared at his mother.

"I know it was hard," I sputtered.

"Hard? Try agonizing. Try earth-shattering. Life-changing." Each word delivered with razor-sharp enunciation.

"All for the better, I hope," I muttered.

"I hope so, too, but only time will tell. And if you think I'm taking this too lightly, well..." She pushed her chair out, stood. "I'm going to lie down. Come on, Kevin."

He took his time getting to his feet, a weird expression on his face. Part pride, part confusion, part amusement.

Nicole stood up straighter. "Thank you for all you've done for us, Mess. I really mean that. But I guess it's time to be moving on. We'll be out of your hair by tomorrow morning. I wouldn't want to make you *nervous* by overstaying our welcome."

I was expecting her to stomp off, but she simply took Kevin's hand and they slowly walked out of the café, heads held high.

I pushed my own plate away, appetite gone. Just another situation I managed to screw up.

* * *

Cesar and I sat behind the registration desk going over the week's numbers. I'd postponed this meeting several times, but now that Nicole and Kevin were moving on—without my assistance—I guessed I needed to move on too, although it bugged the crap out of me that things were being left unresolved. The break-in here, the break-in at Nicole's apartment, the whereabouts of Payton, and the crooks after the money. All still a mystery.

I hated not knowing things.

"So our monthly occupancy rate has fallen for the sixth time in the past six months." Cesar glanced up from his computer screen. "If that trend continues, we'll be looking for a new place to live."

"If that trend continues, we'll be able to live in any room here we'd like. Gotta look at the glass as half full."

"If we don't attract more customers, there won't be any glass to look at." He sighed. "I wish you'd take things more seriously, Mess. This may be a hobby for you, but this is how I make my living. My family lives here."

I'd just accused Nicole of not taking her situation seriously, and now Cesar was accusing me of the same thing. Some kind of weird symmetry in the air. But I *did* take the motel business seriously. "My father will not close this place down. Not until the real estate market rebounds, and even then, he's got a sentimental attachment to this place. He'll never get rid of his baby."

"Which baby are you talking about? The motel or you?"

My cheeks got warm. "Ouch."

"What your father does matters, of course, but I take pride in my job. And one measure of success is if this motel does well financially. Plus, I'd like to get a raise sometime. You know it's been a while."

"Let me see what I can do about that." I adopted an *I'm-the-boss-around-*

here tone.

"Phil won't allow that, not with these downward revenue trends."

"Let me handle Uncle Phil, okay? You just keep this place humming along."

"Very well." Cesar's face relaxed. "I understand two of our visitors will be leaving us tomorrow."

"How'd you find out?"

"Kevin came in to say goodbye."

"Really?" Seemed a little out of character for him.

"Really. He's a good kid, once you get past the teenage wall of feigned apathy."

"I guess." I picked up a listing of the past month's expenses. "Let's go over these numbers."

Cesar ran down the previous month's expenses, adding commentary where necessary. Advertising, laundry, maintenance, transportation—did I really need to borrow the courtesy car so often?—and a host of other line items. After a few minutes, I half-tuned him out, mind wandering.

I'd been moping around since lunch, trying to figure out how I could apologize and convince Nicole to stick around. At least until I could get a handle on things and make sure they got their new lives going on a decent trajectory. I hadn't come up with any genius ideas.

"Can I ask you a question?"

He interrupted himself—something about improving the grading of the parking lot. "Sure."

"How were you able to connect with Kevin?"

"Same way I connect with everyone. Be nice. Show an interest in them. Treat them as worthy individuals with their own unique needs."

Thanks, Oprah. "I tried that. There were a few glimmers, but ... I don't know."

"Did you try to engage him in conversation? Ask what he likes to do?"

"He was always playing games on his phone." I exhaled, partly in frustration. With Kevin, but more so with myself.

"Did you ask him what games?"

I shook my head. I didn't care what he was doing on his phone. Until I needed it and took it. Then I cared. Of course, I didn't think Kevin interpreted it as me caring. He considered it duping him and his mom. Not a great way to foster a relationship.

"It doesn't matter so much what you talk about with kids, as long as you get them talking. Once the floodgates open, it's not too difficult to steer the conversation in the direction you want."

"That how you deal with Abie?"

"It's not quite that simple, but in many ways, yes. Half the time you need to be willing to meet them in the middle. The other half of the time, you need to meet them three-quarters on their side. Most kids don't see the world objectively. There's a lot of personal bias going on." He arched his eyebrow the way he did when he was trying to drive home a point. "A lot of adults are like that, too."

This wasn't about me. Was it? I didn't bite but filed it away for a future conversation. What would it be like to be psychoanalyzed by Cesar? I shuddered. "Since you're on a roll, advice-wise, do you have any suggestions as to how I might convince Nicole to stick around and let me help her find a place to go?"

"Why don't you ask her what she's planning? Get her to start talking. Show some compassion in her plight but realize that people sometimes have a difficult time accepting help, no matter how well-intentioned. Look for something of value you can offer her."

I thought I'd tried most of that. "I have the feeling she's more comfortable running from something she'd be better off facing in the long run."

"Many people are. You can only do so much. It's very, very difficult to help someone who doesn't want to be helped."

I put down my sheaf of papers. Difficult wasn't impossible, was it? "Let's put a pin in this and come back to it later, okay? I have something I need to do."

Cesar waved me away. "Go. Go. I'll be here when you get back. Man's gotta have priorities, right?"

* * *

I knocked on Room Six, figuring Nicole had already gotten enough rest. Rude, maybe, but she had the rest of her life to catch up on her sleep. Nobody answered, so I kept knocking. The passkey called to me from my wallet in my pocket but using it and barging in would shred any last bit of remaining credibility. Assuming I had any left.

With each series of knocks and subsequent silence from within, my nerves jangled. Had something terrible happened? Had someone been waiting in their room to ambush them when they got back from lunch? Had Nicole given up hope and done something drastic?

The passkey sang its siren song.

I pounded on the door a little harder, with no success. Tried calling both their phones. No answer. I glanced around the parking lot, but there wasn't any sign of Nicole or Kevin. Had they ducked out for something to eat? Unlikely, we'd just had lunch a couple of hours ago. Gone for a walk? I scanned up and down the street as far as I could see. No sign of them.

If something had happened to them and they were in their room needing assistance, I would be negligent in not at least trying to help them. Right?

I pulled out my wallet and removed the passkey. Jammed it into the slot and when it blinked green, I pushed the door open. "Hello? It's Mess, checking up on things."

No answer.

I flipped on the lights.

The room was empty.

Chapter Twenty

Totally cleared out.

Evidently, Nicole and Kevin hadn't wanted to wait until tomorrow. I did a quick room check, found nothing. Wandered back outside and found Griff standing there, leaning against his doorjamb next door, picking at something in his teeth with a dirty fingernail.

"Have you seen Nicole or Kevin?"

"Yeah."

"And?"

"And they left. About an hour ago. Some lady in a red Ford Fusion picked them up. After they left, I told my buddies they could leave, too. I hope that was okay."

"Yeah, sure." I tilted my head to look up at Griff towering above me. "You didn't think to tell me?"

He looked hurt. "They said you knew."

"You talked to them? Did they say where they were going?"

"The mom wasn't very talkative. She said they were leaving and then she went into her room—it didn't look like she was feeling very well. The kid stayed out here, and we chatted for a while."

"Oh? About what?"

"I dunno. Nothing much. He thanked me for watching out for him and his mom. Good kid. Hope things turn out well for them."

Everyone connected with Kevin, except for me. "Did you get a look at the lady driving the getaway car?"

"Getaway car? Nicole and Kevin didn't seem like they were abducted against their will or anything." He kept working at something stuck in his teeth, but with fingers the size of his, he was having a real hard time.

I tried to ignore his teeth. "Bad choice of words. Did you get a good look at the driver?"

"Boss, all I see are the tops of the cars."

* * *

I trudged to my room. I hated losing and although I hadn't technically lost anything—there was no competition here—I considered not achieving my goal as a loss. I went next door into the office and plopped down at my desk. Picked up the thumb drive Lia had given me and stuck it into the USB port. Opened the directory of photos.

The Eiffel Tower.

The Statue of Liberty.

Big Ben.

A gondola.

I scrolled through the pictures, memories from my youth, until I came to a close-up of the bench in front of the first hole. I remembered sitting on that bench, anticipating the start of a new round.

I played the course a lot as a teenager. Ten times a day during the summer. Pretty soon, I knew every bump and break under the green felt, and I knew where all the dead spots were in the bumpers. I also learned the exact spots to hit my tee shots to give me the best chances for getting an ace.

At one point, I tried to hustle my school buddies for a buck here and there, but my father—or was it Uncle Phil?—nixed that moneymaking scheme before I'd made enough to buy lunch.

When I was fourteen, I set the course record. At least, I claimed it was the course record; I didn't think anyone else was tracking it. Over the next year or two, I improved upon it by a few strokes. I even persuaded my father to put up a plaque in the starter's hut proclaiming that fact.

No one ever beat my score, and I still have that plaque somewhere to prove it.

I moved on to the next photo: the starter's hut. When I was old enough—as determined by my father, anyway—he let me run the place. I spent many hours perched on a rickety stool in the hut where I sold tickets and snacks. Gave out the equipment—putters, balls, scorecards, little pencils embossed with "See the World in 18 Holes."

I'd listen to music on my boombox, and sometimes I'd even pipe it over the loudspeaker system by putting a rubber band around the transmit button and setting the mic on the counter next to the portable stereo.

We sold ice cream from an old chest freezer and on hot days I gave away free Fudgsicles to the next person who'd get a hole-in-one. Of course, I'd wait until a hot girl stepped up to the tee of the easiest hole—number 17, right in front of the hut—before I'd announce the contest over the loudspeaker.

My ploy actually got me a few phone numbers.

Those were the days.

They didn't last forever. When I turned seventeen or so, my interests turned in other directions. I stopped working there and the mini-golf course fast became a fading memory. If my father cared that I no longer sold tickets or inventoried the equipment or cleaned the fiberglass figures, he didn't say a word about it to me.

On one hand, I didn't care that he took it in stride. On the other, it would have been nice if he'd at least let me know I'd be missed around the course. *Hey sport, it's sure going to be hard to find a replacement for you. What will we do without you? How can the course record-holder just up and leave?*

But that was my father.

I pulled the thumb drive out of the computer. There was only so much nostalgia I could handle at one time.

I tried reading some industry magazines but couldn't focus on much of anything. People were struggling to eke out a living in this world, suffering all types of abuse and indignity—and not just Nicole and Kevin. Hard to concentrate on the latest and greatest blackout curtains or the newest three-in-one shower soap dispenser innovations.

I gave up on the magazines and picked up my tablet. Surfed around for a while, but nothing captured my interest. I moved back into my room and spread out on my guest bed—covers still rumpled from where Kevin slept. I flipped on the TV and channel-hopped. Some SportsCenter on ESPN, some news on CNN, some cooking thing on some cooking channel.

An hour passed. Maybe two. Possibly three.

* * *

As much as I tried to put everything out of my mind—or at least distract myself—I couldn't stop replaying the last conversation with Nicole. Had I really aggravated her so much that she'd taken off? Or had she been looking for an excuse to leave, and my insensitivity and boorish behavior had been convenient? Did her abrupt departure have anything—anything whatsoever—to do with Billy Lane's death?

A bad habit of mine, second-guessing every single decision I made, especially when things didn't work out the way I wanted. What difference did it make? They were gone, and really, it wasn't my problem. I'd stuck my nose into her affairs from the beginning—with a heavy assist from Mama and Vell—but I wasn't sure if Nicole had actually ever wanted my help. Or anyone else's, for that matter.

I clicked the TV off. Sitting around here, wallowing in self-pity wasn't a ticket to happiness. I needed to get out. And it was about dinnertime.

I called Lia. "Hey there. I know it's super late notice, but I was wondering if you'd like to grab something to eat."

"I'd love to, but I'm on deadline for something, and I can't spare a minute. Sorry, Charlie."

"Raincheck?"

"Absolutely."

Next I tried Vell. No dice, he had other plans. I worked my way through a few other friends, all busy, and finally decided to call Cesar. A little outside-of-work bonding might be beneficial, if not exactly fun. "Hello, Cesar."

"Hello, Mess."

"So, um, what are you and Diego—and Abie—doing for dinner tonight?"

"Dinner? Tonight?" He paused, then came back with a suspicious, "Why do you ask?"

"Well, I'm not doing anything, and I thought it might be fun to, you know, do something together."

"You mean as a family?" His tone pitched higher at the end of the word *family.* Much higher.

"Something like that."

A pause. "Unfortunately, we are meeting one of Diego's co-workers for dinner." He added quickly, "At his co-worker's house. Sorry. Maybe we could all get together some other time?"

"Yeah, sure." I hung up. Was Cesar feeding me a line? What difference did it make? A no was a no. I was never sure if Diego liked me anyway, and I'd hate to make things awkward for anybody.

I thought about calling Mama, seeing if I could wrangle a last-minute dinner invitation. She was fabulous in the kitchen; I always wondered how Vell stayed so slim growing up. But I didn't relish being there in person when I told her I'd lost track of Nicole and Kevin. I was getting desperate, so I tried my sister. "Hiya, Izzy. How're you doing?"

"What do you want, Mess?"

Her suspicion matched Cesar's. I needed to work on my delivery. "Can't a guy just call his sister to see how things are going?"

"Sure he could. But why are *you* calling? Need some money?"

"I'm a little insulted by that."

"I didn't think you got insulted by anything. But I can't talk now, I'm on my way out. Ballet class. Wanna come see your nieces dance? They'd love to have their cool uncle show up and cheer them on. Eighteen seven-year-olds in tutus, trying to stay in step. What could go possibly go wrong?"

How badly did I want company this evening? Not that badly. "Thanks for the offer, but I have plans. I'll call you in a couple days and we'll catch up, okay?"

"Okie-dokie. Adios, mon frère."

I hung up and set my phone on the nightstand.

Utter failure.

I ordered a pizza and turned to Netflix, planning my triple feature, looking for a category called "Movies for Losers."

I couldn't find one.

Figured.

* * *

Six slices of pizza and two-and-a-half crappy movies later, my phone buzzed with a tweet, from Kevin: *Help me, Mess!*

I sat up straighter in bed and responded: *Where r u?*

Kevin's response: *They got mom.*

Chapter Twenty-One

Texting wasn't going to do it. Having already pulled the fake texter routine myself, I needed to be sure it was Kevin on the other end of the phone. More importantly, I needed to know what was happening, ASAP. I hit the send button and Kevin picked up on the first ring. "What's going on?"

"They took mom. They got her."

Kevin's words spilled out in a panic. "Slow down and tell me exactly what happened. First, take a deep breath."

He started talking again, but I couldn't make out a word. "Kevin, unless you calm down, I can't understand you. Now, please, take a deep breath."

I gave him a moment to gather himself. "Now, are you okay?"

"Yeah." A few gulps of air.

"Good. Where are you?"

"At McDonald's."

"Which one?"

"I don't know. I ran here."

I got out of bed and started looking for my shoes. "Are you safe there?"

"Please come get me. Please, Mess. Please."

"Sure, sure. Right away. As soon as you tell me where you are."

"Okay."

I heard movement and heavy breathing. A moment later, he gave me an address, along with a couple of landmarks he spotted out the window. He was only about two miles away, just inside the Beltway. "Don't go anywhere.

I'll be there in five minutes."

I got there in four.

Kevin huddled in a booth in the back corner, near the restrooms, with a view of the side doors and the parking lot out the window. The hood of his hoodie was drawn over his head and a baseball cap further hid his face. Pretty much all you could see were his jittery eyes scrutinizing everyone who walked past.

When he saw me, he put down his drink and tipped his head. Even scared to death, he was too cool to wave. *Teenagers.*

I slid into the booth across from him. "You sure you're okay?"

He glanced around then leaned forward and down, as if he were whispering something to a napkin on the table. "I'm okay. But they took Mom."

"Who did?"

"I don't know who. Men. Big men."

I glanced around the restaurant instinctively. No big men lurking. "Where did this happen?"

"We were staying in an apartment of one of Mom's friends."

"Where is she now? This friend?"

Kevin shrugged. "She didn't stay with us. She was out of town. That's how we could use her apartment."

"That apartment near here?"

"Yeah." Kevin's eyes darted all around.

"So where were you, exactly, when these men took your mom?"

A sheepish look appeared. "On the back patio."

"At midnight?"

He nodded.

"Smoking," I said. Not a question.

He nodded again.

"Okay. So you were outside on the patio. Any idea how these men got in?"

"Knocked on the door?"

"And your mom just let them in?"

He shrugged again. "I don't really know. I was outside."

"Go through what you know, then. Run down the time from right before you went outside until you texted me, okay?"

Kevin took a big slurp of his soda, then jumped right in. "Angie, Mom's boss, picked us up from your motel and dropped us off at this apartment. Mom said it belonged to a friend of hers, Helene something, who was out of town."

"Do you know her?"

"No. Never heard of her. But the apartment was nice, so ... For dinner, we ordered Chinese and ate it while we watched TV. Then Mom went into her room and got on the phone, I think. For most of the night. Then she went to bed."

"What time was that?"

He shrugged. "Maybe eleven?"

"And what were you doing during that time?"

"Nothing. Watching a movie. Playing on my phone."

The usual. "Okay. So your mom went to bed. Then what happened?"

"Then I went outside. On the patio." He stopped, picked up his cup of soda and I noticed his hands shaking a little.

"And?"

"I wasn't out there very long when I thought I heard something inside."

"What?"

"I don't know. Like maybe Mom going to the bathroom or getting something to drink in the kitchen. But about a minute later, I heard louder noises. Deep voices. At first, I thought maybe she couldn't sleep and turned the TV on, but it didn't sound like a TV show or anything. I cracked open the patio door so I could hear better. They were all arguing. Something about money and kicking someone's ass. My mom sounded pissed, you know." He looked at me for reassurance.

"I know."

"One of the guys asked about me, and Mom said she'd dropped me off at a friend's house. The patio door was off the dining area, on the far side of the kitchen, so they couldn't see me, but I hid farther in the shadows on the patio, in case they decided to search the apartment."

"Did they?"

"I don't know for sure. I guess they believed her."

"Okay. Go on. What happened next?"

"These men were definitely angry, but I didn't think they were going to take her. If I did, I would have done something, I swear..." Kevin put his head down on the table. His back rose and fell with his sobbing. I wanted to reach over and console him, but I didn't want him to get the idea I thought he was a baby.

So I just sat there, watching, as my insides knotted. Kevin wasn't even my child, and I felt like total crap, unable to provide what he needed. I could only imagine how Izzy or Cesar might feel if Olivia or Emma or Abie was as torn up as Kevin.

A few people in the restaurant glanced our way, but for the most part, the world kept rotating on its axis. Wasn't that the whole problem? People in trouble, all alone in the world, everyone else too busy or preoccupied with their own troubles to get involved.

After a few moments, Kevin raised his head, trying subtly to wipe his eyes. I pretended to follow something in the parking lot to give him a chance to get it together.

I turned back. "I know this is hard, but I need to know what happened if I'm going to be able to help. Okay?"

Kevin nodded.

"For the record, you did the right thing. You were outnumbered, and it sounded like these men meant business. Most likely, if you had tried to help your mom right then, you would have been injured yourself. Or worse."

He stared at me, swallowed.

"And I'm not just saying that to make you feel better. It's the truth." I flashed him a reassuring smile. "After you heard them arguing, then what happened?"

"Then...then...then it sounded like they grabbed her. Mom sorta shrieked and there was scuffling. One of them said to be quiet. So they were all quiet. Then it sounded like they left."

"Was your mom quiet too?"

He nodded.

"After they left, then what?"

"I waited some, just in case they came back, or if it was some kind of trap to get me to come out. After a while, I peeked around the corner of the dining area. They were gone. The apartment door was open, but they were gone." A few tears dripped down his cheeks.

"There was nothing you could have done, Kevin."

"I don't know. My mom told me if something like that ever happened, I wasn't supposed to get involved, under any circumstances. She wanted me to stay safe and get help."

"She told you that?"

"Uh huh."

"When?"

"When did she tell me?"

"Yes."

He bit his lip as he thought. "I guess it was the day we left home. Right before Vell picked us up."

"Okay." Was it simply something you said to your kid when you were about to step into the unknown, or had Nicole had an inkling of what was coming? I thought the answer to this question might explain much of what was going on.

"Mess?"

"Yeah?"

"Do you think Mom knew something bad was going to happen?" Kevin asked, as if he'd just read my mind. Mama had nothing on him in the clairvoyance department.

"I honestly don't know. Probably she just wanted you to be prepared in case something happened, you know, now that you wouldn't have your established support network in place."

Kevin looked at me as if I'd just tried to explain one of Einstein's theories. I wasn't sure where *established support network* came from, either, but I made a note not to use it again. "Have you tried contacting her?"

"She didn't answer my call or my texts."

I'd tried calling her myself—using her old number—on my drive over to

McDonald's but all I got was a robotic voice asking me to leave a message.
"Anything else you can remember about what happened that might help me figure out who might have taken your mother?"

"Yeah. There is something else. One of the guys mentioned my stepdad. Good 'Ol Todd."

Bam!

Kevin stared at me now, and he no longer looked like a scared fifteen-year-old.

Now he looked like a pissed-off, fully mature man.

Chapter Twenty-Two

A million things ran through my mind, but I needed to decide what to do now. Call the cops to report Nicole's abduction?

That would seem like the prudent thing to do.

Except...

My gut was trying to tell me something. Kevin had already deceived me, the night when he claimed his mom "never came back" and he said he didn't know where she was. And his description of the whole abduction just didn't seem right. A little hazy on the details and a little too theatrically delivered, including the punchline: "*Good Ol' Todd.*"

"So, Kevin, we should probably call the police to report this, huh?"

He shrugged.

"I know a detective. He'll come get your statement. He'll need that before he can help find your mom."

Kevin licked his lips. Then he half shrugged and said, "I didn't really see anything, you know."

"I understand. But you heard them, right?"

"Their voices were kind of muffled. So I'm not sure I heard them clearly." He didn't meet my eyes.

"Are you saying your mom wasn't taken against her will?"

"I think she was, but...but I can't be sure. Not sure enough to tell the cops anyway. Maybe we should wait a while. I suppose it's possible she left with them. You know, on purpose."

"Wouldn't she have told you?"

He nodded. "Well, she probably thought I was sleeping and didn't want to wake me. Then when she tried to call, maybe her new phone wasn't working right."

"So maybe she would go back to the apartment to tell you?"

"Maybe."

"Okay. Let's go. Direct me there."

We left McDonald's and headed back to the apartment where Nicole had gotten snatched. But it was dark, and Kevin hadn't been paying attention when they'd gotten dropped off and many of the garden-style apartment complexes looked similar. After about twenty minutes driving around in circles, we gave up and I pulled over to the side of the road.

"Okay." I took a big breath and exhaled deeply, giving Kevin the impression I'd weighed all the factors and come up with a sage decision. "How about this? How about we sleep on it and see how things look in the morning. Maybe your mom will have her phone working by then."

"So no police?"

"Not just yet. That okay with you?"

He tried to mask it, but I read relief on his face. "I guess so. If you think that's best."

"For now, I do. Let's go get some sleep." I started the car and headed for home, but as we got closer, I had second thoughts. Although I didn't really believe Kevin's story about his mother's abduction, I couldn't absolutely rule it out. And if it was true, then whoever had taken Nicole was using her for leverage to get the money from Payton. What would stop them from trying to use Kevin as leverage to get Nicole's cooperation, if necessary?

Nothing.

They'd already linked Nicole and Kevin to the motel somehow, so it would be foolish for us to take any risks, even with Griff standing guard. That might have been enough yesterday, but things seemed to have escalated, what with Lane's murder and Nicole's latest disappearance.

No sense taking chances, and certainly not with a kid's life at stake. Especially when I didn't have a clue what was going on.

I kept driving for another mile and a half down Route 50, then pulled into another motel parking lot. If Kevin noticed we were in a new place, he didn't utter a peep. The rooms were laid out in an "L" shape, and I parked on the far end of the lot, on the short end of the L, in front of the manager's office.

The Sleep Tight Motor Lodge was of the same vintage as my motel, and I supposed your typical lodger might categorize them in the same downscale class. But in my opinion, The Fairfax Manor Inn beat The Sleep Tight eight days a week.

Our rooms were larger. Our rates were cheaper. Our service was friendlier. And the guy running the Manor Inn—moi—was a whole lot less crabby than Harrison Utley.

I unlocked the doors. "Come on, Kevin. We're going to stay here tonight."

He looked around, as if he'd just awoken from a nap. "Here? What's wrong with your hotel?"

Even though some people used the terms hotel and motel interchangeably, most people still thought of a motel as being inferior to a hotel. So when people referred to my motel as a *hotel*, I didn't correct them. Didn't want to be rude. "Nothing's wrong with it. But we're going to stay here tonight."

Kevin shrugged and followed me into the office.

Even though it was past one a.m., Harry Utley sat in a recliner watching a small TV mounted close to the ceiling in one corner of the room. When he saw us, he slowly stood and hit the mute button on the remote control. He wore a blue and pink Hawaiian shirt, and I tried to remember if I'd ever seen him *not* wearing one. "Well, if it isn't Baron Hilton," he said.

"If it isn't J.W. Marriott. Or maybe it's Jimmy Buffet."

"Funny, as always." Harry shook my hand. "Who's your friend?"

"Kevin. This is Harry."

"Pleased to make your acquaintance." Harry turned to me. "Come by for some advice on how to run a successful lodging operation?"

"As a matter of fact, no. I need a room."

"Of course you do."

Although Harry and I were technically competitors—not that it mattered much, our real enemies were the economy chains who could afford expensive ads and promotions—we had an informal agreement. If one of us needed a room—to house overbooked guests, if there was a power outage, if we had an especially large event to handle, whatever—the other one would step up to the plate. It didn't happen often—maybe a couple times a year—but it was nice to know there was an option in a desperate situation.

And right now qualified.

"Will the Presidential Suite suffice?" Harry asked. "I just had the hot tub cleaned and new felt put on the pool table."

Kevin's eyes grew.

"Just kidding, kid." Harry winked at him. "Room 114 okay? Right next to the ice machine. Which is handy in case the AC goes out."

Harry got us a key and held it out, but when I reached for it, he pulled it back. "Would you like to tell me why you need this room?"

"No, I would not."

"Will there be anything illegal, immoral, illicit, illegitimate, prohibited, untoward, seamy, annoying, unpleasant, aggravating, disruptive, or disgusting going on in the room?"

"Of course not."

"Do I have your word?" He held the key just out of reach.

"I'll give you two words. The first one begins with the letter F."

"I'll accept that answer." Harry handed over the key. "Enjoy your stay at the Sleep Tight. If there's anything you need, don't hesitate to ask."

"Chocolates on the pillow?"

Harry fished in his pocket, pulled out a Hershey's Kiss. Tossed it to me. "Here ya go. You can stick it on your own pillow, if that makes you happy. Don't ever say this isn't a class operation, all the way."

* * *

First thing the next morning, both Kevin and I tried reaching Nicole, but neither of us had any luck.

Since he'd left his clothes behind at the apartment we couldn't find, I took him to get some. This time, we hit the mall and I bought him a few pairs of jeans, some shirts, and a new pair of kicks. He had his eyes on a pair that cost $140; I persuaded him to settle for a pair for $99. Couldn't have a teenager walking around in a pair of twenty-five dollar no-name shoes from Shoes R Us.

We also picked up another dark hoodie, just in case something happened to the one he always wore.

The doughnut we'd gotten earlier hadn't made a dent in Kevin's hunger, so we stopped at Subway to get him a sub. As Kevin was telling the guy behind the counter what he wanted, I called Lia and asked her if I could swing by her office to ask Shotgun Stokes a few more questions.

"I think he just came in," she said. "It's your lucky day. He usually doesn't roll in until well after lunch."

"I'll be there in about ten minutes," I told her.

"Great. See you then."

After I paid at the cash register, I said to Kevin, "Let's go, sport. Back to the Sleep Tight."

"Now?"

"Right now. You can bring that with you." I pointed to his sandwich. "Just try not to make too big a mess in my car, will you?"

I dropped Kevin off. I told him I'd be back in an hour or so and made him promise not to leave the room, for any reason, and not to answer the door, either. I waited until he'd gone into our room and closed the door before I drove off.

I texted Lia from the parking lot, and she met me at the receptionist's desk just as I'd finished signing in.

She pecked me on the cheek. "What a nice surprise."

"Ah, the pleasure is all mine." And I meant it.

"I'm glad Shotgun can see me."

"I didn't actually tell him you wanted to talk to him. Thought it might be better to just drop in." She lowered her voice. "Harder to say no that way."

I started to ask why he would say no, then swallowed my words and concentrated on Lia as she took me back to his office. She wore a form-fitting skirt and heels and seemed too dressed up for just hanging out at a newspaper office, banging out an article. Not that I was complaining—she looked very nice. The idea that maybe she had a lunch date crossed my mind, though, and my stomach tightened.

Shotgun was in the same position I left him three days ago, at his desk pounding his keyboard. This time, when he picked up his head and saw Lia, his smile could have lit up a dark alley. Then he noticed me standing next to her and his face sagged. "You again?"

I offered my most disarming smile. "Me again."

"What do you want?" Shotgun all but growled.

"Just a few more questions, that's all."

"You know I'm the reporter, right? I'm the one who's supposed to be asking the questions."

I kept the smarmy smile going. "Just a few, really. Won't take long, I promise."

"We'd really appreciate it," Lia added.

That seemed to do the trick. "Okay, I guess I have a minute." His gaze stayed on Lia a little long for my tastes. "Come on in."

We entered his office, but he didn't ask us to take a seat, so we stood. "I know you're busy, so I'll get right to it. Know anything about a guy named Billy Lane—"

Shotgun interrupted. "...found face down in a ditch. Dead."

"Yeah. How'd you—"

"I'm a crime reporter. It's my job to know these things. And I'm very good at my job. Actually, I figured I might be hearing from you. Considering this skell used to run with Todd Payton. The same Todd Payton you seemed awful interested in the other day."

"So you know about Lane?"

Stokes nodded. "Sure. Lane was a dirtbag. I'd heard his name involved in more than a few incidents over the years. Ran with a rough crowd, including Payton. I think the cops believe his death was some kind of deal gone bad or retribution for something ugly. Don't think they've arrested anybody for that yet."

That jibed with what I'd learned from Ostervale.

"What's Payton's story?"

"After you mentioned him, I did some digging. He's been associated, to various degrees, with a variety of low-lifes, but nothing major. I take it he hasn't poked his head out from his hiding place."

"Nope."

"You wouldn't happen to have any idea where he might be, would you?"

"Nope."

"Uh huh." Stokes picked up his pen and started flipping it around with his fingers, like a baton twirler with the tiniest of batons.

"You haven't heard anything about Nicole Payton? Or about a woman who had been abducted?"

"Nicole? She still missing?"

"Well..." I explained that I'd located her, then she disappeared again. I'm sure I sounded like an idiot who had simply misplaced his car keys.

"Hang on." He opened and closed a couple of desk drawers before finding a notepad. He flipped it open and took the cap off the pen he'd been playing with. "Want to give me the details?"

I thought about it, but since I was pretty sure no abduction actually took place, I shook my head. Nicole had run out on Kevin before, so I didn't put it past her to do it again. If I told Stokes and he started asking around, I was afraid Payton might somehow get wind of it and be able to track her down.

Stokes had his pen poised above the paper. "Are you saying Nicole Payton has been abducted?"

"I didn't say that. I was speaking in hypotheticals."

"Okay. Hypothetically speaking, who do you think took her?"

"Forget I said anything. Nobody got abducted that I know about."

"Uh huh." Stokes eyed me.

Lia eyed me, too.

I steered the questioning away from Nicole and back toward Lane. "You said that Lane used to run with Payton. Did something happen?"

"A few months back, I heard there was some, how should I say it? Some internal squabbles in the sphere of low-lifes. Some people got roughed up, took sides. Seemed like there was some splintering going on. Not sure who's loyal to who anymore."

"Here's another question: Have you heard anything about a loanshark, or anyone else for that matter, trying to collect a large debt? And using some severe threat tactics?"

"It always comes down to the money, doesn't it?" Shotgun leaned back and interlaced his fingers behind his head. Tilted his gaze up at the ceiling. Kept staring up there as he thought about what to say—I knew because I could practically hear the gears turning inside his skull. "Why do I get the sense you know more than you're letting on?"

I shrugged.

"If you can't level with me, how do you expect me to level with you?"

"If I knew more, I'd tell you."

"Sure, kid. Sure." Shotgun laughed. At least I think it was a laugh, it came across as more of a snort. "This loanshark could be any of a dozen losers. Sorry I can't be more specific, but the criminals don't keep me informed of their every move. Unfortunately. It would make my job a whole lot easier." He pulled his laptop closer and sat up straighter. Ready to get back to work. "Anything else?"

"This is very important. So if you hear anything..."

"I'll let you know," Stokes said. "After I've written the story, of course. Now, if you'll excuse me, I've got work to do." He reached for his computer, then raised his head and fixed me with a stare. "Take some friendly advice. Butt out, and let the experts handle things. If you don't, you're liable to get hurt. I'd rather not get assigned to write your obituary."

I didn't know how to respond to that, but I didn't need to. Shotgun had started typing and as far as he was concerned, I was yesterday's news.

Lia walked me out to my car. She took my hand in hers before I could climb in.

"Maybe Shotgun's right, Mess. Maybe you should become uninvolved. Report what you know to the authorities and let them handle it. You're not a cop, you know."

"You're probably right."

"I am right. Promise me you won't do anything dangerous."

I didn't answer.

"Please?"

"I'll be very, very careful," I said. "Careful is my middle name."

"Well, Mess Careful Hopkins, you better be." Lia kissed me, then let go of my hands. "Back to work for me. Call me later?"

"Absolutely. Bye." I watched her re-enter the building. I knew she was completely right, that I should butt out and let the cops do their jobs, but my mind kept going back to Kevin. What if Nicole hadn't been taken? What reason could there be that she'd take off and leave her kid behind, again? What if she was involved in something illegal? What if she was scamming me, and was really involved with Payton? Would I be ruining Kevin's life if I helped the cops find her so they could arrest his parents?

On the other hand, what if she had been abducted? Maybe Kevin had seen what he'd described? Could I trust a fifteen-year-old who'd already played me once?

I drove back to the Sleep Tight, thoughts ping-ponging in my mind. Should I follow Shotgun's advice to bail out and let the police take over, or should I stay involved, despite the danger? I certainly wasn't a crime expert like Shotgun, nor was I a family counselor. What, exactly, could I provide to Kevin and his situation? Good intentions?

Regardless of my lack of experience in these matters, my answer always came back to the same thing. I couldn't butt out. A kid's life was in turmoil and at the moment, I was his only advocate. No way was I going to leave Kevin high and dry.

No way.

I'd just keep giving it my best effort and hope it was good enough.

When I got back to our room, Kevin was gone.

Chapter Twenty-Three

I texted him immediately and his phone buzzed. It was sitting on the dresser, charging. Which meant one of two things. Either he hadn't gone far—because he wouldn't go far without his phone—or he'd been abducted, too.

I called Harry at the front desk. "Have you seen Kevin?"

"What, I'm supposed to keep track of all my customers?"

"No, but I thought maybe you'd—"

"Relax. He's across the street. Outside the Burger King. Smoking. He's been there for about twenty-five minutes. Got something to eat first."

My pulse slowed. "You know what he ordered?"

"Of course not. You think I pry into other people's lives?"

"Thanks, Harry."

"You owe me, Mess. No need to worry either, I'm keeping track."

* * *

I locked the room and hustled across the parking lot. Waited for a gap in the heavy traffic along Route 50. Made it to the median, then waited another minute for the westbound side to clear. I dashed across and found Kevin on the side of the restaurant in the exact position he was last time I'd caught him smoking. One foot up, back slouched against the wall. This time, though, he didn't throw away the butt and pretend he hadn't been smoking.

"Hey." It took quite a bit of restraint not to yell at him.

He blew out a mouthful of smoke. "Hey."

I waved the smoke away with my hand. "I thought I asked you to stay put."

Now he tossed aside his cigarette. "Sorry. I didn't think this counted. I'm not allowed to smoke in the room, and I can still *see* our room, right?"

"Yes. And people can see you, too. Don't forget, someone took your mother, and they may want to find you, too."

"They don't want me."

"How can you be so sure?"

A faint smile crossed his lips, and he seemed like he was challenging me. To what, I wasn't sure.

"You know something, don't you?"

The vague smile didn't leave. "Like what?"

Like your mother wasn't really abducted. "I don't know. But maybe you should tell me and let me decide if it's important or not."

Kevin shrugged.

I'd had enough shrugs and evasiveness and teenage attitude. I grabbed him by the shoulders. "Look, this isn't some kind of game. People are getting hurt. People are getting killed. Is that what you want? To end up like Billy Lane, beaten to a pulp and left by the side of the road for the raccoons to eat? You say your mother has been taken. Your stepfather is missing. If you have any information that might shed some light on what's going on here, you better spill!"

Kevin tensed up under my grasp. His mouth opened and he stared at me with glassy eyes. He'd been through stuff that would wither an adult, yet he was still only fifteen. Childhood wasn't supposed to be like that. And here I was grabbing him and yelling at him and piling on.

I let go.

"I'm sorry. I shouldn't have..." I took a deep breath and stepped back, sure that dozens of passersby had congregated and were watching me on the verge of roughing up a kid. When I mustered enough courage to glance around, though, it was just me and Kevin on the edge of a fast-food restaurant parking lot. Of course, Harry was probably spying on us from across the street.

Shell-shocked, Kevin hadn't moved. I wondered how much I brought back memories of him—or his mother—being manhandled by Payton. I was seriously terrible at this child-rearing thing. How bad would I have acted if I actually *didn't* care about Kevin's welfare? That was a scary thought, and my feelings of sympathy for Kevin grew exponentially.

"Kevin?"

His body remained frozen, but his eyes fixed on mine.

"Look, I'm sorry for getting physical and for yelling at you. I got carried away. I think I'm just frustrated with how things are going. I'd hoped you and your mom would be on your way to someplace better by now. Instead, she's gone, and some bad people are involved in your lives."

He seemed to absorb my words, then nodded.

I regulated my breathing. In, out. In, out. The anger and frustration still boiled within, and I needed to get a handle on it, to allow me to think straight, and to prevent me from flying off the handle again and lashing out at Kevin. I didn't want to transform into my father, or worse, his. "Will you accept my apology?"

A tiny nod.

"Okay. Good. Thanks." A part of my knot untied, but I knew I had a long way to go before I was at peace for what I'd done—and more so, for what I was about to do. I nodded at the Sleep Tight across the street. "Why don't we go back and figure out what our next steps should be?" I started to walk away, but I didn't turn my back, not sure if Kevin was going to follow.

He didn't.

I turned back. "Kevin, look. I'm sorry. I hope you can forgive me, if not now, then eventually. But we really should put our heads together and come up with a plan. I think I'm about ready to call my friend with the police."

"Don't do that."

"Why not?"

"Because...just don't."

I was getting the feeling again that Kevin knew something—something damn important. "That's not a good enough reason, I'm afraid."

Kevin chewed on his lip. "I do have some information that might be useful."

"You know where your mother is? Did she text you?"

"No, she didn't text me."

"So what's this information?"

He stared at the traffic going by for a moment. "I might know where my stepfather is."

"Where?"

"I'll have to take you there. I don't know the address."

"Can you give me a ballpark estimate? Around here? Baltimore? South Beach?"

Not even a hint of a smile from Kevin. "Not too far from here. I think I can direct you."

"Do you think he's responsible for taking your mom?"

Kevin didn't answer, just gave me the ubiquitous shrug. But this time, I caught a hint of a smile which I took for a "yes."

This sounded like a wild goose chase, this felt like a wild goose chase, and this sure smelled like a wild goose chase, but we really didn't have much to lose. I hoped. "Let's go."

* * *

We picked Vell up before we began our quest to find Payton. I figured we could use another set of eyes and ears. And fists, if it came to that. I called Griff, too, but he didn't answer his phone. Probably at the junk yard bench-pressing old cars.

I'd already told Vell Kevin's story about Nicole being abducted, of course, along with my immense skepticism. I was pretty sure he agreed with me that Kevin was, most likely, yanking our chains for some reason, but I was hoping to get a more definitive opinion from him after he spent some more time with Kevin. Unfortunately, I had no idea exactly *why* Kevin would want to deceive us. Nor did Vell.

Only thing to do was to play it out and see what happened.

Kevin couldn't give us an address, and he had trouble remembering some of the street names, so we pulled a lot of U-turns and did a lot of backtracking. I forgot that, until you actually drove places, navigating wasn't so easy. And for a kid like Kevin, who always had his head in his phone, all of the streets must have looked similar.

"You think we're in the right neighborhood now?" Vell asked from the backseat.

"I think so," Kevin said. "I recognize that RV."

We drove past a Gulfstream which dwarfed a tiny house on the corner, and Kevin directed me to make the next left. Then a right. Then the second left. We were on the other side of the George Mason University campus, where many of the modest houses overflowed with college kids. I wasn't sure if it was my imagination, but the area smelled vaguely like stale beer.

"There." Keven pointed to a brick house, even smaller than the rest. At some point—more than ten years ago, if I had to guess—it had been painted white, but the paint was now chipping. "That's the place."

"Are you sure?" I asked.

"Yeah. I remember that fire hydrant." He pointed to a red hydrant in front of the house that inexplicably extended about three feet in the air.

"Okay." I eased up on the gas and we slowly rolled past it.

"How come we're not stopping?"

"Just taking a look. See what's going on."

Nothing was going on. There was a single car in the driveway, but nobody was visible. The curtains were drawn and a stand-alone shed at the back of the driveway was shuttered tight. No menacing pit bulls on chains lurked in the front yard.

At the end of the block, I pulled over and swiveled to face Vell. "What do you think?"

"Seems pretty quiet. If Payton is here, he doesn't seem to have his posse around. Just the one car."

"Yeah." We could still see the house from where I parked. Nothing about it screamed danger. Yet...

"Tell me again why you think your stepfather is here?" I asked. Kevin told me earlier, before we'd picked Vell up, but I wanted to make sure his story hadn't changed.

"Like I said, he stopped here once to get something, after picking me up from soccer practice. Said a good buddy of his lived here, and that he travelled a lot. Said this friend would give him the shirt off his back. Or something like that. I got the idea he'd stayed here before."

"Did you see this friend?"

"No. He wasn't even home. My stepdad got the key from under a planter by the front door. I sorta got the idea this was some kind of clubhouse or something. That he would come here when he wanted to get away from my mom for some reason."

"Okay. Good to know."

"What are we waiting for?" Kevin asked. "My mom could be in there."

I could understand his impatience. He just wanted to see his mother again. Unharmed. So did I.

"If those men who took her are here, we want to make sure they're not going to hurt her if we barge in. Or us, either."

Kevin nodded. "There's three of us. And they don't know we're coming."

"You've been watching too many movies," Vell said. "Real life doesn't work like that. These guys could have guns."

"They didn't have guns last night," Kevin said.

"I thought you didn't really see them."

"I didn't. Not really. But I'm pretty sure they didn't have guns."

"How could you tell, though, if you didn't see them?" Vell asked, hammering home my point.

Kevin shrugged. "They would have said something, or my mom would have. You know, to warn me. She knew I was out on the patio. I could hear them, I just couldn't see them."

"And you're sure your stepfather wasn't with them?"

Kevin blinked rapidly. "Pretty sure. I mean, I didn't hear him or anything."

Vell looked at me and I recognized the expression on his face. I'd seen it before as we dealt with people trying to put one over on us. "Okay, then. Let's go see if we can find your mom, shall we?"

Kevin reached for the door handle, but I put a hand on his shoulder. "I think you should stay here, just until Vell and I check it out first."

"What?" Kevin wriggled under my hand, but I held firm.

"We're just going to make sure it's safe. You can watch from right here."

He opened his mouth to argue but closed it after realizing I wasn't going to budge. He slumped back in his seat.

"Okay. Here's the plan. Vell and I will go to the door. See if anybody's home. If your mom is indeed there, and it seems safe, one of us will wave you in. Got it?"

Kevin nodded, a scowl on his face. I'm sure he had visions of kicking down the door and racing in, kicking the crap out of some bad guy—or his stepfather—as he saved his mother.

I had a vision of him getting socked in the mouth by some thug. Luckily, I was the adult.

"This won't take long. If we're not back within ten minutes, call the cops." I unbuckled my seat belt. "Come on, Vell." I pointed to Kevin. "You stay put, okay?"

A curt nod.

"I mean it, Kevin."

No nod, just a glare.

Vell and I got out, and I glanced over my shoulder as we headed for the house. Kevin had moved into the back seat to get a better view, and he stared at us crossing the street.

"I'm with you. Kid's story seems a bit far-fetched. What are the odds we're going to find Nicole here?" Vell asked. "Or even Payton, for that matter?"

"Infinitesimal."

"You always were the optimistic sort."

We kept a steady pace as we approached. Not too fast, not too slow, not wanting to arouse suspicion in case someone happened to be watching. Every few strides, Vell had to shorten his step to keep from getting ahead of me. Nothing seemed amiss in the neighborhood; most of the college kids were probably either at class or sleeping.

"If Payton is here, do you think he's going to be happy to see us?" Vell asked.

"No."

"Now's a time I wished we believed in guns." Both Vell and I had seen too many of our friends suffer from gun violence, but his point was well-taken. I didn't think Payton would shoot us, although there were many other painful deterrents he could employ.

A sidewalk path went directly up to the door. We paused for a second, glancing around to see if we were alone, then headed up the path. A lone planter, full of red flowers, stood next to the door.

Vell got there first. "Knock or bell?"

"Go big or go home."

Vell poked the doorbell button. We stepped back, preparing for the worst—Payton and his posse, out for blood—but expecting something more like a befuddled resident wondering who the heck we were.

Nobody came, so Vell poked the button again. After another minute, I elbowed Vell aside and started banging the door knocker. Faint echoes bounced around the neighborhood.

"Payton is never home when we come calling," Vell said.

I touched the planter with my toe. "Should we see if the key's here?"

"We don't even know if this is the right place. Kevin isn't what I'd call a reliable witness."

"Exactly. If the key *is* here, that would be more proof this is the place Kevin remembers."

"Touché," Vell said.

I bent and tipped the planter to one side.

A key.

"Well, I guess this is the place." I retrieved the key and set the planter down.

"A lot of people keep keys under their planters," Vell said.

"Maybe. But since we're here..."

"Sure. What's a little breaking and entering between friends, right?" Vell scanned the street, up and down, checking for nosy looky-loos. "All clear."

I was about to put the key in the lock when we heard the whirr of a power saw coming from around the corner. Vell and I tiptoed to the edge of the porch, and I peeked around the edge. The sound seemed to be coming from the stand-alone structure.

It was deeper than I'd guessed at first glance, and with the rolltop door facing out onto the driveway—closed at the moment—it could serve as a garage.

Although the house had been built from solid brick, the garage looked like it had been slapped together in about two hours with leftover cinder blocks and mismatched lengths of vinyl siding lashed tight with duct tape. Or maybe not so tight.

On the side, there was a single door with windowpanes that had been blacked out with paint.

Vell and I stepped off the porch and onto the driveway. As we crept closer, the whirring noise stopped and started. The thought of Payton with a power tool didn't thrill me.

I motioned for Vell to stay by the rolltop door, while I approached the side door, considering my options. I could knock. I could barge in. I could knock and run, to get Payton away from the saw.

But if it wasn't Payton, I didn't want to freak out some poor schlub, especially if he was working with power tools. I didn't want to get sued if I frightened him and he accidentally cut off a few of his fingers.

I stepped up to the door and tried the doorknob. Unlocked. Maybe if I peeked in quietly, he wouldn't hear me, and I could confirm whether or not it was Payton.

I turned the knob and opened the door just a crack. A man had his back to me, and he was hunched over some kind of woodworking project stretched across a couple of sawhorses. In his hands he held a circular saw. The odor of pot hung in the air.

All I could think of was *Don't Get High and Saw.*

The guy shifted position, and I caught sight of his face.

Payton.

Chapter Twenty-Four

I eased the door closed and went to confer with Vell.

"It's him," I whispered. "He's working on some woodworking project. I think if we spread out, we can talk to him without him getting violent."

"Didn't work at Gerry's."

"He doesn't have his posse behind him now. We'll see what kind of backbone he really has. When I count to three, we'll barge in, and I'll go to the far corner, and you stay by the door."

"If something goes wrong, be sure to tell Mama I love her."

"Come on."

Vell followed me, and we got set outside the door. I held up a finger, and then two, and when I hit three, I flung open the door and raced across the length of the garage into the far corner. Vell stepped in behind me.

Between his concentration, the sound of the saw, and the haze of pot smoke lingering in the air, it took about twenty seconds for Payton to notice he had company and an additional twenty seconds to place our faces. When he did, he stood straight up. Unfortunately, he didn't put the saw down. "What do you want?"

"We just want to talk," I said.

"Talk, huh? How about you answer a question for me first? Do you know where Nicole is? I really, really need to talk to her." Payton looked at Vell, then at me. We'd strategically spread out enough so if Payton made a run at one of us, the other would be able to counter-attack from the offside.

"No. That's one of the questions we wanted to ask you."

"Don't know where she is." Payton's eyes had a little trouble focusing.

"Did you kill Billy Lane?"

His face soured. "Hell no. We used to be friends you know. You have any idea who did it?"

"Cops want to talk to you."

"Oh yeah? Let 'em. I had nothing to do with it." Payton hefted the saw again, pulling its yellow cord tight.

"I thought you two had a falling out."

"So what? Doesn't mean I killed him." Payton squinted at me. "How'd you find me, anyway?"

"Word's out, Payton. Whoever's looking for you won't be far behind."

"What do you know about someone looking for me?" The muscles in his forearm bulged as he held the saw.

"I know you owe a lot of money. And I know you've been taking some, uh, interesting jobs to try to pay it back."

"You don't know crap." Finally, he set the saw down on the floor next to a sawhorse. I wasn't sure, but it looked like he was building a gun rack. "I had the money. Someone took it."

"Sure. I bet the Coach bought that line."

"If he'd bought that line, I wouldn't be hiding out here, would I? I'd better pack up again. If you jokers found me, you're right, they'll be along soon. And I'm not anxious to see them right now."

"Who is this Coach dude?" I asked.

A primal yell grabbed my attention. Vell stumbled forward, pushed from behind, and Kevin came roaring into the room, screaming like a banshee. He charged at Payton, who stepped aside, bumping Kevin with his hip. Kevin spun ninety degrees and sprawled across a workbench. He reached up and grabbed a chisel from a pegboard full of tools.

Now armed, he whirled around and brandished the chisel.

Payton crouched into a fighter's stance. If Kevin charged him, I had no doubt who would win the fight. "Easy now, Kevin. Let's talk this over."

"Nothing to talk about. He hit my mom. He deserves a little payback."

Kevin held the chisel like an experienced knife fighter would hold a blade. Underhanded and to the side.

There were three of us, so we instinctively spread out, surrounding him.

"Put that down, Kev," Payton said. "Don't make things worse for yourself."

"Listen to your stepfather," Vell said. "You cut somebody people will think you're the bad guy. If you put that thing down and we talk it out, people may get a different idea."

Kevin's wild eyes darted around, and he danced back and forth, jabbing the chisel in the air at Payton. "You hurt her. You ruined what we had. You made us leave." He wiped a few tears away with his free hand. "It's all your fault."

Vell had worked his way closer to Kevin, but he was moving very, very slowly. Couldn't be too careful, dealing with a distraught teenager wielding a very sharp object.

"My fault? First of all, I never did anything to your mother. It was her fault catting around like that. Disrespecting me. If I wanted to have hurt her, she wouldn't be walking right now." With his head held up—keeping an eye on Kevin—Payton bent over and picked up the circular saw. Depressed the trigger a couple of times, and the metallic whir filled the garage with dread.

I felt like grabbing the saw and giving Payton a close shave with it. A very close shave. "Everybody take a deep breath, okay?"

"Hey, kid," Payton said. "Did your mother take my money? It isn't hers, it's mine. And I aim to get it back. If I find her..."

Kevin didn't answer. His knuckles were white as he held the chisel in a deathgrip. Nobody moved. Payton held the saw at waist level. Vell and I held our breath and hoped nobody did anything rash. An observer might have thought we were playing a twisted game of Statues.

I broke the spell. "I think it's time we were leaving. Come on, Kevin."

I stepped toward Kevin and held out my hand for the chisel. He ignored me and lunged for Payton. Somehow, Vell grabbed the back of Kevin's shirt collar and reeled him in before he did any damage. Advantage of being a collegiate-level athlete. "No you don't," Vell said. "We're going to leave your stepfather alone now. Don't worry, he'll get what's coming to him, one way or another. Karma's a bitch."

Payton bared his teeth and ran the saw. Vell maintained his grip on Kevin, and I carefully pried the chisel from his hand. The fight seemed to have drained from his body, because he gave it up easily. Poor kid. Just another reminder that the adults in his world were always getting the best of him.

Hard to believe in karma when you were fifteen years old, and all you've been dealt in life have been deuces.

I spoke to Payton. "I know a detective you can talk to about Lane. Tell him you're innocent. It would be easier, and better for you, if you came forward on your own volition. And if you're with the cops, it's a lot less likely Coach will get to you."

"You're insane. The cops aren't going to believe me, not when they can pin Lane's murder on me and clear their case. Besides, as soon as I find my money, I'm outta here. Going to start over in Texas."

"Where do you think your money is?"

Payton glared at me as if we were both sharing some secret. "I bet Nicole has it. Why she ran off." He held up the saw and pulsed it on and off. "Now get the hell out of here."

We didn't have to be told twice. Vell took one of Kevin's arms and I grabbed the other, and we escorted him swiftly from the garage, down the driveway, and out onto the street, as fast as we could without looking like we were fleeing the scene of a crime. When we got to the car, we stuffed Kevin into the backseat and Vell got in with him. The last thing we needed was for Kevin to break free and try another kamikaze run at Payton.

Before I got in, I called Ostervale and told him where Payton was. I also told him Payton probably wouldn't be there when he arrived. Ostervale thanked me and hung up.

I climbed into the driver's seat and shifted around so I could see Kevin in the back. "I thought we told you to stay put."

He was still breathing hard, and I figured it was only partly due to the physical exertion. Threatening someone with a sharp tool was bound to get the juices flowing. "He ruined my mother's life. And mine, too. He deserves some payback. If you hadn't stopped me..."

He didn't finish his sentence, and I didn't think adding, "...he would have killed you" was the considerate thing to do. "Kevin, violence doesn't solve anything. Just gets people hurt and ruins lives."

"You sound like my mother."

"Speaking of which, you think it's possible your mother has the money?" I asked Kevin.

He pressed his lips together, looked away, the definition of petulant.

"You didn't bring us here to find your mother, did you?"

Kevin looked out the side window.

"You thought your stepfather might be here, and you wanted us to bring you here. So you could attack him. Am I right?"

Kevin glanced back and from the twinkle in his eye, I knew I'd pegged it. And he was proud of his accomplishment. I wished I'd known ahead of time what the deal was so I could have alerted Ostervale. If Payton didn't have anything to do with Lane's death, then the cops wouldn't hold him, despite what he thought.

Unless they wanted him for something else, too. Which wasn't entirely out of the question.

"Next time, I think we'll be leaving you behind."

I got the car started and we turned around at the end of the cul-de-sac. As we approached the house, Payton's car peeled out, tires screeching, rubber burning. He hadn't been kidding about taking off ASAP. I called Ostervale back and told him not to bother sending a cruiser. I also told him what kind of car Payton was driving; unfortunately, I didn't get the license.

Ostervale hung up. This time, he didn't bother thanking me.

I parked at the curb in front of the house, and since I still had the key in my pocket, Vell and I searched the place, just to make sure Nicole wasn't locked in a closet somewhere.

She wasn't.

We returned to the car, where Kevin continued to sulk in the back seat. I turned to Vell. "I could use a snack. How about you?"

"Took the words right outta my mouth, bro. I can taste it already."

"Luckily, I know just the place."

Chapter Twenty-Five

When we walked into Mama's living room, she was at her desk in front of her webcam, dressed for business. In her case, this meant a colorful caftan, an equally colorful bandanna on her head, and eight or ten strings of even more colorful beads around her neck. Every finger displayed a ring, and huge dangly earrings hung from each lobe.

She held up a finger off to the side, indicating she was almost done with her call.

I whispered to Kevin to keep silent, and the three of us watched her in action.

"So I'm feeling some very strong energies, with regard to your close family members. The elderly one, she's doing okay, isn't she? Despite what the doctors have predicted?" Mama said to her client over Skype.

A tinny voice came through the speakers. "Yes. Yes, that's right! She's hanging on longer than they thought."

"She's got your spunk, all right. But say your goodbyes soon anyway. The passing time will come eventually."

"Yes, yes, I will. Thank you so much. You've given me hope."

"I'm just the conduit, Sharlene. You're the one doing all the hard work," Mama said. "Same time next week?"

"Absolutely."

"Goodbye then." Mama clicked off, and in one smooth motion, removed the bandanna from her hair and got up. Came over to give Vell a big hug.

"Hey baby. Nice to see you." She let him go and engulfed me. "Hello, Mess. Every time I see you, you get more handsome."

"What about me?" Vell asked.

Mama scrunched up her face, reached out, and pinched Vell's love handles. "You getting enough exercise, son?"

Vell opened his mouth to respond, but Mama had moved on to Kevin. "Who's your friend?"

"This is Kevin."

"I'm Vell's mama. Pleased to meet you."

For a moment, I thought Mama would try to hug Kevin and crush him like a paper cup. But she stuck out her fist, and Kevin bumped it.

"I bet you boys are hungry." Without waiting for an answer, she left the room.

"Mama needs to come out of her shell," I said.

"She comes out any farther, she'll be in everyone else's shell," Vell said.

He and Mama might have a complicated relationship, but their underlying love held it together. "What do you think, Kevin? This is where Vell grew up."

Kevin just nodded absently. He wandered around the room, attention drawn to all the fortune teller trappings set about. He picked up a little figurine and examined it. "Is this a voodoo doll?"

Vell took two big steps and practically snatched it out of Kevin's hands. "Let's not be playing with this stuff, okay?" He placed it gently back where it belonged.

"Sorry," Kevin said with a tone. He glanced at me, and I gave him a little shrug. I'd never known Vell to be superstitious. But the way he rushed over to grab that voodoo doll made me wonder. I stored the observation away, to be brought out next time I wanted to, uh, needle Vell about something.

Mama returned to the room, carrying a silver tray. She set it down on the coffee table in front of the couch. "Have a seat and eat."

Vell plopped down in the middle of the couch, but Mama waved him aside. Reluctantly, he scooted over. "That spot is for guests. Kevin, dear, why don't you sit there?" She gently guided Kevin down into the place of honor. Once he was situated, Mama waved to me. "Go ahead, sit down."

Mama eased down next to Kevin, and I took a seat on a chair next to the couch.

There were several plates on the tray. A big one held three distinct foods—some beans and rice, something that looked like chicken curry, and something else I guessed was shrimp and grits. Next to it, two small plates held a few saltine crackers and a dollop of peanut butter. There was only one fork on the tray.

"Kevin, the plate in the middle is for you," Mama said. "Sorry, I didn't have enough of everything. Vell and Mess, I know you won't mind. After all, you like peanut butter, right?"

Usually, I held the position of Most Pampered Guest in Mama's house, and as such, I got the preferential treatment. Looked like I'd been usurped by Kevin. Vell must have been used to being a secondary citizen because he grabbed a small plate without a comment. Either that, or he knew complaining wouldn't change a thing.

Kevin picked up the fork and poked at the food as three adults stared at him. He scooped up a little of the beans and rice and tasted it. It took a few seconds to register, but when it did, he smiled and went back for a big forkful.

Mama's grin widened.

I dipped a cracker into some peanut butter and crammed it into my mouth.

After Kevin finished the beans and rice, he moved onto the shrimp, gaining momentum as he plowed through the food. He didn't even hesitate when he got to the curry and kept going until the plate was clean.

Just as he swallowed the last bite, Mama rose. "Can I get you some more?"

Kevin nodded and Mama scooped up his plate and swooped out.

"I thought she didn't have enough for us," I said to Vell.

"She doesn't." He popped another cracker into his mouth.

Mama returned with another plate heaped high with food. This time it only took about three minutes for Kevin to devour it. When he did, he put his fork down. "Man, I'm stuffed. That was delicious."

I'd never seen Mama's smile so big. "Glad you enjoyed it, honey."

Kevin sagged back into the couch and his expression looked a lot like Uncle

Phil's used to look after the Thanksgiving feast when I was a kid.

"So," Mama began. "Tell me a little about yourself, Kevin."

Aha! I should have known there was a method to Mama's madness. This whole thing started with Mama steering Nicole and Kevin my way, so she knew Kevin's basic story, but I wasn't sure how much Vell had updated her about the latest developments. I sat back, eager to watch a master interrogator at work and hoping to pick up a few pointers.

Kevin shrugged. "I'm just...I don't know. Nothing much to tell."

"Tell me something." Mama smiled. "I know I'm curious, and I don't mean to pry, but this one here don't tell me much of anything." She jerked her head at Vell. "And I so like to know what's going on in people's lives."

Kevin swallowed, clearly on the hot seat. But Mama did just feed him... "Well, my mother and I just moved out."

"That's a big change," Mama said. "Sometimes changes are hard."

"I guess."

"Where are you moving to?"

"I don't really know yet."

"Just you and your mom, right?"

Kevin looked down into his lap. Mumbled.

"What was that, dear?"

He picked his head up, eyes moist. "Yes. Just us two."

"What can I do to help?" Mama asked.

Kevin seemed to focus right on Mama's face, on her words. More importantly, he seemed to be focused on her meaning. It was a far cry from his usual evasiveness and practiced apathy, and I felt honored to be in the living room of Mama, the master.

"I don't really know."

"But you do know you could use some help, and there are people, good, trustworthy people, who want to help you, right?"

A small, not-quite-convincing nod from Kevin.

Mama had been leaning quite close to Kevin, but now she shifted away to give him a little more space. "You know, I have a special gift. Some call it the sight, others call it the shine. Others say it's more like ESP or fortune telling. Whatever you call it, though, my gift allows me to connect with other people. To sense things going on with them, with their lives, with their loved ones. It's not 100% accurate, I will admit, but it's uncanny—to others, anyway—how close I get to the underlying truths. Present, past, future." She reached out to me. "Give me your hand, Mess. Let me show Kevin that there's nothing to worry about."

After sitting there quietly for so long, Vell finally spoke up. "Come on, Mama. Leave Mess alone. You can save your magic tricks for your *customers*."

Mama whipped her head around. "Hush!"

I couldn't see her face, but from the expression on Vell's, I knew she was mighty pissed, something that didn't happen often, but when it did, mortals better watch out.

Vell frowned, then folded his arms and slumped back into the couch cushions, staring at the far wall. I got the feeling he'd done the exact thing dozens of times growing up in that house.

Mama swung back toward me, extending her hand. I took it, and she closed her eyes. Next to her, Kevin wasn't missing a beat.

Mama bobbed her head up and down a few times. Inhaled dramatically, then tipped her head back. "This here is a good man. An honest man. He truly cares about others. And not just friends and family. Strangers, too. He'd go way out of his way to help someone in need."

I liked to think Mama was right, but she knew me, and so far, she hadn't unearthed any sterling nuggets with her sight.

"He's a skeptical sort, sometimes, and he's not always the neatest or most punctual person, but if he says he'll do something, he'll do it." She paused and cocked her head funny, eyes still closed as if she were getting a direct data download from some mystical place. "Eventually. But he's a man you can always trust."

She exhaled, then let her chin drop down to her chest. She remained inert for a few seconds, then started shaking her head like she was waking up in the morning. Her eyes fluttered open, and she appeared surprised at where she was. Blinking rapidly, she took a few quick breaths, then slapped on a tired smile.

Kevin's mouth hung open.

"Now it's Vell's turn to be read."

Vell kept his head turned away.

"Come on, now. Don't be stubborn. I'm sure Kevin wants to know if he can trust you, too."

I wasn't sure if Kevin was buying into Mama's shtick. Just because some old lady said someone was trustworthy didn't make it so. But Mama cast a large spell—maybe in more ways than one—and if anyone could pull it off, she could.

"D'Marvellus Jackson, I'm speaking to you."

Vell slowly turned his head, resignation on his face. I'm sure he thought this whole thing to be ridiculous—he told me he'd always been ashamed of Mama's shenanigans, especially when his friends ribbed him about it—but I knew how much he too wanted to help Kevin.

"Okay. But how about the condensed version?" Vell asked.

"Stop fussing. This won't take long. Now give me your hand."

Vell reached across Kevin's lap from one side, Mama from the other, and they clasped hands, creating a Kevin sandwich.

Mama repeated her machinations and tipped her head back. "Another fine human being. Kind to a fault. Generous with both time and money. Always putting the needs of others in front of his own."

Vell's sour expression had softened.

"He helps anyone he can, and he can be trusted completely."

Now a tiny smile emerged on his face.

"Of course, no man is a saint. It wouldn't hurt him to be a little kinder to his Mama. The women who raised him, sacrificed—"

Vell yanked his hand away, and Mama's eyes flew open. For a moment, I thought she might lash out at Vell again, but she actually winked at him, over Kevin's head.

"Thank you, hon, for cooperating."

Vell muttered something that sounded like, "You're welcome."

Mama put her arm around Kevin, pulling him close, and if it had been any other person on the planet, save for his mother, Kevin probably would have slapped it off. But Mama had her way with people, even the most resistant. "I hope you got the picture that you can trust others—even if you don't know them well—to help you out in times of need."

Kevin nodded, slowly, seriously. "I do. I trust you. Thank you. Thank you all."

I eyed Kevin, wondering how good an actor he was.

Chapter Twenty-Six

Mama had a long list of chores for Vell to do, so Kevin and I headed back to the Sleep Tight. On the way, I called Cesar to see if anything at the motel needed my attention.

"Everything is fine here, Mess," Cesar said. "As usual."

"Good to hear. Not that I doubted it or anything."

"Of course not. Although..."

"What?"

"There was something that seemed a little suspicious. Or I should say, more suspicious than the normal suspicious activities that many of your guests—"

I cut him off. "What happened?"

"About an hour ago, two guys came by, knocked on a few doors. Hung around a while. Mostly sat in their car and watched the place. When Griff asked them who they were looking for, they mentioned a few names—probably made-up—then took off."

"Hmm. What were they driving?"

"Black Suburban."

"They come back?"

"Not that I've seen. I think they saw the size of Griff and decided they should harass someone else someplace else." Cesar didn't always speak fondly of Griff, but this time, he sounded happy to have the big guy around.

"Okay. Thanks. If they should return, let me know?"

"Certainly," Cesar said.

"Thanks. Talk to you later."

"I shall await your—"

I hung up on him.

When Kevin and I got to the Sleep Tight, Harry came bounding over as soon as we parked by our room. "Can I talk to you for a minute?" he said.

"Sure."

He side-nodded at Kevin, who leaned against the car playing with his phone. "Alone?"

"Sure, sure." Harry and I walked out of Kevin's earshot. "Okay, what?"

"Coupla guys came around asking about you. And the kid."

Crap. "What did you tell them?"

"Whaddya think I told 'em? I told 'em to pound sand."

"You did?" I tried not to let my amazement seem obvious.

"Well, not exactly in those words. But I did tell them I hadn't seen you."

"Thanks. I owe you another—"

"Already wrote it down in my book," he said.

"When were they here?"

Harry glanced at his watch. "'Bout forty-five minutes ago."

"They ask for us by name?"

"Naw. But they described you both pretty well. One guy was normal looking. Jeans, windbreaker. The other guy was pretty scary. Walked with a limp. Wore a sweatshirt, cut off at the shoulders and wristbands, like some musclebound gym rat. Weird. But scary weird, you know?"

"These guys drive a black Suburban?"

Harry's eyes popped out. "Yeah? How'd you know?"

"Lucky guess. I don't suppose they told you why they were looking for us?"

"Oh yeah, we had a long discussion about that. And then we talked about our favorite movies, favorite restaurants, our most intimate dreams and desires. You know, the works."

"I'll take that as a no."

"A big fat one." Harry leaned in close. "I'd swear on a two-inch stack of Benjis that these guys are bad, bad men."

"Thanks, I'll keep that in mind." I scanned the parking lot for any black Suburbans that may have snuck in while we were talking. Nada. "Anything else, Harry?"

"No," he said. "Except I got the license plate. You know, if you're interested."

"You aren't as stupid as you look," I said. "I owe you yet another one."

"Already logged in."

Harry handed me a slip of paper with the license number on it, and I thanked him again and let him get back to his running-a-motel business. Kevin and I hustled into our room, and when the door was closed—and the deadbolt thrown—I broke the bad news to him. "Pack up your stuff. We're moving to a different place."

He flopped down on his bed. "Seriously? I'm tired, Mess. I just wanna stay in one place and watch TV or play video games. Can't we do that?"

"Sorry, but we've gotta go." I pulled my duffel bag out from under a chair. "Now."

Kevin slapped his hands on the mattress a few times. When I didn't react, he hoisted himself up, found his own duffel bag, and started cramming his stuff into it.

I finished packing first, so I took a minute to call Ostervale.

He answered right away. "Hey, man. What totally inappropriate favor do you need now?"

Ostervale wasn't off base, but it hurt me a little that he thought I was just a taker, taker, taker. "Some guy hit my car and sped off. I need you to run his plates." I paused. "If you don't mind."

"He hit your car? How can you tell, amid all the existing damage?"

A fair point. "I saw him. Heard the sound of twisting metal."

"You want to file an official report? Because that's how we roll here at the po-leece department. If the form's not filled out, it didn't happen."

"I was hoping I wouldn't have to go to so much trouble. I don't care about my car; I'd just like to keep this from happening to some other law-abiding citizen. Next time, it might not be only the car that gets bashed."

"And how is *me* telling *you* who this guy is going to prevent that?"

"I don't have all the answers. I'm not a cop, you know." I rattled off the license plate number from the scrap of paper Harry gave me. "Do what you want with it. My hands are clean on this one now."

"If I had more friends like you, Mess, I wouldn't have a minute to myself. Later."

Kevin finally finished packing, and after a final inspection to make sure we didn't leave anything behind, we went outside and threw our bags into the backseat.

"Where are we going now?" Kevin asked.

It was my turn to shrug.

* * *

We drove around for a while, in and out of neighborhoods, west on I-66 and back again, then onto the Beltway for a couple exits. When I was sure we weren't being followed, we headed back to the City of Fairfax. Since I didn't know who was looking for us, I couldn't very well know where to go where they wouldn't find us. And I needed to stay in the area if I wanted to have any shot of finding Nicole and figuring out what the heck was going on.

I also figured it wouldn't hurt to stay in familiar surroundings, where my friends—and Griff and his friends—were nearby. It also wouldn't hurt to be in a public place.

So I parked in the library parking garage and we walked across the street to a new-ish park the City had built. We were sitting side-by-side, watching a couple of kids play in a fancy water jet display fountain. Every so often, some of the jets would shoot into the air, straight up, while others would gurgle down to knee-height or turn off altogether. This water ballet was accompanied by a colored light show, and it seemed like the kind of place that could occupy a kid for an hour.

Maybe that was why it was so popular with parents and nannies.

"You get enough to eat at Vell's?" I asked.

"Yeah."

"Mama knows how to cook, right?"

"Yeah."

"What did you think of her?"

Kevin didn't answer at first, just kept watching the kids chase the undulating water streams. I was pretty sure he heard me, and since I didn't get a blow-off answer or a blow-off shrug or a blow-off grunt, I assumed he was thinking of his reply. After a short while, he answered. "I'm not sure I believe in her fortune-telling stuff, but I believed in *what* she said, you know?"

Very astute. "I feel the same way. Vell's a lucky guy to have been raised by her."

"Yeah, I guess. Although she was giving him a hard time." A wisp of a smile graced Kevin's lips, then receded into teenage stoicism.

I laughed, a little too hard on purpose. "They have quite a relationship. I think that's how they express their affection—through lighthearted teasing. I'm sure you and your mom go at it like that sometimes, huh?"

"I guess so. I don't know how I'd feel if my mom told fortunes, though."

"I hear you. Can you imagine Vell, when he was your age, having friends over and meeting his mom?"

This time, Kevin actually chuckled. Now we were just two guys, shooting the breeze on a sunny afternoon, watching the kids frolic in the fountain.

"What wacky things do you do that your mom gets on your case about?"

"I never clean my room. And I put a Nerf hoop over my trashcan, so the floor around it is littered with my misses." He quickly added, "Not that there are many of those."

"Of course not. Did you know I've got a Nerf hoop, too? In my office. I miss more than I make though. Maybe we should play a game of H-O-R-S-E? I bet I could take you." I pantomimed a few ball fakes, then a fadeaway shot. Pretended to watch the shot through the air, then threw my hands up in the air and imitated crowd noises when the game-winner dropped through the hoop. "Yesssss!"

"What? No way, dude. No way. I'd kick your butt." Kevin was more animated than I'd seen him, which wasn't saying a whole lot. But the morose teenager had left the building, at least for a little while, and it was great to see. Great to know that underneath the angst generated by the upheaval in his life, a regular kid lurked.

"We'll just have to see about that, won't we?"

"Anytime."

Neither of us spoke. We'd started to bond a bit, but I didn't want to press my luck. I also had a theory that sitting together in silence was good for bonding, too. I felt a budding relationship had reached a certain plateau when my girlfriend and I could share time and space without succumbing to the pressure to say something clever or endearing.

Although Kevin didn't utter a word, I could almost feel that change in our relationship. A charge of electricity between us. I'd gained a little trust. Come up with some common ground. Related to him on his terms.

A girl, about four or five years old, slalomed through the water jets, spray making her hair wet. She giggled as she ran, and when she got to the end of the row, she kept coming our way, until she stopped two feet in front of Kevin.

Across the concrete deck, her mother got up from her bench and walked our way, not in a big hurry, but not lolly-gagging, either.

"Hello," the girl said to Kevin. "What's your name?"

"Kevin."

"I have a friend Kevin. He likes trains."

"I like trains, too."

"I like trains, too," the girl said. "And airplanes. And ice cream cones."

The girl's mother arrived. "Come on, Grace, let's leave these people alone."

"Oh, it's no bother," I said. "Grace was just telling us she likes ice cream cones."

"Banilla is my favorite." She turned to her mother. "Can we get ice cream? I'm hungry."

"We'll see," said the mom. "Say goodbye now."

"Goodbye," Grace said.

"Goodbye. Nice talking to you," I said.

The mom took one of Grace's hands, and with the other, the little girl kept waving goodbye to us all the way back to her bench.

"Ever wish you had a little sister?" I asked Kevin.

"Not really."

"They're pretty great." I paused. "Most of the time."

Kevin nodded.

"I don't mean to pry, so if you don't want to talk about it, that's fine. But I was wondering about your real father, or I guess I should say your biological father."

I waited for Kevin to tense beside me, to clam up and pull out his phone and shut me out, but none of that happened. "I didn't know him. He left mom when I was two. I think he was a bus driver or something."

"He ever try to contact you?"

"Nope."

"Your mom?"

"I don't think so." Kevin started fidgeting next to me. "At least she never said anything to me about it. She doesn't talk about him at all. So I don't ask."

"You ever see the grandparents on that side?"

"No. Never. Don't know if they're alive or dead. Don't care, either."

I understood Kevin's reaction completely. Families were complicated creatures. Multi-headed beasts who could breathe fire, or loving angels who could buoy you up with a smile. What was that saying? You could pick your friends, but you couldn't pick your family members. So true.

"Is there anything you can tell me that might help me find your mother?" I asked.

As before, Kevin stared off into the distance. When he finally faced me, his eyes were moist, and it wasn't from the water jet spray. "I'm sorry, Mess. I am. I really screwed this whole thing up." He choked up and turned away.

I put my hand on the back of Kevin's shoulder. "What do you mean?"

His back rose as he took a big breath. Then he turned around. "This entire thing is my fault. If I hadn't..."

A dozen questions ran through my mind, but I started with the most obvious. "If you hadn't what?"

Kevin put his head in his hands, sobbed. It wasn't the first time Kevin had gone off blaming someone in an emotional tirade—first his stepfather, now himself. Heck, it wasn't even the first time today.

I gently put my hand on his shoulder and waited until he calmed down. No need to say anything. When he did, I suggested we go to Baskin-Robbins and get some ice cream.

Banilla.

That brought a small smile to his lips, but it was fleeting.

* * *

We ordered our cones—neither of us had chosen vanilla, not with so many other intriguing choices—and found a bench outside the store, underneath the *31 Flavors* sign and overlooking the parking lot of the sketchy shopping center. There was a carpet store, a drug store, and a Hooters on the other end, and every time I'd ever driven by, the lot was never more than a quarter full.

Sometimes I wondered how so many retail stores and restaurants stayed in business.

I'd started to ask him several times for an explanation and managed to wait until he had finished his cone. But not a second longer. "What do you mean it's all your fault?"

"It is. I'm sorry."

"Why don't you start at the beginning?"

"Why bother? There's nothing you can do about it." A truck rumbled by on the street, and he followed it with his eyes.

"Try me. If nothing else, maybe you'll feel better getting it off your chest. Sometimes holding in a secret is pretty stressful."

He snuffled, then began. "Okay. My stepdad lost his job last year sometime. Mom said he'd always drank and gambled, but things seemed to get worse. And worse. He hit Mom once, and..."

"Must have been very difficult to watch."

"I didn't see him hit her. Not that first time. Just saw the bruises." Kevin looked away from me as he talked.

"I was speaking in the larger sense. Watching things fall apart must have been very difficult. Bad for your mom, bad for you."

"Yeah."

"So then what?"

"It just got worse and worse. I begged her to leave him, and she wouldn't. I begged her to call the cops, and I threatened to call myself, a bunch of times, but I never did. I should have."

"Why didn't you?"

"Mom didn't want me to. Said she loved him, that he was going through a rough time. Told me to be patient, that Todd was a good man." Tears welled in his eyes. "Good men don't hit women."

"No, they don't." I thought back to my childhood. My overbearing parents. My jerky uncle. The usual sibling squabbles with my sister. Nothing even approached—not even close—anything Kevin had endured. I knew how my life had been affected by my upbringing, and I could only wonder how the terror in Kevin's life would manifest itself as he grew up and started his own family. "Did he ever hit you?"

His eyes sparked. "He tried once. He was drunk and I said something about it to him. He swung at me, and I ducked. I should have clobbered him right then, but I just ran away. If I had, we wouldn't be here talking. And he wouldn't have continued to terrorize us."

"I doubt that. If you'd hit him, things probably would have escalated, and we might not be sitting here talking. You might not be sitting anywhere talking. Your stepfather is quite a bit larger than you. Meaner, too." I let that sink in for a moment. I'm sure that thought had crossed his mind at some point, but to hear someone else say it, to confirm your worst-case scenario as being plausible, was an entirely different thing.

And how must Kevin have felt, forced into the position of being his mother's protector, and failing time after time? Probably tore him up inside, seeing his mother being mistreated like that and being powerless to stop it. I tried to imagine what I would do—as an adult—if Russell ever started banging Izzy around. I'd want to throttle him, make him suffer, but I'd probably call the cops. Would I if Izzy begged me not to? Would I? I honestly didn't know.

"I still don't see how any of this is your fault."

"I threatened to run away if she didn't leave him. I *made* her leave. If I hadn't, we wouldn't be on the run, hiding out, and those men never would have taken her."

"Trust me, it's not your fault. Do you honestly think things would have been better if you stayed and your stepfather kept hitting your mother?"

He shrugged.

"Things would have come to a head eventually." I gripped his shoulder. "This is not your fault, Kevin. This is Todd's fault. Don't ever forget that."

"If I hadn't said I was going to run away, this never would have happened."

I didn't answer. Trying to talk someone out of feeling guilty wasn't easy, especially when that someone was a teenager with a missing mother. Hopefully, with time, Kevin would realize the truth, namely that Todd Payton was the monster in this story. We sat there in silence for a while, watching the traffic. I tried to come up with a plan of action, seven steps to success or some such crap, but I only got as far as step one.

I patted Kevin on the thigh. "Okay, then. We need a place to stay, don't we?"

"I guess."

"Can't go back to my place. Can't go back to the Sleep Tight. Can't go to your old apartment. Got any ideas?"

Kevin shrugged. I didn't expect him to have any, but I thought I'd at least try to include him in the plans.

"How about Mama's? I'm sure she'd love to have houseguests. I sorta got the idea she likes to cook for people."

Kevin's faint smile was a rare thing of beauty.

Chapter Twenty-Seven

Part of me felt bad barging in on Mama—especially without running the idea past Vell first. But I knew Mama really did enjoy having guests, and those she liked having most were lost kittens and puppies who needed a little help—and a home-cooked meal or three. She had a savior complex as big as her heart. And voice.

When she opened the door, her face lit up. "I knew you were still hungry, child. Come on in."

We went in and explained our predicament. Before I had a chance to finish giving her the rundown, she hushed me. "Okay, okay. I'll just take Kevin here and show him where he'll sleep. Mess, you can bunk in with Vell. Just try not to let his snoring keep you up."

I'd heard Vell snore before, and I thought I might have a better shot at getting a good night's sleep if I slept in my car parked on the side of the highway. But I'd worry about that later. "Where is the man of the house, anyway?"

"Going through some boxes of keepsakes in the basement. Go on down, I'm sure he could use some encouragement."

I left Kevin in Mama's very capable hands and found Vell in the basement, surrounded by a dozen boxes and plastic bins.

"Did you forget something?" Vell asked. "Like taking me with you?"

"Change in plans."

"I didn't know you had any plans in the first place." Vell stood tall, clapped his hands together which created a small cloud of dust.

"Figure of speech. We need to find Nicole, before Kevin explodes with guilt. He's convinced this entire thing is his fault."

"Where is he?"

I grinned.

"What?" Vell eyed me.

"Kevin needs to be safe. So I brought him here. Mama can watch him."

A flash of panic crossed Vell's face. "What? Here? I don't think that's such a—"

"Come on, Mama will love the chance to shower someone—other than you—with attention. She'll have a blast fussing over him."

At that, Vell softened. "Might be nice for her to have another person to nag. Take a little pressure off yours truly. At least for a while. Okay, I'm down with it."

"Besides, I didn't really have any other choice. I can't be babysitting him anymore. I've got to get this thing settled."

"You mean *we* have to get this thing settled" Vell all but winked at me.

"I was hoping you'd say that."

"Well, I want you to stay safe, and the only way I can see to that is if I tag along." He pushed aside the box he was working on. "Besides, we'll just be in the way of Mama trying to spoil Kevin."

"That sounds more dangerous than what we have planned."

"You don't know the half of it," Vell said, dead serious.

"Okay then."

"Okay then," Vell echoed.

I exhaled. "Now what?"

"You're the brains of our little team. I'm just the brawn," Vell said.

"I thought you were Vellipedia."

"Oh, right." Vell stared at me for a moment, thinking. Then he glanced at the time on his phone. "We can make it before closing. Come on, let's go talk to a buddy of mine."

He gave me directions while I drove, and our little journey ended in a strip shopping center not far from the Dunn Loring Metro station. I parked next to a red Tesla and Vell and I walked across the lot to a gigantic thrift store.

"We're not going clothes shopping, are we?" I opened the door for Vell.

"We're going information shopping," he said. "Come on. Pudding works in the back."

We wove through the aisles of second-hand merchandise. Utilitarian metal and wood racks held all sorts of household goods, and clothes and linens and towels were strewn on long tables running the length of the store. The store wasn't crowded, but it wasn't empty either. Customers browsed, looking for bargains amid the mountains of stuff piled high and crammed into every available nook and cranny.

It was like an enormous garage sale.

When we reached the back of the store, Vell knocked on a door that said, "Employees Only." A moment later, the door cracked open, and a head poked out. "Yeah?"

"Whassup, Pudding?" Vell said.

A look of surprise, followed by a warm smile. The door swung open. "Hey, hey, hey, if it isn't my man, D'Marvellus Jackson!" He accentuated the Jack in Jackson as if he were introducing Vell at an NBA game. "Come on back."

We followed Pudding into the back room, which, surprisingly, was a lot neater than the sales floor. He directed us to a few folding chairs surrounding a metal, government-issue desk. "Take a load off. Or more specifically, two loads."

We all sat.

Pudding had one of those timeless faces. Could have been thirty years old. Could have been sixty. Skinny. Dark food stains on his t-shirt. Maybe that was why he was called Pudding.

"How's business?" Vell asked.

"Steady. Always people looking for quality goods at a fair price. When they can't find that, they come here." Pudding smiled, and a gold tooth glinted. "Of course, I just work here. Get paid the same no matter how many old jeans get bought. How have you been? How's Mama?"

"Good and good."

"Nice to hear." Pudding jutted his chin at me. "Who's your friend?"

Vell clapped me on the shoulder. "This is Mess. Solid dude."

Pudding nodded and smiled. Smiled and nodded. I guessed all the pleasantries were finished. "So?"

"So. How come you haven't answered my texts or calls the past few days?" Vell asked. "I need some information."

Pudding squirmed in his chair. Shrugged. "Busy. Real busy. Plus...you know, I prefer to conduct business in person."

"Okay. I'll let it slide this once," Vell said. "But please try to be more considerate in the future, will you?"

"Sure. Sure." Pudding licked his lips. "Sorry, man."

"You know any bad dudes named Coach?"

Pudding swallowed. Then he bit his lower lip. He didn't say a word, even though it was clear—crystal clear—he heard Vell's question.

Vell glanced at me, then turned back to Pudding. "Where can I find him?"

Pudding closed his eyes and moved his lips, as if he was negotiating with himself. Eventually, the eyes opened, and he spoke aloud. "You didn't hear any of this from me."

"Never do." Vell smiled patiently.

Pudding held out his hand, palm up.

Vell nodded at me. "Information ain't free, Mess."

I looked at Vell, then at Pudding. Both waited expectantly.

It took me a second to figure out what they were waiting for. "Oh, I get it." I pulled out my wallet, fished out a twenty. Placed it in Pudding's hand.

He observed it for a long moment, then raised his head and looked back at me, expression blank.

Vell nodded at me again. "You get what you pay for."

I removed another twenty, put it on top of the first one in Pudding's hand. "Better?"

He didn't move a muscle.

Vell spoke to me, slowly and clearly. "Let's show my friend Pudding some respect, okay, Mess?"

I took the remaining money from my wallet, forty-seven dollars, and slapped it down onto Pudding's palm. "That's all the respect I've got left."

He smiled and stuffed the cash into his pocket. "Coach is a dude named Camarillo. Rafael Camarillo. If it's shady, Camarillo's into it. He runs a pretty big crew, but somehow manages to stay out of prison. He's got some blue-chip lawyers on his side and he's got some friends in very high places."

"Where can we find him?" Vell asked.

Pudding glanced around the back room as if one of Camarillo's men was waiting to jump out of the shadows and cut out his tongue. "For a guy like that, he's pretty accessible. Takes a 'hands-on' approach to his activities. I've heard he usually works out of a small office at the Annandale Y. In the back, across from the outside pool entrance. He actually runs their youth basketball programs, providing a shining role model for our next generation. Some kind of Renaissance man—thuggery and sports, all in one tidy package."

"We need to appeal to him," Vell said. "Any idea what soft spots he might have?"

Pudding stroked his weak chin. "Without any specific knowledge, I'd have to think money might work. I mean, doesn't money work with most people?"

After a little more chit-chat, Vell and Pudding chest-bumped goodbye—I just nodded— and we headed out of the store, leaving Pudding to count the dough I'd just given him.

"Why do you call him Pudding?" I asked.

Vell shrugged. "'Cause that's how he introduced himself to me. Want to know more, I guess you'll have to ask him."

"I would, except I'm all outta cash."

Chapter Twenty-Eight

Back at the car, I called Shotgun Stokes and put it on speaker. "Hello? This is Mess Hopkins. Lia's friend?"

"I know who you are. I'm a reporter, remember? I don't forget names or faces. Whaddya want?"

"I know who Coach is. Guy named Camarillo. You heard of him?"

"Sure. Everyone knows Camarillo. Heard him called a lot of things, just never Coach. Cold-hearted crime boss. Thinks he's the big kahuna when it comes to all things illegal, and frankly, that's not too far off. The police have been after him for years."

"I'm going to talk to him. Get him to call off the dogs chasing Nicole and Kevin."

Shotgun paused so long, I thought maybe he'd nodded off. "Lia thought you were smart. I guess she was wrong."

"Don't worry, I've got back-up." Next to me, Vell snorted.

"Unless your back-up is a SWAT team, I'd think again. Camarillo doesn't fool around. Should I waste any breath trying to dissuade you?"

"No. But the record will reflect you tried. What more can you tell me about him?"

"He's got a hand in virtually all illegal business in Virginia, starting at the Potomac, west to Leesburg and south to Manassas. Drugs, gambling, theft, prostitution, even movie pirating. Despite his, ah, wide range of activities, he tries to maintain a low-profile."

"Sounds like a charming guy."

"Oh, he is. I don't think he much likes me, considering what I write about him. He once called me to complain when I described him in an article as being 'a treacherous scumbag lowlife who would kill his mother for a doughnut.'"

That didn't sound very journalistic to me, but what did I know? "Thanks for the info, Shotgun."

"I'll pray for you."

"Thanks again, but I don't think that's necessary."

"I'll make sure to spell your name right in the obit. Good luck." He clicked off.

Vell said, "Maybe we should stop and bring some coffee and doughnuts with us. Put a smile on Camarillo's face. He might be less likely to kill us."

"Unless he's on a diet. Then he just might kill us for bringing doughnuts."

Vell grinned. "So you're saying six of one, half a dozen of another?"

The butterflies in my gut flapped their wings.

* * *

I glanced at my phone, and it was closing in on nine o'clock. We could try to take care of business, but it would be dark real soon, and the combination of being in unfamiliar territory in the dark wasn't very appealing.

"What do you say we get a start in the morning?"

Vell smiled and his body seemed to relax. "That's a brilliant idea. Always nice to get a good night's sleep before entering the lion's den."

"Absolutely. If we're going to die tomorrow, I'd like to die well rested."

We drove back to Mama's and found her and Kevin in the kitchen. He was eating brownies—fresh-baked, by the smell—and she was watching him intently, making sure he didn't miss a crumb.

"You boys find out what you needed?" she asked us.

"Yeah," Vell said. "You happen to know a guy named Camarillo?"

Mama scrunched up her face, thinking. "Doesn't ring a bell. Good guy or bad guy?"

"Bad guy. Very bad guy."

"And you're going to meet with him, aren't you?" Mama asked.

I didn't believe in her powers, but she'd read our minds this time. Of course, maybe she just knew how Vell and I operated. We didn't answer, just nodded.

"Then please, be careful, okay? That's all I ask."

"We will, Mama. We will," Vell and I said, in almost perfect unison.

* * *

The next morning, we stuck around long enough for Mama to cook us a fabulous breakfast. Eggs, bacon, waffles, muffins. If we were indeed going to die today, at least we were well-rested *and* well-fed.

Vell and I left Kevin with Mama, along with a suggestion—you didn't give Mama *instructions*—that Kevin shouldn't go anywhere. Then we set off to find Nicole.

We drove in silence to the Y, each of us making peace with ourselves, just in case.

The small front lot of the Y was crowded, so we parked around the side. Went in through the front double doors, and we were funneled past the reception desk. Two ladies in front of us, both carrying rolled-up yoga mats, flashed their IDs and pushed through the swinging metal gate.

An old guy in a gray YMCA T-shirt looked up from where he sat. "IDs?"

"We're not members," I said, adding. "Not yet, anyway."

"Interested in joining?"

"Maybe."

The old guy spun in his chair, looked over his shoulder through a glass window into an empty office. "Fiona isn't in, at the moment. She shows the prospects around. Answers questions, you know. Can you come back in about fifteen minutes?"

I opened my mouth, ready to offer a plea, when he waved us through. "Aw, go on. Look around. Just don't cause any trouble, okay? If you have any questions when you're through, Fiona can help you out."

We didn't have to be told twice. Vell and I pushed through the gate, then kept on going down a long hallway. Smaller hallways branched off in both directions, and we got glimpses of different activities underway: exercise classes, arts & crafts, chess and checkers, a book club. Most of the participants seemed to be of a certain vintage, which made sense at 10:30 a.m. on a weekday.

When we came to an intersection of large hallways, we turned right, following a sign that said POOL. Thirty yards later, we found ourselves peering through glass walls at the indoor pool. On the far side of the pool deck were more windows, these facing the great outdoors, where the blue of another pool beckoned.

They must have opened a few weeks early, because we hadn't yet hit Memorial Day.

"Can you swim?" Vell asked.

"Sure." I took in his slightly panicked face. "Can't you?"

"Oh sure, I can swim. Like a hammer."

"For your sake, then, I hope Camarillo doesn't throw us in the pool."

We kept going down the hall, and after a few dead-ends, we found a small office near what we deduced was an exit leading out to the pool. A beefy man in a neon green tracksuit sat at a tiny student desk outside the closed door of the office. His completely shaved head reflected light from the harsh fluorescent fixtures above. A carved wooden plaque above the door read "Coach."

We stopped about five yards away in front of a bulletin board and pretended to read fliers about swim lessons, swim meets, and rooms for rent. The guy didn't look up, too busy scratching away at a puzzle book with a yellow pencil.

"Now what?" Vell whispered.

"We talk with Camarillo." I tapped one of the fliers. "Unless you're finally ready to take some swimming lessons."

"Camarillo it is."

We casually strolled over to the guy doing a word search puzzle. He circled a word, then looked up and pointed behind us. "Locker room's back that way."

"We'd like to speak with Mr. Camarillo for a minute."

He squinted at us, seeming to notice Vell for the first time. "I'm not saying

I know who or where this Mr. Camarillo is, but what matter would you wish to discuss with him, if he were so available?"

It took an extra couple of seconds to parse the question, and I tried to mirror the thug's language, having once read that it improved communication. "The matter we wish to discuss with Mr. Camarillo involves a certain sum of funds that he has and will be seeking in comprehensive reimbursement from an earlier transaction or series of transactions with certain non-present parties."

Vell snorted, then tried to turn it into a cough. The big oaf didn't seem to notice; he was too busy trying to untangle my explanation. Finally, he said, "Who are you guys?"

"I'm Cole. This is Pike."

He frowned. "If you guys are screwing with me, you'll be sorry."

I held up three fingers, Boy Scout style. "No sir. We just need a few minutes of Mr. Camarillo's time. Then we'll be gone, and you'll never see us again."

"Okay. Wait here." The word search aficionado unfurled himself from the tiny desk with some effort. Taller than Vell by a couple of inches, he was wider in the shoulders and narrower in the hips, too. Vell was a former basketball player, but this guy could be a current athlete—in any number of sports. I just hoped he wasn't skilled at mixed martial arts, if it came to that.

He rapped on the closed office door.

"Yeah?" A deep voice bellowed from inside.

"Couple grunts want to see you."

"They cool?"

Camarillo's gorilla looked us up and down again, wrinkling his nose as if he'd just gotten a whiff of some spoiled yogurt. "Not even close. But they seem harmless enough."

"Come on in."

Camarillo's bodyguard swung the door open and stepped aside to let us through. He followed us in and closed the door behind us, then leaned against it, arms and legs crossed.

The office was bigger than I would have guessed, and if the odor of chlorine hadn't hung in the air, I never would have guessed we were in an old YMCA building. The walls were freshly painted, and sleek, modern furniture made the place seem more like a CEO's office than a youth basketball coordinator's.

Behind a fancy desk—with absolutely nothing on it—sat Camarillo. He hadn't bothered getting up when we entered. He had shortly cropped hair, just starting to gray, and wore a teal performance T-shirt—the hi-tech stretchy kind—that accentuated his physique. I guessed when your office was in the Y, you could squeeze in some weightlifting now and then.

Naturally, a whistle on a lanyard hung around his neck. *Drug dealer, loan shark, pimp, boy's basketball coach?*

"I'm Rafael Camarillo and this is my associate Z-Ray," he said, gesturing at the lug leaning against the door. "Who are you?"

"Our names aren't really important," I said.

He was about to reply—not in a nice fashion, it seemed—when he noticed something about Vell and nodded. "I know you."

"Oh? I don't think we've met before," Vell said.

Camarillo smiled suddenly. "No, we haven't met, but I know who you are. Dee-Marvelous Jackson?"

"Uh, I usually go by Vell. If I may ask, how do you know me?"

"I saw you play, man, and you *were* marvelous. Sweet stroke from three. Could take it to the rack, too, against guys much taller. I watched you tear up all comers in the City Challenge Cup some years back. You dropped thirty points in the final, if I recall."

Vell's grin threatened to break his cheekbones. "Thirty-three, actually."

"You had some talent, yes sir. Too bad about the knee."

The grin ebbed. "Stuff happens."

Camarillo's smile also disappeared. "Okay, Vell and nameless friend. What do you want?"

I stepped forward. Now that we'd shared some good memories with Camarillo, I figured the direct approach might work best. "We understand Todd Payton owes you a lot of money, and we just wanted to let you know his wife, and his kid, have absolutely nothing to do with it. In fact, they've left Todd and she plans to divorce him and start fresh in a different state. So going after them probably isn't a good thing to do. I mean, it'd be a better use of your resources if you concentrated on finding Payton himself."

Camarillo sat motionless, but his eyes blazed. If I wasn't mistaken, that was raw fury I saw. I wondered if it was just because I'd mentioned Payton, or if it was because I dared to tell him what to do. His jaw clenched and he began breathing rapidly through his nose.

I glanced at Vell, and Vell glanced at the door, and I had a feeling we were both calculating our odds of overpowering Z-Ray and getting out the door before Camarillo pulled a gun from who knew where and shot us both, leaving us to bleed to death on the floor of his office in the back of a downtrodden YMCA building. It's amazing what goes through your mind when you envision your last seconds on this good green earth.

A shudder rippled through me. And another. For a moment, I feared I'd go into full spasm mode. But as Camarillo's breathing slowed and his jaw eased, my tension also abated, but that wasn't saying a whole lot, because it was still sky high.

After a moment, Camarillo spoke in a fairly measured tone. "Dee-Marvelous, you and your friend came in here, and we had a little shared moment as I remembered watching you light it up, one weekend years ago. That was pleasure." He opened his hands, palms up, and gestured around his office. "This is business. I never mix the two. Never. So don't be under the impression that you can enter my world, my inner sanctum, and tell me what I should do. I haven't achieved what I have by being soft. Do you think I should be soft?"

Vell shook his head. I followed suit and made sure I used my indoor voice. "We're not asking you to be soft. We—I—was just trying to make your life easier and my friend's life a little less worrisome. She really has nothing to do with this. Just in the wrong place at the wrong time with the wrong guy. A really wrong guy."

Camarillo opened his top desk drawer, and my pulse shot up as I tensed. Surely he wouldn't really shoot us here. Too many people would hear the gun go off.

He pulled a teak letter opener out of the drawer and began cleaning his fingernails with it. I exhaled.

"She has nothing to do with it, huh? That's what you're telling me?"

"Exactly," I said. Next to me, Vell nodded to bolster my claim.

"She told you that, right?"

"Yeah. Said she didn't know anything about any money." Something wasn't sitting right. No doubt Camarillo was smug, but he seemed a bit too smug. Like a tenth grader who's somehow managed to see the answers to the final exam before the test.

Camarillo pointed his letter opener at me. "That's not what Payton himself says."

"What?" I felt like I'd just gotten an elbow to the solar plexus.

"I think you heard me." He turned to Vell. "You heard me, right? Your knee may be screwed up, but your hearing still works, don't it?"

"I heard you. But you can't believe Payton," Vell said. "Man's a liar, among his other nasty traits."

"That could be true. In this case, however, I believe him. He says she took the money right out from under his nose. Then the bitch took off." He slapped the letter opener into his other palm a few times. "What do you think about that theory?"

I had a hard time believing Nicole had taken the money. I was pretty sure that Payton, being the scumbag that he was, told Camarillo that Nicole had taken the money to buy himself some more time. But Camarillo seemed to entertain the possibility that Payton was speaking the truth. Unless he was just shining me on so he could try to get me to give up Nicole.

I quickly weighed my options. I could tell *my* truth, namely that we had no idea where Nicole was, but I doubted if Camarillo would believe me, and he'd probably torture me to tell the truth. Or I could lie and tell him I did know where she was. In which case he might just torture me for the information. Rock, meet hard place.

I took the wishy-washy, hopefully self-preserving, middle ground, which happened to be closest to the real, honest-to-goodness truth. "I don't know exactly where she is, but I can contact her. I'd be happy to deliver any message you might want to give her. Maybe some communication can clear up this whole misunderstanding."

"Oh, I don't need you to do that. You see, I've been in contact with her."

Another shot to the gut, and this one hurt more. Could Camarillo have abducted Nicole? "When did you talk to her?" I sputtered.

"She claims she didn't take Payton's money, and that she has absolutely no idea where it might be."

"Do you know where Nicole is, right now?" I asked, desperate to know if she was okay.

"For the moment, she is fine. And, as long as I get my money back, she will continue to be fine. But if I do not get my money back, and soon, she will not be fine much longer."

"I told you she has nothing to do with this. Your beef is with Payton, and only Payton."

Camarillo went back to cleaning his fingernails with the letter opener, working it this way and that, stopping to admire his work every so often. Tension hung in the air, right alongside the faint odor of chlorine. Finally, Camarillo looked up and said, "Nicole says she doesn't know where my money is—and I was pretty persuasive. But I think you two clowns might know where it is."

Next to me, Vell made a noise, halfway between a snort and a whimper. I glanced at him, and it seemed like his eyes were pleading for me to say something brilliant, something that would make Camarillo realize that we didn't have anything to do with this either.

Unfortunately, I had nothing.

"So here is what I am thinking." Camarillo tapped the point of the letter opener against the top of his desk. "If I get my money back, all of the money I am owed, then no harm shall come to her." He paused and narrowed his eyes. "Or her son."

"He's completely innocent," I said. "There's no need to drag him into this."

Camarillo shrugged. "If I do not get back what is rightfully mine, I am not responsible for what happens to thieves. Or their family members."

"Look, we have no idea where the money is," I said.

Camarillo smiled, but I might as well have been looking into the face of a wolf. “If that is true, it is a shame, for everyone involved.”

Somehow, I think Camarillo lumped me and Vell into that group, too.

“You have twenty-four hours.”

Chapter Twenty-Nine

No further threats were made, and Z-Ray let us leave without incident. As we passed the front desk, the old check-in guy spotted us.

"What did you think?"

"Facilities are nice," I said. "But there's a pretty nasty stench coming from that back office, near the pool."

By unspoken agreement, Vell and I didn't talk about what had just happened as we left the facility and headed across the parking lot. We weren't sprinting, but we were hustling along at a pretty good clip, afraid Camarillo might change his mind and instruct his muscle to jump us, just to teach us a lesson. After all, we could still deliver his money with a broken collarbone or two.

Except for the fact we had no idea where his money might be.

We made it to the car unharmed, and I didn't waste any time getting us back on the road.

"We, my friend," Vell said, "are screwed."

I was about to come up with a clever retort when I noticed a silver Beamer on our tail. It lagged a few cars behind, and the guy driving it wore wraparound mirror shades. I couldn't be sure, but I thought he was shaved completely bald.

"Don't turn around, but it looks like we've got company."

Vell shrunk down in his seat and tried to get a glimpse behind us in his side-view mirror.

"Silver BMW. Three cars back. I think Z-Ray's driving."

"Probably thinks we're going directly to retrieve his money."

"Let's have some fun, shall we?"

"Always up for a laugh," Vell said, totally serious.

We drove slowly, so we wouldn't lose him, which wasn't hard to do in the ever-present DC-area traffic. I checked the gas gauge, expecting it to be almost empty—as usual—but it was close to full. Avia must have filled it up after her interviews. Nice gesture, and one I wouldn't forget. "Been to Maryland lately?"

"Nope."

"Have to be anyplace in the next hour and a half?"

"Just by your side, singing sweet melodies."

"Perfect, but let's skip the sing-along." We could use the time to decompress and regroup. Our meeting hadn't gone as expected, to say the least.

In half a mile, we left Route 7 to head north on the Beltway. In the past ten years, the traffic that had been only terrible during rush hours was now terrible most of the time, and today was no exception. You expected things to get snarled due to an accident or because of construction, but what confounded me most was traffic that jammed up for no discernible reason.

I checked my rearview mirror. Z-Ray was right there. I wondered how full his gas tank was. I guessed we were about to find out.

As traffic ebbed and flowed, twenty miles per hour up to fifty, Vell and I discussed our meeting with Camarillo. We both assumed he had, in fact, abducted Nicole, and we figured he'd come up empty when he'd squeezed her for information about the money. Given that scenario, we concluded he was still holding her to use as a bargaining chip to get his money back. Which was pretty much what he implied.

So, our task was simple. Find a boatload of missing money and give it to Camarillo. In twenty-four hours.

No problem.

Our conversation didn't go much beyond that. Mostly because neither Vell nor I had a clue about what to do next.

We drove in silence and watched the exits creep by: the Dulles Access Road, Tysons Corner, GW Parkway. Then into Maryland. River Road, I-270 and points north, Bethesda, past the Mormon Temple, through Wheaton. We stayed in the right lane and chugged along. I kept an eye out for the Beamer and for once, I wasn't too pissed off by the traffic. I fully intended to waste a couple hours, while Z-Ray had no idea where we were going.

Past the exit for I-95 and Philly and New York. Into Prince George's County. College Park, the home of the University of Maryland. Greenbelt. Lanham. If Camarillo's muscleman didn't get out much, we were giving him a nice driving tour.

We'd been on the grand circle tour about an hour and a half as we approached the exit for FedEx Field, home of the Washington professional football team. I toyed with the idea of getting off the Beltway and driving around the stadium parking lots but decided against it. Driving on the Beltway was plenty annoying.

We kept going, over the Wilson Bridge back into Virginia. Through Alexandria, Springfield, and back to Annandale, where this whole fiasco started. I read somewhere that the Beltway was sixty-four miles in circumference. With all the traffic, it had seemed like one hundred and sixty-four. I would say it was nice to be back home, but we weren't exactly home. Not yet.

I got off the Beltway and drove back toward the YMCA. I passed the building and swung into a Wendy's drive thru and got into a line that snaked around the back of the restaurant.

Three cars were ahead of us. The Beamer had not gotten into line after us.

"You see him?" I asked Vell.

He casually put his arm across my seat, looked through the rear window. "Nope. He's probably waiting on the other side by the pick-up window. There's only one way out of here, and he probably doesn't want to get caught behind us, waiting on his food."

After the lady in the car ahead of us ordered her food and pulled up, I made a sharp right turn to leave the line. The back of the Wendy's parking lot abutted the rear of another parking lot, belonging to a gas station. I bumped my Civic right over a substantial curb, across a small grassy area, and barely missed an air machine as my car thumped down in the gas station's lot.

I quickly maneuvered past the gas pumps and out onto the main drag.

"Company?"

"No, we're clear. Nice job," Vell said. "But I think you owe me a double cheeseburger. Can't get a guy's hopes up like that, dude."

We headed back to Mama's but not until we'd criss-crossed and double-backed through half of Northern Virginia to make sure we weren't being followed. Camarillo might know who Vell was, but Mama had a different last name, and it wouldn't have been fair to lure Z-Ray there; he wouldn't have a chance against Mama if they faced off.

Our first order of business was to make sure Kevin was okay. Camarillo had given us a day to get the money, but I didn't really trust the word of a crime boss, especially one who kidnapped people.

When we got to Mama's, no one was home.

Vell went directly to the fridge, where Mama sometimes left notes figuring it was one place Vell would always look. No note.

We searched the house, found nothing—Kevin's stuff was still there—and met back in the kitchen.

"Well?" I asked Vell.

"Maybe she took him to Bible study," Vell said.

"You think?"

"No." Vell leaned his butt against the counter.

My insides constricted. Something was off. "Text her."

Vell pulled out his phone, tapped a few buttons. "Sometimes it takes her a while to respond."

"Okay. The door was locked, no evidence of foul play or forced entry. It's unlikely Camarillo could locate Mama, especially so quickly. I mean, Z-Ray might still be waiting for us to emerge from the Wendy's drive-thru."

"Maybe Payton found them? She opened the door to let him in, you know, just to talk to his step-kid, and—"

"You know Mama better than that. No way would she let him in. No way. We need to relax. I'm sure we're just jumping to conclusions," I said.

Vell nodded but looked ten miles from relaxed.

The front door banged open, followed by Mama's booming voice. "Vell? Mess? Are you two here?"

She came charging into the kitchen. "He's gone. Kevin's taken off."

So much for jumping to conclusions.

We got Mama to sit in the living room and calm down, and she told us what happened. "After you two left, Kevin and I chatted a bit. He was a bit disturbed he'd lost his phone charger—I think he wanted to play games or something—so I said he could use my computer. He seemed to be content, so I went to take a shower and do a few things upstairs. When I came down, he was gone."

"And he didn't say he was going out?" Vell asked.

Mama fixed him with a withering stare. "I've just been out searching the neighborhood. No sign of him."

I patted Mama's considerable shoulder. "It's not your fault. Kevin pretty much does what he wants."

"It *is* my fault. I'm the adult around here. You asked me to keep an eye on him. I'm sorry, Mess. I screwed up."

"Any idea where he might have gone? When you were chatting, did he say something that might give us a clue?"

"Not that I can recall. We talked about his mom—how much she sacrifices for him. We talked a little about his stepfather. That boy sure don't like him, and with good reason. He's a bad man. But I don't remember him talking about someplace he needed to go. Boy that age shouldn't carry so much anger." Mama closed her eyes and leaned back on the couch.

I almost suggested she try using some of her gifts to get a bead on him but didn't want to be seen as mocking her. If she had an inkling where Kevin had gone, she would have said so.

"Oh, Vell," Mama groaned, eyes still shut.

"What?"

"There's something else." Her voice cracked and I don't recall ever hearing Mama so worried. And that worried *me*. A lot.

"After I realized Kevin had taken off, I checked my purse. It seems Kevin borrowed some of my money."

Vell snorted. "Borrowed?"

"And..." Mama's eyelids fluttered.

"And what?" Vell asked.

"He got into that box I kept in the hall closet."

"What box in the closet?" Vell asked, his voice strained.

"Your grandfather's box."

"I don't know anything about any box in the closet." Vell glanced at me, eyes wide, and shrugged.

"I'm sure I told you about it."

"What's going on? Mama?" Vell gripped her arm. "Take another deep breath and tell us what's so important about this box."

"The box contains stuff from your grandfather. Stuff I didn't just want to throw away. And..."

"And?"

"And your grandfather's pistol is missing."

Chapter Thirty

After five more minutes of Mama hyperventilating, we got her settled down.

"Gun? We had a gun in this house?" Spittle flew from Vell's mouth. Laid-back Vell had gone apoplectic.

"It was your grandfather's. I kept it in case..." Mama's face hardened. "This wasn't always such a good neighborhood."

"You know what guns have done to our community. To our friends," Vell said.

"To tell you the truth, I'd forgotten about it. I was in the middle of spring cleaning, so I'd moved the box out while I cleaned the bottom of the closet, and he must have..." She sighed, and even her sigh had a slight rumble.

Vell swatted the air and spun around, saying something that sounded like, "Yeesh." He walked over to the window, pushed the drapes back, and peered out.

"Was it loaded?" I asked.

Mama nodded. "If I needed it in a hurry, I didn't want to be fussing with bullets."

I supposed if you *had* a gun that made sense. "Mama, why don't you go upstairs and lie down. Rest."

"Okay."

I grabbed both of her hands and hoisted her up from the couch.

"I really am sorry." She wiped a few tears away as she lumbered from the room.

I waited until the stairs creaked before speaking. "She's gone, Vell."

Vell let go of the shades. Turned around. "That gun was in my house for years."

"It was hidden away. A keepsake. A reminder of her husband. That's all. It's not like Mama was planning to knock over a 7-Eleven."

Vell shook his head. "I don't expect you to understand. White boy from the suburbs."

"This is kind of the suburbs, too."

"You know what I mean."

"Yeah," I said. "I do."

He expelled a big breath through his mouth. "I can moan about the injustices of life later. Right now, we got a problem."

"You mean an emotionally unstable fifteen-year-old on the loose with a gun?"

"Yeah, that."

Although Vell had shifted gears intellectually, he still seemed a little shell-shocked, so I took him by the shoulders, guided him to the couch, and eased him down, right into the depression where Mama had been sitting. Then I took a seat in the chair opposite. "Okay. We need to find Kevin, and fast. If you were a fifteen-year-old boy, an angry fifteen-year-old boy, where would you go?"

"I'd go after who I was mad at."

"That's what I was thinking, too." For the most part, since I met him, Kevin had played the part of the sullen, disengaged teenager. Except when he'd been acting distraught about his mom being missing, the only time I'd seen any fire from him had been when he'd gone after his stepfather with a chisel. We'd saved them both then, but I had a feeling Kevin did not take that defeat well, and given the chance, he'd go after Payton again.

And now he had a gun.

"You think he may know where Payton is? He knew he was at that dude's house."

"Yes, he did. You think he just called or texted Payton to find out? Boy reaching out to his stepfather?" Vell asked.

"Hell, anything's possible."

I caught sight of Mama's computer across the living room, amid all the fortune-teller accessories. "Mama said Kevin was playing computer games." I got up and went over to the computer. "Maybe he wasn't playing games."

I plopped down into Mama's chair and with Vell staring over my shoulder and breathing down my neck, I checked the recent browsing history.

Kevin had been busy.

And Kevin seemed to know a lot more than we'd given him credit for.

Behind me, Vell whistled softly as he perused the list of locations typed into the mapping site Kevin had accessed. The house where we'd found Payton. His old apartment. My motel. The Sleep Tight. Another ten addresses I didn't recognize, each of which could have been a possible hangout of Payton's.

I found a piece of paper on Mama's desk and started jotting down the addresses. "Why don't you go check on Mama, tell her we're going to find Kevin, okay? I'll call Lia, see if she wouldn't mind coming over to sit with her."

"Sure." Vell left and a moment later, I heard him clump up the stairs.

I reached Lia at work and explained the situation.

"Sure, I'll grab something to do and be right over."

"I wouldn't worry about having something to do. Just get Mama talking, and you'll have enough material for five feature articles. Maybe you'll even win a Pulitzer," I said. "And Lia, thanks."

I hung up and finished copying down all the places Kevin had located, then I went through the rest of the sites he'd visited. The county bus schedules. A taxicab company. A website teaching beginners how to fire guns. A Wikipedia article on Swiss bank accounts.

A search of all the McDonald's restaurants in Northern Virginia.

Kid's gotta have some priorities. Of course, that just underscored how sad this whole thing was. A fifteen-year-old kid, on the loose, with a gun, looking for his brand of justice against his stepfather, and he was mapping out his strategy based on the availability of Big Macs.

"Come on, Vell," I yelled upstairs as I grabbed the lists of addresses and headed for the front door. "We've got to get moving."

* * *

We had no way of knowing what was going through Kevin's mind, so we made the assumption that he conducted his address searches in order of priority. That meant our first stop was the house where Kevin had directed us to before, where we'd found Payton in the detached workshop/garage.

When we turned the corner, everything looked quiet. No car in the driveway, no sign of Payton attacking Kevin with a saw nor of Kevin chasing Payton with a chisel. I had trouble believing Payton would return there, as scared as he was of Camarillo tracking him down, but maybe Kevin had some inside knowledge.

We drove by the house slowly and continued down the street, making the first right turn we could. I pulled to the curb and cut the engine. "You see that guy?"

"You mean the gray-haired dude in the beat-up Chevy scoping out the house?"

"That's the one. Who do you think he is? One of Camarillo's guys?"

"Dunno. Didn't really seem the type." Of course, I had an extremely small sample size to judge from—Z-Ray was the only guy I'd actually seen who worked for Camarillo. But Griff's descriptions of the intruders, and Harry's descriptions of the two guys sniffing around, all described a certain type of guy. Young. Muscular. Brutish. The guy we'd passed in the car had thinning gray hair and a slim build, from what I could tell from our drive-by.

Of course, he had the stone-dead eyes of a killer.

"Be nice to know who he is and why he's here." Vell said.

"Yes, it would."

We got out. I opened my trunk, retrieved a Nationals cap, and put it on backward. Pulled my jeans down a little so they sagged. Vell got the message, and he tugged his jeans down too, and untied his sneakers.

"Ah, youth" I said.

We walked back toward the house, sporting a bit of a pimp roll. I wasn't sure if we fit into the neighborhood vibe or not, but I figured two chuckleheads out for a stroll would be less likely to draw any serious attention from a guy looking for Payton.

As we neared the guy's car, we confirmed he was alone, and that he was simply sitting there, staring at the house across the street. He held a cigarette out the open window with one hand and a Coke in the other. He gave us a quick glance—those dead eyes again—then went back to his surveillance. He reminded me of a hired killer in a Quentin Tarantino movie.

We passed the car, and when we were in the blind spot of his mirrors, we ducked. Vell crept back along the passenger side of the car, and I swung around behind the rear, and came up on the driver's side.

After a silent count of three, I popped up and stuck my face in the open window, careful to avoid his cigarette. "Hey, man."

The guy withdrew his arm, and recoiled in the seat, eyes wide. Some soda splashed from the can and landed on his pants. "Jesus H. Christ! What the hell do you think you're doing?"

Without making a noise, Vell stuck his head through the open passenger window, reached under a folded newspaper on the seat, and grabbed the guy's gun.

"This yours?" he asked, holding it up.

The guy jerked his head in Vell's direction. "Hey!"

"I'll take that as a yes." Vell turned and tossed it on the ground outside the car. "We'll keep it there for safekeeping."

The guy set his soda in a cup holder on the console and flipped the cigarette butt right by my ear out the window. "You two geniuses know who you're messing with?"

"Why don't you tell us?"

"You know if I get out of this car, someone's going to get hurt."

I leaned against the car. With my leverage, I didn't think he'd be able to get the door open. "We just want some information."

"It's sunny outside. That enough information for you?"

His voice had that two-pack-a-day quality, and his nose had been broken—several times, if I had to guess—and hadn't set right. Any of the times.

"Actually, we were hoping to get some of our questions answered."

"What do you think this is, Jeopardy?"

"What are you doing here?" I asked.

"Just enjoying a smoke and a soda. What are you doing here?"

"Same as you. Looking for someone."

A glint of something in the dead eyes. "Oh?" He squinted at me, made a show of looking me over. "Well, he ain't here."

"Who's not here?"

The guy opened his mouth, then closed it and broke into a smile as cold as his eyes. "Whoever you're looking for."

"Actually, we're looking for a kid. About fifteen. Kinda skinny."

This time, there was more than a glint in the guy's eyes. "Who's this kid?"

"We're the ones asking questions. He came by here, didn't he?"

The guy shrugged.

I felt like reaching through the window and slapping this guy silly until he told us. But I had a strong feeling that, although I might feel better, it wouldn't help us find Kevin. "Maybe we could work together. Cooperate."

"Why would I want to do that?"

"We're trying to locate this kid, and we think he's going after Payton. And that's who you're looking for, right?"

"Yeah," he said, this time not even trying to play it coy. He glanced at Vell, then he stared at me. Doing some sort of calculus. "You cops?"

"Us? Do we look like cops?"

"You look like skateboard punks."

"We're two concerned citizens," Vell said. "Trying to keep our community safe."

The guy gave Vell a strange look, then turned to me. "What does the kid want with him? Payton owe him money too?"

"Not exactly. Let's just say it's a family matter."

"Okay. Seems like we have coincidental objectives."

I didn't expect the words *coincidental objectives* out of this guy's mouth. But when you're right, you're right. "Exactly."

"Kid came by here, not too long ago. In an Uber. Banged on the door. Banged on the door to that shack. Gave up after about five minutes. Got back in the car and took off."

"You didn't think to stop him?"

"Stop him from doing what? Selling Boy Scout cookies?"

"He has a gun."

The guy shrugged. "Lotta punks have guns. When it comes down to it though, when you're facing another guy, mano a mano, they all don't have the rocks to use them. This kid? Didn't seem like a killer to me. Besides, he'll just have to wait in line for Payton."

"Anyone ever tell you how charming you are?"

"I told you about the kid. Now you tell me something about where I can find Payton."

I gave him the address of Payton's apartment.

"Yeah, that's the first place we looked. We ain't stupid."

"Wasn't sure. That's all we got. Sorry."

"You don't sound very apologetic."

"Who do you work for? Camarillo?" I asked.

"None of your business."

"Well, tell your boss to watch out for collateral damage. There are some innocent people involved, and they don't deserve whatever it is you're going to do to Payton."

"I'm no messenger boy."

"Fair enough. When we see him, we'll just tell him about our little conversation. And about how we managed to get the drop on you. And get your gun. He might not give you such a glowing recommendation when you apply for your next job."

"I don't like you," the guy said. "But I kinda like your style. You remind me of me when I was just starting out."

"Thanks." Not sure I liked being compared, favorably, to a thug, by a thug, but I took the compliment in the spirit it was intended. "We'll be going now."

"Ta ta," Vell said. He bent down and picked up the gun by two fingers, and we hustled away from the guy's car, after hitching up our pants so we could move faster. I didn't think he'd get out and try something. After all, we didn't have anything he wanted, besides his gun, and we didn't have that for long because Vell dropped it down a sewer we passed.

We made it to the car without incident, and we left the neighborhood a different way, not wanting to pass some old guy climbing down into a sewer.

As we drove to our next stop, Payton's apartment, I handed my phone to Vell. "Call Lia. See how Mama is. And see if maybe Kevin has returned."

"Don't you think she would have called if he showed up?"

"Just grabbing at straws, my friend."

"I hear you."

Vell called Lia. No change: Mama was still lying down, and Kevin was still AWOL.

"Try tapping into your network. See if anyone's spotted a teenage boy running wild with a gun."

Vell took to texting, fingers flying. He mumbled as he did, shaking his head, stabbing at his phone. Now we were chasing longshots, but really, what else could Vell do while I drove?

"Anything?" I asked after a few minutes.

He grunted and kept at it, but I figured it was far too little, far too late.

We didn't find anyone of interest—Kevin or Payton—at Payton's apartment, and we checked with neighbor Betsy. She hadn't seen or heard anyone—resident or intruder from the apartment next door.

We criss-crossed much of Northern Virginia, visiting the addresses Kevin had searched on Mama's computer. After a few fruitless hours, we headed back to Fairfax and the last place on Kevin's list, the Sleep Tight.

I figured if something was happening at my motel, Cesar would have let me know, but since it was right on our way, we stopped in, just to be sure. I left Vell in the car while I went into the office to talk with Cesar. When the above-door bell dinged, he looked up from his spot behind the counter with a big smile. When he saw it was me, the smile dimmed.

"I don't suppose you've seen Kevin around? Or Todd Payton?"

"Hello, Mess. I am well. Thank you for asking. Things are going fine here at the motel you are supposed to be overseeing. Thanks for asking about that, too."

"Sorry." Sometimes I got a little preoccupied by whatever was going through my head at the moment. As a kid, my mother was always telling me to stop and smell the roses. I always responded that I didn't want to get thorns up my nose. "I have complete confidence in you, Cesar. I don't have to ask how things are going, because I *know* things are going well if you're here."

Cesar rolled his eyes. "To answer your question, I have not seen Kevin nor his stepfather. However, those two young ladies—the sisters—checked out. Took the bus, I believe."

Without saying goodbye to me? Unfortunately, it happened a lot. I never expected to hear from most of my guests again, their stop with me just a reminder of terrible times. Left me a bit sad, however. "Okay, thanks. I'll see you later." I headed for the door, calling back to Cesar. "If you do see Kevin or his mom or his stepfather, please let me know ASAP."

I banged through the door, sending the bell jangling.

* * *

In the car, I told Vell that Cesar hadn't seen anyone, but would be sure to let us know if he did.

"He's got a certain je ne sais quoi, doesn't he?" Vell said. "You could take some lessons from him."

I ignored Vell's jibe and was about to put the car in gear when a thought hit me. Sometimes ideas snuck up on me; other times they smacked me in the face. This was one of those other times. "We're doing this wrong."

"Huh?"

"We're going about this thing the wrong way. I mean, what are the odds we're going to find either Kevin or a hundred thousand dollars today?"

"Slim to none."

"Exactly. So maybe we should take a proactive approach." I drummed my fingers on the steering wheel.

"Keep talking, boss," Vell said.

"Look at it this way. Camarillo's got Nicole. Camarillo's the one who's going to come after us when we don't deliver. Camarillo's the one who's scouring the countryside for Payton."

"All true." Vell paused. "And?"

"Keep your friends close and your enemies closer."

Vell turned in his seat to face me. "I don't know, that sounds—"

"Come on. If we follow Camarillo around, he'll lead us to Nicole. And maybe Payton, too. Plus, if we're following him, he'll never find us."

Vell stared at me, chewing on his bottom lip. After a while, he exhaled loudly. "Sure. Whatever. Way I see it, this thing is likely to end badly no matter what we do. Might as well go down swinging."

"Ah, that's the spirit, Mr. Optimist," I said.

"I try."

"Next stop, the Y. We'd better buckle up." And I wasn't referring to the seat belts.

Chapter Thirty-One

We didn't have a plan, but that never really stopped us before. I called the Y and asked the front desk if Coach was there, hanging up as soon as the lady confirmed his presence. Then we hightailed it through traffic and parked in the big lot in front of the Y, making sure we had a clear view of the door.

I repeated my routine—calling and asking for Coach—in case he'd ducked out while we were on the road. He hadn't.

"So now we just wait here?" Vell asked.

"*I* wait here. You need to cover the back door. Call me if you see him leave. I'll do the same."

Vell glared at me for five full seconds, then got out, slammed the door, and trudged away across the parking lot without glancing back.

For a while, I watched the people enter and leave the building. They came alone, in pairs, in small groups. Young, old. Skinny, obese. Black, White. Bored, I pulled out my phone and pored over every box score for every baseball game played yesterday. Then I hit a few social media sites, a few news sites, and then, bored with that, I went back to people watching.

The random flow of people had picked up, and there were now a lot of boys wearing team T-shirts, many with basketballs, some dribbling them through the parking lot.

Another wave of kids went by—this time wearing lime green T-shirts—and I was about to go back to my phone when I spotted a familiar face slicing through the parking lot, only a couple cars away: Shotgun Stokes. I slouched a little in my seat, hoping he hadn't noticed me.

For a second, I expected him to turn on his heels, come over, and rap on the window, asking me what the heck I was doing there.

Of course, I could ask him the same question. I tracked him as he entered the building.

Here for a workout?

He wasn't carrying a gym bag. And really, Shotgun didn't seem like the type to go for a midday swim or a schvitz in the sauna.

If Shotgun was doing a story on Camarillo, would he come here to conduct an interview? Possibly.

But something wasn't sitting right. My thoughts drifted into conspiracy-land. Was Shotgun on Camarillo's payroll? Through his police sources, he probably had some inside information of great value to Camarillo. Maybe Shotgun goes drinking with some cops, gets a few advance tips about raids. Passes them on to Camarillo in exchange for some compensation.

Made sense.

I texted Vell and told him to meet me back at the car. A minute later, he came jogging around the corner of the building. He crossed the lot, trying not to look suspicious, then hopped in, breathing heavy. "Camarillo on the move?"

"No."

"Then why am I running?"

I shrugged.

"So why'd you summon me? Need an answer to a crossword puzzle clue?"

"Shotgun Stokes just went inside."

"The reporter?"

"That's the one."

"Maybe he's researching a story."

"Could be." I paused dramatically. "Or maybe Shotgun works for Camarillo."

Vell let out a long, low whistle. "Holy crap. And you went to him about Camarillo. No wonder Camarillo wasn't surprised when we showed up. Shotgun had tipped him off."

I thought back, trying to remember if I'd told Shotgun anything else Camarillo might have found useful. Had we talked about Kevin? Or Nicole? At least beyond mentioning their names? I didn't recall. Either way, I felt betrayed. Maybe even a little bit violated. Shotgun working for Camarillo? Now that I thought about it, the set-up was brilliant.

Hell, it probably worked both ways. Camarillo could get Shotgun to print falsehoods—or the truth, for that matter—that would hurt his competitors. No wonder Lia and the higher-ups at the newspaper were so impressed with all his crime-related scoops. He was in bed with one of the biggest criminals around!

"So why do you think he's here, in person, rather than just talking on the phone? If Stokes worked for a criminal, you wouldn't think he'd want to be seen together."

Vell had a point. "Well, maybe it is just an interview. Get the word straight from the horse's mouth." When Lia had interviewed me, she'd come to my office, so it was logical that Shotgun would come here to interview Camarillo.

"I have an idea," Vell said. "Maybe we should start up the car, go back to Mama's, and get her to fix us a nice meal. Then you and me can go to a movie, kick back, relax, and forget all this nonsense."

"We can. After we finish what we came here to do."

"Always a technicality with you."

"Let's not take our eyes off the prize here. Shotgun's presence doesn't really change our goal. If anything, the fact that the media is on to him will force his hand. We need to get Nicole back safely. Find Kevin. Anything else is just noise." It sounded pretty easy, just two people to find.

The trick would be to get it done without anyone getting hurt. Or worse.

Why we got paid the big bucks.

I jerked my thumb out the window. "Maybe you should go back to your post. Just in case Shotgun slinks out the back."

"I don't know what he looks like," Vell said.

"Picture an old newspaper guy with a nickname of Shotgun. That's what he looks like," I said. "He was wearing a tan windbreaker and a Detroit Tigers cap. Going incognito, I guess."

"Never much liked the Tigers." Vell took off and I tracked him as he loped around the corner of the building. Nice to see someone getting some exercise.

I kept tabs on the front door and didn't recognize anyone else. I wasn't sure what I expected, but it would have been nice if Kevin or Nicole, or hell, even Payton, came strolling by. Would have made our job a little easier.

After about five more minutes, Stokes stepped out of the building, stopped, surveyed the parking lot in front of him, then sauntered back to his car, just another old dude leaving the gym. I texted Vell and told him he could forget about Stokes and go back to waiting for Camarillo.

We didn't have to wait long. Three minutes after Stokes left, Camarillo and Z-Ray came out of the building and went directly to an SUV parked in the first row.

I called Vell and told him he had thirty seconds to get his ass back to the car.

Camarillo's muscle hopped in the driver's seat while Camarillo got in the back. They pulled out. I started the engine, then ducked down as they passed.

When I lifted my head, Vell was sprinting across the lot. When he got to my car, he whipped open the door and jumped in, and I jammed it into reverse. Then slapped it into drive and peeled out, hot in pursuit.

My panicked actions weren't really necessary, because Camarillo was still at the lot's exit, waiting to turn onto the main street. I slowed, and hung back in an aisle, not wanting to get right behind him. Next to me, Vell sounded like a panting German shepherd.

"You need to work out, my friend," I said. "I thought you were an athlete."

"I made it, didn't I?"

"Barely."

He waved me off. "Who's in the car?"

"Camarillo's in the back and the big guy we met the other day is driving."

Vell nodded between gulps of air.

Camarillo turned onto the main street, and we followed suit, careful to stay far enough behind to avoid being spotted. They drove so as not to draw attention to themselves, and we mirrored them. A few miles per hour above the speed limit, keeping up with traffic, no crazy lane changes. We made a few turns until we were headed vaguely northeast.

A few more turns, down increasingly smaller streets, and we found ourselves on a leafy street in a modest neighborhood, not too far from Bailey's Crossroads. Camarillo's SUV slowed, then swung into a driveway. We stopped about sixty yards away and I tucked the car behind a gray minivan, but we still had line-of-sight with Camarillo. At least I did. Vell's view was obstructed.

I kept the engine running. You never knew when a quick getaway would be in order.

The driver got out and went inside the small two-story house, leaving Camarillo alone in the back seat.

"What's going on?" Vell asked.

"This is just a stop," I said. "The driver got out and went inside the house, but Camarillo's still in the car."

We waited.

Nothing moved on the street. No cars. No people. I didn't even think there was a breeze. Finally, the door to the house opened, and Z-Ray emerged. Holding Nicole by the arm. She tried to break free from his grip, but he jerked her arm so hard she almost lost her balance.

"Oh shit," I said.

"What?" Vell leaned over until he was almost in my lap so he could get a good look.

He was in time to see Z-Ray manhandle Nicole down the front walkway and stuff her into the backseat with Camarillo.

"Doesn't look like she's a happy camper," Vell said. "Or that she's a voluntary participant in this little adventure."

An understatement.

"Maybe we should ram them right now," Vell continued. "Plow this heap into theirs and then you and me could snatch Nicole before they knew what hit them."

I was a bit miffed by what little regard Vell had for my car. Of course, that same exact thought had occurred to me. "Don't think I'm not tempted, but they probably have guns. And they strike me as the 'shoot first and ask questions never' type of guys."

"They may have guns, but we have justice on our side."

If only justice were bulletproof. "Let's keep following them and see how this plays out. We can always ram them later."

"Okay, then," Vell said.

"And would you mind returning to your side of the car?"

Vell shifted back into his seat without commenting, unless you counted a little snort as commentary.

The SUV took off, continuing down the road. We stayed behind it, always keeping within sight, but never getting too close. Tailing someone was pretty easy if the person you were following didn't have a clue they were being followed.

We left the development and found ourselves going north on Route 7. Then we made a left, west, onto Route 50. We drove past shopping centers and restaurants—many Korean and Vietnamese—aiming for the Beltway.

A mile later, we breezed right past the Beltway interchange.

"Looks like we're headed to Fairfax," Vell said.

Truth was, there were dozens of towns we could have been on our way to: Vienna, Oakton, Chantilly, Centreville. But Vell had a point, we *were* heading to Fairfax. I picked up my phone and called the motel.

"Hello?"

"Good afternoon. This is the Fairfax Manor Inn. How may I help you?"

"It's me, Fareed."

"Hello, Mess. What do you need?"

"Is anything going on there?"

A pause. "Nothing unusual. Why?"

"Is Cesar there?"

"No. He went to Abie's school for a play or something."

"Thanks." I hung up.

"You think he's going to the motel?" Vell asked.

"Why would he?"

I caught Vell's shrug out of the corner of my eye. "That's a good question. Where do you think he's taking Nicole?"

"Hopefully, we'll find out sooner rather than later."

We were now only about a mile east of the motel. A bad feeling grew in my gut. I called Griff. No answer.

"Coming up to it, Boss," Vell said.

Ahead of us, the SUV slowed. Instead of turning into the motel's parking lot, it changed lanes, into the middle lane.

I exhaled, and it was so loud, I almost expected Vell to cover his ears.

"I guess we're going someplace else," Vell said.

"Just a scary coincidence." I exhaled again. The last thing I needed was for something to be going down at the motel.

"Maybe we're headed all the way to West Virginia."

Suddenly, Camarillo's SUV moved into the left lane.

Unease rippled through me.

Then he veered into a left-turn-only lane, at a stoplight.

"Shit." My stomach knotted. Looked like they *were* heading to the motel. They'd just been doing a drive-by to see if something was going on, much as I'd done when I'd gone to see Payton. I stomped on the brakes, but after a split-second calculation, I realized I couldn't very well come roaring up to a stop right behind him without calling attention to ourselves so I eased off the brake, stayed in my lane, and kept going.

As we passed through the intersection, Camarillo made his U-turn and headed back in the direction of the motel.

"That ain't good," Mr. Understatement said.

I ignored the No U-Turn sign at the next available spot and spun us around, wheels screeching. We reached the motel just as Camarillo was pulling into a parking spot.

I kept going another fifty yards and parked on the other side of Hole Lotta Love. Might be better to keep out of sight for now, at least until we figured out what the hell was going on.

Vell and I piled out of the car and hustled to get a peek around the corner of the café. Camarillo's SUV had parked along the row of rooms, in front of Room Eight or Nine, if I had to guess, but it was hard to get an exact bearing from our angle.

"Think he's after us?" Vell asked. "Come to break our kneecaps a little early?"

A logical assumption, but why come all this way unless you knew we were going to be there? I had a strange—bad—feeling about this. "No. Something else is going on."

Vell shrugged. "Maybe he's simply returning Nicole to us."

We stared at the car. Nobody got out. Nobody got in.

"If he's returning Nicole, how come she hasn't gotten out yet?" I asked.

"Good question. Maybe we should call the cops. Let them sort all this out."

"We should." I pulled out my phone. Started to punch in 9-1-1. Stopped after the first 1. Hit cancel and put the phone back into my pocket. "Let's see what's going on first. I'd hate to get Nicole mixed up in something she doesn't deserve to get mixed up in."

"I hope you know what you're doing," Vell said.

I hoped I did, too.

Chapter Thirty-Two

I noticed movement from the far side of the parking lot. A single person walked along the row of rooms, heading for Camarillo's car. I recognized the gait a beat before Vell, but he spoke first.

"Kevin."

Kevin hiked up his jeans as he got to the car. It looked like he said something to the driver, then shifted his attention to the back seat, driver's side. Where Camarillo sat. We were on the other side, so we didn't have a clear view of what was transpiring, but a million thoughts raced through my mind. Had Camarillo lured Kevin here for some reason? To capture another hostage to use as leverage against Payton? Or was Camarillo threatening Kevin, trying to get him to do something, using Nicole as leverage? Or maybe he was trying to set up some kind of scheme to trap Payton?

All I really knew was that my head hurt trying to think this through.

Z-Ray got out and Kevin walked him to a room, pushed open a door, then stepped back as Camarillo's goon went in. Kevin returned to the SUV, this time going to the rear window where Nicole sat. The window rolled down, and Nicole's arms shot through, grabbing Kevin in an awkward hug.

"The hell is going on?" Vell asked.

I pulled out my phone and called the office. Fareed answered. "Good afternoon. This is the—"

"This is Mess. I need to know who's checked into Rooms Eight and Nine?"

"Just a sec." Fareed mumbled to himself as he looked up the info.

"Nobody's in Room Nine. And the lock in Room Eight is still busted, so nobody's in there, either."

"Okay. Call Griff, tell him we have a situation. And then call the cops." I hung up and turned to Vell. "Now or never. Let's go."

I grabbed an old baseball cap from the backseat, pulled it down over my face as much as I could, rolled up one leg of my jeans, and half-tucked my shirt in. Then I set off, lurching across the parking lot, not directly toward Camarillo's car, but in that general direction. As I got closer, I began warbling *Aqualung* as off-key as I could.

Kevin glanced my way, but dismissed me as a homeless, and harmless, drunk. I shuffled along, as unsteady on my feet as I was in voice. When I got even with the SUV, I took a hard right and began staggering toward it, arms outstretched, hollering unintelligibly about spare change, careful not to let anyone get a good look at my face.

Circling around to Camarillo's side, I stopped about ten feet from the car and began spouting snatches of random song lyrics and past-memorized monologues, hoping to keep Camarillo's attention fixed on me.

It was working. He stared at me through the window with an expression of disdain. Or maybe it was disgust. Kevin had come around to the back of the vehicle, and he was gaping at me too.

Through the car windows, I could tell that Nicole also was watching my antics with interest.

As I hammed it up, Vell sprinted toward the SUV from the other side.

I shuffled closer to the car and made a roll-down-the-window pantomime to Camarillo. He shook his head. I shambled closer and kept motioning for him to open his window, now swinging my head back and forth to keep him from getting a good look at my face. I wasn't positive he'd remember me, here, out of context, acting like a derelict, but no sense taking any chances.

I rapped on the windows with my knuckles. Hard. Harder. Even harder. In my peripheral vision, I saw Kevin observing the entire farce. If he recognized me, he didn't let on. I kept rapping, harder and faster.

Finally, Camarillo gave in and rolled the window down. Before he could say a word, I reached through the window and grabbed his shirt collar and pulled him against the window as hard as I could. He didn't fight back. In fact, he seemed rather calm for the situation.

Kevin came up beside me. "Let my mom out."

"Sure, kid. I was planning to anyway." Camarillo hesitated, and a creepy smile formed. "Just like we agreed. Assuming, of course, that you kept your end of the bargain."

"Your guy is still inside, isn't he?" Kevin said, sounding a lot older than his fifteen years.

"Point taken," Camarillo said to Kevin, then he addressed me. "Please let go. You're wrinkling my clothes."

I released him and stepped back, tugging on Kevin's shirt to get him to move away from the SUV, too. I didn't have a clue what bargain Camarillo was referring to, but now didn't seem like the right moment to discuss it with Kevin.

On the other side of the car, Vell was extricating Nicole, having to first open the front passenger door to unlock all the doors. A moment later, he and Nicole came around the front of the SUV.

Kevin looked at me, then at Camarillo, then at Vell. He seemed as if he'd just woken up from a trance. Then he took four big steps and flung himself into his mother's arms.

"We'll be on our way now," I said to Camarillo. "Don't even think about trying anything."

Camarillo simply tipped his head at me.

I half expected him to get out and try to prevent us from taking off, but we had him outnumbered. And I had the feeling that Nicole no longer figured in his plans. Something about his bargain with Kevin.

I didn't want to ruin the Hallmark moment between Kevin and his mom, but I knew Z-Ray was less than fifteen feet away, just on the other side of a motel room door.

"Come on, guys. Let's get out of here." I pried Kevin free from Nicole. Both their faces were damp. I grabbed Kevin's arm and Vell took Nicole's, with the intention of guiding them toward the office, and relative safety, when the door behind us flew open and Z-Ray burst out, holding an unwilling victim at gunpoint.

Payton.

Everyone froze. I did a quick tally. There were four of us, five if you included Payton. There was one of him. But he had a gun. Advantage: man with the gun.

Z-Ray recovered from his surprise first. "Okay, nobody move. Or I blow his head off."

We didn't move, and a moment later, Camarillo emerged from the car to join us. He spoke to his guy. "You get the money?"

"Claims he doesn't have it."

"And you believe him?"

"I, uh, worked him over pretty good. Nothing."

Payton did look like he'd been through quite an ordeal. Face bloody. Shirt ripped. Holding his arm at a funny angle.

"A liar, huh?" Camarillo stepped toward Payton, and I thought he was going to deliver a vicious backhanded slap right across Payton's already-battered mug, but he swiveled toward Kevin. "You lied to me, kid. You said he had the money. We had a deal, and I don't think you're holding up your end."

"He does," Kevin said, in a voice so small and fragile that no one could possibly believe him. That didn't prevent him from doubling down on his lie. "He has it. I saw it. In a black duffel bag with the word Everlast on it."

Payton's eyes popped. "You little shit. You took it. You took my money." Payton lunged for Kevin, but Z-Ray clamped a beefy hand on Payton's shoulder and drew him back.

Camarillo stepped forward, sticking his face two inches from Kevin's. Dark eyes burned hot. "Where's the money? Fork it over and no one gets hurt. Don't and my friend here's going to get serious. With your pals here. With you. With your mother."

To Kevin's credit, he didn't back down. "I don't have it."

Camarillo stared at him another beat, nose to nose, then turned toward Payton. As he did, Kevin reached behind his back and whipped out his gun.

Mama's gun.

Chapter Thirty-Three

"Don't move!" Kevin screamed.

Camarillo spun around, and Kevin aimed the gun right at his chest. The boy's hand shook, the boy's arm shook, the boy's shoulder shook.

The corners of Camarillo's mouth turned upward. "It takes a big man to shoot someone, kid."

"Get out of here," Kevin said to Camarillo. "Or I'll pull the trigger."

Camarillo didn't move; Z-Ray had shoved Payton to the ground and was now leveling his gun at Kevin.

Shootout at the Fairfax Manor Inn wasn't a headline I wanted to see. I eased into the middle of the standoff, eyes glued to Kevin's wobbly hand. His gun pointed at me from one side, and Z-Ray's gun pointed at me from the other. Harm's way, all right.

But neither really had a beef with me. At least that's what I told myself.

"Look, nobody wants to shoot anybody, so why don't we put the guns down?" I smiled, as if I were asking for the time of day.

The guns didn't move. Still trained on me.

"Just give me my money, and we'll be on our way," Camarillo said.

"I called the cops, you know," I said.

"Then we'd better settle this quickly." Camarillo took a step toward me.

As if on cue, the faint sound of sirens could be heard in the distance.

Camarillo took another step toward me.

Out of the corner of my eye, I saw Payton, still on his knees, grab Z-Ray's legs and try to topple him. Z-Ray didn't fall, so Vell entered the fray, whirling and nailing him with a crazy roundhouse kick to the side of the head, sending the gun flying and knocking him over, right on top of Payton.

Camarillo dove into the melee.

Chaos had descended on the Fairfax Manor Inn.

I quickly retrieved Z-Ray's gun and while the others wrestled, I engulfed Kevin in a bear hug, careful to pin the arm holding the gun to his side. He fought me, but I held tight and whispered in his ear, "We got your mom back. Don't do anything that will wreck your life. For your information, shooting someone will do that. Do you hear me?"

He stopped resisting and nodded. I let go and focused my attention on the scrum, which had all but settled down. Z-Ray had Payton neutralized in a headlock, and Vell had Camarillo's arm twisted behind his back, face mashed against the wall. A double stalemate.

Except now I had the gun.

I walked over to Z-Ray and pointed it at his sweat-slicked forehead. "Enough."

His skull wasn't too thick to get the message, so he released Payton. Next to him, Vell relaxed his hold on Camarillo. I motioned for Camarillo and Z-Ray to stand together, so I could cover them more easily. "And now, we wait for the cops."

At the mention of cops, Kevin bolted. A flat-out dash away from us. His mom yelled for him to stop, but he kept right on going. Twenty seconds later, Payton took off in pursuit. I couldn't very well shoot him in the back as he ran, and I doubted he'd listen to me if I yelled for him to stop any more than Kevin listened to Nicole.

"Well?" Vell asked.

Shit. I handed the gun to him.

Vell didn't take it from me. "I don't want this thing."

I pressed it into his hands. "Think of the greater good. And keep an eye on these clowns. I'll chase them." The last thing I wanted was for Payton to get his hands on Kevin, especially if he thought the kid had stolen his money.

I took off. Kevin was long gone, but Payton was just rounding the corner of the motel, gaining steam.

Behind the motel was a paved accessway, wide enough to allow garbage trucks to reach the dumpsters. When Kevin got back there, he could either go right, toward the Toyota dealership and the Denny's beyond, or he could loop around behind the motel and the office. Once he decided to loop around, he wouldn't have any options; a tall fence ran the entire length of the property, which kept trespassers away. And fleeing teenagers from escaping that way, too. In this case, a good thing.

The sirens grew louder, closer.

I needed to catch Kevin and disarm him before the police arrived. If they saw a boy running with a gun, bad things—very bad things—were liable to happen. I also needed to catch up to him before Payton did. Kevin didn't stand a chance going up against his stepfather, and I was afraid the gun he wielded would only make things worse.

And irrevocable.

I barreled around the near corner and eased up a bit, hoping to spot Payton, if not Kevin, too, but they'd left me in the dust. I fought to catch my breath as I increased my pace. I really needed to get into better shape.

When I got to the rear of the building, I stopped. Glanced right. Nothing. Glanced left along the rear of the motel, and saw Payton, just disappearing around the far end, where Kevin had been smoking the first night he'd come to the motel.

Seemed like ages ago.

I continued my pursuit. Once Kevin got in the clear, back on Route 50, he could go in a dozen directions. Payton might be close enough to track him, but if I lost him, I'd have little hope of catching them.

Although I'd run probably only about a hundred yards, my lungs burned, and my right hamstring was screaming at me. I ran through the pain.

As kids, Izzy and I used to run laps around the motel, with our mother timing us. I used to give Izzy a huge head start, but I'd always manage to catch her by the finish line. Then, it was for fun, exercise, and bragging rights. Now, I had a strong feeling that Kevin's life was at stake, and I harbored no illusions I'd beat him to the finish line.

I kicked it into overdrive.

When I reached the far end of the motel, I'd lost Payton. But the gate to the mini-golf course hung open. And it was still swaying, as if it had just been opened.

I jogged over and stepped through the gate, pulling it shut behind me. If they were on the grounds, they'd have to go through me to get out. I called out, "Kevin. Payton. I know you're in here. Come on, let's talk this through."

No answer.

Slowly, I walked toward the starter's hut and the first hole. Nothing there but the Eiffel Tower. Moving toward the center of the course, I called out again. "Let's settle this thing like adults. Calmly. Coolly. Kevin, I know your mother would want that."

Again, no answer, but I thought I heard some scuffling behind the Statue of Liberty, which stood about fifteen feet directly in front of me. Sixty yards away in the motel parking lot, I could hear the shouts of the cops, who'd just arrived. I thought about yelling out to them, letting them come over and defuse the situation, but, again, I didn't want to take the chance that they'd just throw kerosene on the fire instead.

Better handle this myself.

I crept up to the Statue of Liberty and peered around it.

The first thing I saw was Payton, arms up. Then I saw Kevin, pointing the gun right at his stepfather's heart.

I came out into plain sight. Held up my hands, too. "Okay, Kevin. Time to put the gun down. You've made your point."

Kevin didn't put the gun down, though. He held it straight out and sideways, like in a stylized action flick, and the strain was making his entire arm shake.

I kept advancing, hands held in front of me, careful not to make any sudden moves. "Kevin. Your mom is worried about you. She sent me to make sure you're okay." I smiled. "You're okay, aren't you?"

His eyes burned with hatred. Pretty far from okay.

He still had the gun trained on Payton—who hadn't moved—and I wasn't even sure he was hearing a word I said, but I kept up my patter. "Well, I know you're angry. And you have every right to be. But the best thing we can do is talk about it. Get everything out in the open. You, your mom, your stepdad. Clear the air. Getting violent isn't going to help anyone."

He glanced my way for a split-second, then re-focused on Payton. The arm holding the gun wavered.

What would Kevin do when the cops realized we were here and came over to investigate? Would that force him into making a rash decision? "Kevin, let's take a deep breath and talk about this."

Kevin continued to ignore me. He inched forward, emboldened by the gun. He screamed at his father. "You beat Mom. Hurt her so bad I could hear her crying herself to sleep."

Payton didn't answer.

"You forced us to leave. You ruined our lives."

I tried again. "Kevin. Please. What am I going to tell your mom? She asked me to bring you back, unharmed. She wants to make sure you don't do anything that would ruin your own life. She loves you."

"Where's my money?" Payton asked.

"That's all you care about, isn't it?" A few spit bubbles gathered at the side of Kevin's mouth. "You never cared about Mom. Or me. All you care about is yourself."

Payton took a small step forward. "Not true. I love your mother. She walked out on me, you know."

Kevin waved the gun. "Bullshit. We had no choice. Remember that night last week. You came home shit-faced and called one of your stupid friends from the kitchen. I heard you. Bragging about some job you pulled. Said you made enough money from that 'deal' to solve all your problems, set yourself up for good." Kevin's voice broke. "And then you said you were going to dump my mom and find someone else."

"I never—"

"Shut up! I heard you. I fucking heard you!"

Payton shuffled forward.

Kevin instinctively took a half step backward. "The next day, you came home, pissed about something, hit her. It was the worst time ever. Later that night, I begged Mom—begged her—to leave you. So, when you went off to work the next morning—Mom and I packed up and took off."

Payton's hands balled into fists. He tensed, and I had the feeling he was exercising every ounce of restraint he possessed to keep from charging Kevin.

"You were always snooping around the apartment, sticking your nose where it didn't belong. You found my money, and you stole it. I want it back," Payton said. "Now."

"I don't have your money! And even if I did, what good would it do you?" Kevin's eyes grew wide, and his maniacal grin rivaled the Joker's. He steadied his gun hand. "Dead men don't need money."

I edged closer. "Kevin! Don't shoot!"

He cut his eyes in my direction and the gun dipped. Payton leaped forward and grabbed Kevin's arm. The gun went off, but neither one stopped struggling. I put my shoulder down and threw myself at them, linebacker-style, just as I'd laid Payton out in Gerry's parking lot.

The three of us fell in a heap onto the remnants of the 12th hole. A pile of thrashing knees and elbows. Payton managed to wrest the gun from Kevin, but I grabbed Payton's wrist with both hands and twisted, twisted, twisted until he let go. With the combined weight of Kevin and me on top—and with Kevin flailing away at him—Payton couldn't do much more than cover up and try to protect himself.

Kevin kneed Payton in the groin, and I picked up the gun. I didn't have to say anything; Payton flopped back on the faded green felt and closed his eyes. Defeated.

Next to him, Kevin cried, no longer an adult in a teen's body.

Chapter Thirty-Four

The cops hauled away Camarillo and Z-Ray, and we all gave statements to my buddy Ostervale. Nicole had the courage to describe her abduction, and Kevin chipped in with what he knew about it. The cops also carted Payton off into custody after discovering a variety of outstanding warrants. I was sure he'd be doing time for something—even if Nicole declined to press any kind of domestic abuse charges. I supported her decision whichever way it went—after all, it had to be incredibly difficult to open yourself up like that—but I sure hoped he'd get what he had coming.

Hours later, after the proverbial dust settled, Nicole, Kevin, and I had dinner at Sandy's—she insisted on staying open late just to serve us.

Nicole still seemed a bit shell-shocked—understandably—although she claimed Camarillo and his men treated her reasonably well. No surprise that the dinner conversation was muted, hard to act cheery given all that had transpired. And Kevin was so down in the dumps, too, that he passed up an opportunity to get dessert.

With no place to go—their apartment had been trashed, even if they'd wanted to return—Nicole and Kevin were stuck at the motel again. Cesar and I got them set up in Room Four, and I said goodnight to them, knowing it would take some time, patience, and a good deal of therapy to put all this behind them, if that were ever totally possible.

I wandered back to my room, thought about calling Lia to fill her in on the crazy events. I'd called her earlier, to let her know Nicole and Kevin were safe, although I hadn't gone into all the gory details. But I was too exhausted now to answer her inevitable questions. Instead, I just sent her a text to let her know Kevin and Nicole were holding up well and that I'd talk to her in the morning.

I watched an old episode of Seinfeld, hoping it would calm my nerves, but after it was over, I was still wired. Too much residual adrenaline pumping through my system. I decided to get some fresh air.

I stepped out of my room, into the night air. Pulled up a molded plastic chair and had a seat in the shadows on my "porch." Cars whizzed by on Route 50, but every once in a while, a chorus of crickets broke through the traffic noise.

So many people in this world—and in this very City of Fairfax—needed help. And not just a cup of sugar or a hand moving a heavy sleeper sofa into the basement. Serious, life-changing help. Unfortunately, I had a feeling the vast majority suffered without it.

I thought about Nicole and Kevin's situation, happy theirs didn't devolve into utter tragedy, but it was disheartening to know there were so many more people who wouldn't—or couldn't—find the wherewithal to seek help. Pride, circumstances, ignorance, delusion. There were many reasons those in need stayed silent, most just excuses. Some things, I clearly didn't understand.

The sound of a door opening jolted me from my philosophical funk.

I watched a dark figure emerge from Room Four. Kevin.

He glanced around, but I stayed still, and it was dark, and he gave no indication that he saw me. He pulled his hood over his head and slinked away.

I got up and followed.

Kevin didn't go far. I tracked him to the mini-golf course next door, where he opened the gate and ducked inside. I slipped in behind him, thirty seconds later. The streetlights from Route 50 shining on the fiberglass landmarks cast creepy elongated shadows on the concrete paths.

I spotted Kevin near the fourteenth hole. The Windmill Hole.

He dropped to his knees and crawled inside, just as I used to do, all those years ago. I stood there, watching. He'd discovered what I had. A refuge. A hiding place. Had he holed up here when he'd gone missing? Right under my nose?

A moment later, he emerged carrying something.

A black duffel bag. When he moved into a beam of light, I could make out the words on the side of it: Everlast.

Kevin came down the path, heading for the gate, oblivious to my presence.

"Hey there."

He whirled in my direction.

"It's me, Mess." I stepped out of the shadows and leaned against the Statue of Liberty.

"You scared the shit out of me." He gasped for breath.

"Whatcha got there?" I pointed to the bag in his hand.

"Uh..."

I found it amusing that I'd caught Kevin so red-handed he couldn't even force out a lie. Maybe he *was* maturing.

"What are you going to do about it?" Kevin's voice wobbled.

I didn't need much time to think before I answered him. "Do about what?"

He eyed me, silently. Trying to tell if I was serious, or just stringing him along, like many of the adults he'd crossed paths with in his life.

I put my arm around his shoulder. "Come on, I'll walk you back to your room. Tomorrow's the first day of the rest of your life, and I'm sure you'll want to be well rested."

* * *

Two days after Camarillo was arrested, I said goodbye to Nicole and Kevin as they embarked on their way to a new life in Asheville, North Carolina. As promised, Angie had put in a good word with the folks running the Ford dealership down there, and they had a lead on an affordable apartment in a safe neighborhood. Of course, their nest egg would be able to help smooth out any rough edges associated with the transition.

I made Kevin promise to look out for his mother—and to look out for himself. I also promised to come by for lunch the next time I found myself in

Asheville.

Yesterday, I got a nice email from Avia, thanking me for my generosity—for both the room and the use of the car. She landed a warehouse job in Manassas, and she and Rona had found a place to stay in some lady's converted barn in exchange for doing some chores around the farm. I never *expected* to be thanked, but it sure did feel nice to know I helped some people during their darkest hours.

Uncle Phil flipped out over the press coverage the motel got. I told him not to worry, that people had short memories and it would all blow over soon. Now, a week later, it almost had.

At least for the time being. I had the strong feeling the other shoe was about to drop. Although I didn't tell that to Phil. No sense riling up the old guy.

I drove down to the newspaper building to meet Lia. After checking in with the receptionist and getting my stick-on nametag, we went directly back to Shotgun's office. This time, he wasn't at his desk typing. He was standing at his window, gazing out at the Town Hall building.

I knocked on the doorjamb, quietly, trying not to startle him, but he spun around with a wild, feral look in his eyes, as if he were a raccoon and I'd flipped the outside light on suddenly, catching him with his snout in the garbage can.

"Sorry," I said.

Shotgun waved me off, forcing a smile. "Too much coffee this morning." He raised a lupine eyebrow at Lia. "Good morning."

Lia hit him with a cold smile. "Morning, Shotgun."

"Come in, come in." He moved away from the window and eased into the chair behind his desk. "Have a seat."

Lia sat in the chair in front of his desk, and I grabbed a chair from against the wall and dragged it over.

"Let me again offer my congratulations. Helping to capture Fairfax Public Enemy Number One. Very impressive."

"Thanks. Nice article. Or should I say articles."

"Thank you, sir." He touched his finger to the brim of an imaginary cap.

After the news broke, Shotgun had called me for information—and a few choice quotes—for his story. Then he'd followed up each day with an article about some other newsworthy aspect of Camarillo's criminal activities. If Shotgun had his way, I'm sure he'd write an article about Rafael Camarillo every day for the next month.

"So what can I do for you?" Shotgun asked. "Or maybe you want to do something else for me? I know, you've got a line on another major local crime figure. Don't tell me, Mess Hopkins has decided to give up his hospitality career and go into law enforcement." From his tone, he thought he was being very funny, and to emphasize his point, he bared his teeth, in what I'm sure he thought was a smile.

Lia leaned forward. "Actually, you're not far off. About us exposing a local crime figure, I mean."

"Oh?" His toothy smile dimmed.

She leaned back, crossed her legs. "I'll let Mess fill you in."

"Since everything went down, I've had some time to think. And a few things don't make sense to me. Maybe you can help me out here."

"Uh, sure." Shotgun picked up a pencil and started playing with it.

"I was at the Y on the day Camarillo was arrested. When you waltzed in there, it seemed like you'd been there before."

"I'm not following."

"You'd met Camarillo there before. On more than one occasion."

"I don't recall. What's your point, anyhow?"

"You don't recall? Well, I went back and talked to the desk staff there. Showed them your picture—you know, the one that sometimes runs with your stories—and they remembered you showing up. Multiple times. They remember letting you in without a membership card, just because you were a so-called celebrity."

Shotgun waved it off. "Okay. So what? I was there. *Multiple* times. Doesn't prove anything. I used Camarillo as an anonymous source. Every reporter does that."

"Then how come you didn't know people referred to him as 'Coach'? Huh? There's a sign that reads COACH *right on his door*."

"You're crazy, Hopkins."

"And what about Billy Lane?"

"What about him?" Shotgun's voice had gotten shrill.

"You knew he was dead before the police had even released that information. I asked you if you knew him, but you told me he was dead before I told you."

"I don't know what you're talking about." He tapped the pencil eraser on his desk, faster and faster. He turned to Lia. "What's going on here, anyway?"

"At first, I thought that maybe you were working for Camarillo."

"Hah! Ridiculous. I would—"

I interrupted. "Now I know Camarillo was working for *you*. You've been the criminal puppetmaster."

Shotgun sprang to his feet. "Get the fuck out of here. Both of you."

Lia smiled. "Oh there's more, *babe*. For the past couple of days, I've been researching all your stories, trying to find any instances when you've abused the power of the press to your own advantage. Stories that have pointed the finger at rival operations. Stories that seem to have exonerated Camarillo. I know police investigations are independent, but I have a feeling that you might have an insider or two on your payroll. I think I've discovered a pattern. It'll take more research, of course, but I think I'm dead on."

"You're crazy, too." He pointed the pencil at Lia.

I reached out and grabbed it from his hands. Tossed it across the room. "The DA doesn't think we're crazy."

"You went to the DA with this already?" Shotgun sputtered.

"We wanted to make sure we were on the right track," Lia said. "Went to Harold, too. Pitched my idea to write up a series on this whole thing. Your criminal involvement, your abuse of power, whatever else I can dig up. You get the idea." Lia's eyes blazed with delight, and I enjoyed seeing her so fired up. "If I were you, I'd start packing up your office now."

Shotgun Stokes, crime reporter extraordinaire, slumped in his chair, now looking like an old grizzled loser, panhandling on the corner. "There's no concrete evidence. I'll never be convicted."

"Maybe not by a jury," I said, rising. Lia got to her feet beside me. "But you'll get your trial in the press, and I think your readers are smart enough to figure things out for themselves. I can see the headline now, *Local Crime Reporter Secret Crime Boss.*"

Stokes swallowed hard. "They'll believe me over you, eight days a week. The people in this county love me."

"The people in this county don't love crooks. Once the truth gets out, they'll despise you. They trusted you, and you've betrayed them. You're finished, Stokes." Other criminals, when facing a similar situation, might flee, to Mexico or South America, or some country without an extradition treaty. But Stokes's enormous ego would never let him act like a common criminal. He'd rather go to trial and bank on the Shotgun Stokes reputation rather than run and tacitly admit guilt. Ditto for any kind of plea deal. His hubris would make his punishment worse.

"When I'm done with you, they won't be calling you Shotgun Stokes anymore," Lia said. "They'll be calling you *Inmate* Stokes."

Stokes opened his mouth to respond but closed it before speaking. He turned away quickly, gazing out the window like when we'd first arrived. Afraid to let us see defeat and despair on his face?

Lia and I exchanged smiles, and a crystal-clear image of the future formed in my mind. Lia looked spectacular in a sleek black dress as she stood on stage in front of a fancy banquet hall, accepting the Pulitzer Prize for her articles exposing Stokes. She delivered a speech that was articulate, funny, and inspirational, and when she finished, the entire crowd jumped to their feet, clapping and cheering.

I was there, too, cheering the loudest.

About the Author

Alan Orloff has published ten novels and more than forty short stories. His work has won an Anthony, an Agatha, a Derringer, and two ITW Thriller Awards. He's also been a finalist for the Shamus Award and has had a story selected for THE BEST AMERICAN MYSTERY STORIES anthology ("Rule Number One," first appearing in SNOWBOUND from Level Best Books). Alan's next novel, SANCTUARY MOTEL, will be released in October from Level Best Books. He loves cake and arugula, but not together. Never together. He lives and writes in South Florida, where the examples of hijinks are endless.

You can connect with me on:

- https://alanorloff.com
- https://twitter.com/alanorloff
- https://www.facebook.com/alanorloff
- https://www.instagram.com/alanorloff

Also by Alan Orloff

Novels

Diamonds for the Dead, Midnight Ink 2010 (Agatha Award Finalist)

Killer Routine, Midnight Ink 2011

Deadly Campaign, Midnight Ink 2012

The Taste, 2011, self-pubbed

First Time Killer, 2012, self-pubbed

Ride-Along, 2013, self-pubbed

Running From the Past, Kindle Press/Amazon Publishing, 2015

Pray for the Innocent, Kindle Press/Amazon Publishing, 2018 (ITW Thriller Award Winner)

I Know Where You Sleep, Down & Out Books, February 2020 (Shamus Award Finalist)

I Play One On TV, Down & Out Books, July 2021 (Agatha Award Winner, Anthony Award Winner)

Short Stories *(40+ including one in five consecutive Best New England Crime Stories anthos)*

Notable ones:

"Rule Number One" appeared in Snowbound and was selected for Best American Mystery Stories 2018.

"Dying in Dokesville" appeared in Malice Presents: Mystery Most Geographical and won a Derringer Award.

"Rent Due" appeared in Mickey Finn: 21st Century Noir, Vol. 1 and won an ITW Thriller Award.

Printed in the USA
CPSIA information can be obtained
at www.ICGtesting.com
CBHW030715270923
1145CB00018B/111